CW00517095

A Moth to the Flame

Dougie McHale

Azzie Bazzie
Books

Prologue

The second he sees him, Brodie Lucas knows the young man is going to jump. Dusk is falling, there is no one else around. The last of the walkers, shrinking from him, have already reached the other side of the Forth Road Bridge, a 2.5 km suspension bridge that runs over the River Forth.

Brodie freezes. The young man, muttering to himself incoherently, paces up and down, staring at his shoes.

It is common knowledge the bridge is a suicide spot, but in all the years Brodie has walked over it, he has never witnessed an attempt.

Brodie's dog stops walking and sits down, as if it, too, senses the gravity of the situation.

Brodie edges forward. His mind races. He has no idea what he is going to do or say. The young man looks up, and before Brodie can take another breath, the young man has climbed over the railing and is precariously standing on a steel beam, with the choppy and dark water below him.

The young man's demeanour has changed. Distressed, he is now shouting, but to Brodie's relief, not at him. Good, he thinks, at least I can still try and connect with him, find something, anything. Brodie can feel his body tense as he inches towards the railing and rests his hands on its cold surface. His eyes rotate towards the water, it looks angry and forbidding. What state of mind can compel anyone to jump? A sharp sensation spikes through the middle of his body and he shudders.

'My name's Brodie. What's yours?'

The young man is crying now.

'Tell me your name.' Brodie tries to keep his voice steady; it needs to be audible, controlled, but he just feels desperate, out of his depth.

'My name's Brodie,' he repeats. 'And this is Jasper.' Jasper has poked his nose through the railing.

The young man moves to the edge of the beam. Brodie is aware of his body shaking. He doesn't dare shout out. Instinctively, he wants to, but mutes the words before they rise from his tongue.

The young man's body sways, like a tree about to fall. Brodie is convinced he will witness him jump and then, to his immense relief, the young man sits down, hunched over, his legs dangling over the beam precariously.

'Isaac,' he says.

For a moment, Brodie is startled, confused, then his mind clears. 'Hello, Isaac. You're making me nervous sitting over there. Why don't you just come back up here, and we can talk. I'm not good with heights. I'm fine if there's enough space between me and the drop but this… well, it's about my limit, really.'

Isaac bends his head forward and cradles it between his hands. 'My head hurts. You're making it hurt.'

'I'm sorry. I didn't mean to upset you.'

'This shit shouldn't have happened. I couldn't stop it. They made me do it.'

'Listen, Isaac. We can talk about it if you want to?'

Isaac starts to pull at his hair, his emotions fluctuating wildly from sobs to intense anger. 'I had no choice, no choice. They would have killed her. I hate myself. This has to end.' Isaac turns his face away from Brodie. His words muffled, caught by the wind.

Brodie fears he is losing him. He knows that one of the many security cameras strategically placed around the bridge's structure will have caught them, alerting the others. He won't be on his own for long.

'Where do you live Isaac?'

'What?'

'Do you stay local? That's an English accent. London? Further south, maybe?'

'Why should that matter to you?'

'It just does. I'm from Edinburgh. Jasper and I walk the bridge quite often and then we head down to South Queensferry for something to eat. You get a great view of the Rail Bridge. In fact, we were just on our way down there.' He is trying to fill the time; he needs to find something that will bond them. 'It's one of my favourite places. I'd strongly recommend it. If you like your food, there's some lovely restaurants and bars. Jasper often gets his bowl of water.'

Brodie tells him he has a son about his age, who now lives in London with his partner. He doesn't get to see him as much as he'd like, and it plays on his mind. He needs to arrange to visit him. He misses him. Time slips by so quickly. He tells Isaac, we all have people we care about, whom we love and who love us in return.

Isaac covers his face with his hands.

'What about you, Isaac? Is there someone you care about?'

Isaac wipes his eyes with his palms. 'She'll be better off without me. They both will. It will be over.'

'Who? Tell me their names.'

'Cheryl, she's my girlfriend and Zak, my son.'

For the first time, Isaac looks at Brodie, a smile crossing Isaac's face. Brodie can feel the tension drain from him. At last, he's getting somewhere, he is talking. Where are they? Why is it taking so long for someone to come?

'How old is Zak?'

'He's two. It's his birthday today.'

'Then surely he'd want to see his dad.'

Isaac covers his face with his hands.

'Do you want to hurt them, cause them unimaginable pain? Think about it, what this will do. You can stop it. You can stop it right now. All you have to do is come up here with me.' Brodie gestures with his hand, trying to coax Isaac.

'You don't know what you're talking about. It will be over.'

'What will be over?'

'It ends here.'

'What does?'

'Everything.'

'Please… Please don't do this.'

'I'm already dead.'

'Let me help you.' Brodie is startled by the abrupt direction the conversation is taking. 'It doesn't have to be like this.'

'No. It doesn't. I could have taken pills, but I didn't want some poor housemaid to find me at that hotel.'

'What hotel?'

'The Dakota.'

'I know it well. They serve the best fish I've ever tasted.'

'I never tried it.'

'You still can. We can do it together.'

'You don't understand. This is the only way.'

'No. You're right. I don't understand. But I know this is not the only way. You have a choice. Please, Isaac. I want to understand, I really do.'

Isaac is staring at the dark water below him.

'The police found drugs in my flat. You see, I distribute class A drugs all over the country for these bad motherfuckers. They do everything; drugs and people trafficking, prostitution, you name it. Nothing's below them if it makes lots of money.

'I had a load of shit on me. I was about to go to St. Pancras Station, and then head up north to Manchester when the pigs kicked down my front door. They found the drugs, confiscated them and I was let out on bail. Someone was talking to the police; how else would they know?''

Isaac continued to tell Brodie his story. It felt like he had to tell someone. All Brodie could do was listen. Isaac said he knew that retribution was coming. Two nights later there was a drive-by shooting in Camden. The drug dealers had their honour to defend. Isaac knew he needed to escape that life, but how could he? In Camden, it's 24/7 drug tourism. On his last trip, he was badly beaten by dealers in Bedford, hospitalised with serious head injuries.

'They took the drugs and now I'm in debt to my suppliers, fucking thousands. I've got a son; he's only two. If I die, the debt dies with me. If I stay alive, I fear for Cheryl and Zak. Those bastards wouldn't even blink over harming them. I've put them in so much danger.'

'Then why are you here? Why are you not with them?'

'I'm putting everything right. She needs to get out of London. Those bastards won't find her. I fucked them over. Took some of their money, not much, but enough to secure a lease on a flat for six months.

'There's some leftover for her, not much, but it'll be a new start and my son will be safe. That's all that matters, and with me dead, those fuckers will have bigger fish to fry. Death will descend upon me and sweep me away.' Isaac inches forward.

'No! No! Isaac don't do this. You can change your life. You can watch your son grow.'

Isaac rummages in his jacket pockets, one after the other. Brodie can see him panic. 'I had an envelope. It should be here. I knew I should have burnt it.'

Brodie pulls his hand through his hair. He glances at Jasper. The dogs head is bent forward, its ears twitch as it sniffs at an envelope. Brodie reaches down and swipes it from Jasper's intrigued nose. 'This must be it. It must have…'

Just then, Brodie feels a slight touch on his arm.

'We'll take it from here.' It is a police officer and his eyes are telling Brodie to move away. 'Just step away, move over to the vehicles.'

Brodie turns his head, another police officer is behind him, a woman, who smiles at him. Behind her, Brodie can see several vehicles standing stationary, one still has its passenger door open.

'I've been talking to him. His name is Isaac. I think I can get him to stop...'

'It's our job, sir. Just move away.'

'Come on Jasper, this way.' Brodie gestures to the dog who follows him, as he moves from the railing, the hunched figure of Isaac disappearing from his view.

And then, Brodie is jolted by an almost inaudible cry. The police officer's voice is alarmed and defeated, and Brodie's stomach sinks and curdles inside him. His mind freezes and all he can see and will continue to see is the desperation on Isaac's face.

Brodie gives a statement to the police. They ask if he would like to speak to a counsellor. He says it won't be necessary and drives back to Edinburgh in his car.

He turns the key in the lock of his front door and closes it behind him, into a familiar silence, a stillness that accompanies him as he moves through the house. It is the same each time, it crashes into him, like hitting a wall head-on; he is alone, his world has shrunk.

Jasper sets off down the hall, tail wagging. Once Jasper eats and settles in his favourite spot, sprawled on top of the sofa, Brodie slumps into a chair and watches the news on television. Although he tries to focus on the newscaster, her mouth moves but her words are meaningless, his thoughts remain on the bridge and the face of Isaac, now tattooed on his mind. He runs a hand over his chin; he is exhausted to the bone. He realises he still has his jacket on. As he slides out of it, his eye snags an envelope. And then he remembers.

Brodie takes the envelope from the pocket and turns it in his hands, inspecting it. It had slipped from his mind. He was going to give it to police but then, as the young man, Isaac, jumped from the bridge, and panic ensued, unconsciously at some point, he must have put the envelope in his jacket pocket.

Brodie stands and walks into the kitchen. He places the envelope on a work surface and considers whether to open it. It is sealed. There is no address written on it and no stamp attached. There is a letter, or at least, something inside it.

He runs his fingers across the brown paper. His instinct is to leave it unopened, but then what? His heart begins to pound at the thought of such a prospect. Finally, smiling at the absurdity of his indecision, curiosity finally tugs at him.

He has always found the garden to be a place where he can go to be alone with his thoughts. After his wife's death, he found it to be a still and calm space of comfort. His favoured spot is at the far end where an old wooden bench sits under the branches of a tall Sycamore tree. Brodie lights a cigarette and leans his back against the bark of the tree. He watches the next-door neighbour's cat disappear into a row of hedges that badly need trimming. It is a pleasant evening and he can smell the charcoaled scent of a barbeque drifting on the warm air. Somewhere not far off, the sound of a siren, an ambulance or police car maybe, announces that, unlike his garden, not everywhere is as peaceful. The sun is beginning its slide into the horizon, washing the sky in flushes of scarlet and orange.

He has left the envelope on the kitchen table; the letter it contained lies next to it, where it dropped from his fingers. He takes a long drag on his cigarette and pushes his hand through his hair. He remembers Isaac's expression, his face contorted in blazing anger, but there was also fear in his eyes and an air of resignation.

Brodie has read it twice. It is not a letter, but rather a collection of notes, Isaac's notes. A list of things to do. Buy train tickets, set up a bank account. Several names. An address. The words, *South Queensferry*, bore into Brodie's eyes. It is the small town that sits between the bridges that cross The River Forth where Isaac ended his life. There is a street name, a house number and the phone number of an estate agent, with the name *Alan Ferguson* underlined twice.

Brodie's thoughts are rapid and intertwined. Isaac has leased a flat or a house in South Queensferry for his partner and son. What was he thinking? Every day they'll see the bridge he jumped from. Isaac wasn't thinking, was he? Maybe, initially, he didn't intend to do it and it wasn't until after he secured the lease that he set his mind to end his life. Who knows? And would he have just decided there and then? Brodie has no idea how these things work; he has never had to think about the psychology of it, until now.

Did Isaac get in touch with his partner and explain everything to her? Isaac was desperate that she left London. She may already be on her way. Brodie remembers mention of train tickets in Isaac's 'to-do list.'

They're getting a train. They'll arrive in Edinburgh, probably. Poor woman. Brodie gives a protracted sigh. Does she know Isaac is dead? It's not unusual to find the body weeks later. Some are never discovered, washed out into the open sea.

Brodie can feel a shawl of obligation shroud him. For some reason, he feels responsible for this woman and her child's safety. He interweaves his fingers on both hands and rests his forehead on them as if he is about to pray. He taps his two thumbs against his brow. Why does this matter to him? Because he found himself confronting a man about to take his own life? Or because Isaac revealed the story that led to that moment? Maybe it was both?

He feels ludicrous. What has any of this to do with me? There is no onus on me to do anything or to feel anything, especially for someone I don't know. Thinking back, standing on the bridge and trying to convince a stranger not to take his life, now feels like a dream. Let's get this nonsense out of my mind. Even as he is thinking this, Brodie is unconvinced. It does not satisfy him.

He stands and walks solemnly towards the house. Doing nothing would make him desperately unhappy. He stands still and looks towards the sun, now disappearing. Everything changes in an instant. It leaves a transformational impression on him, urging him to do what he knows is the right thing and, at that moment, probability and certainty reassuringly focus him. His mind is set.

Once on the outskirts of Edinburgh, and outwith the rush hour traffic, the drive along the M90 takes less than fifteen minutes to reach South Queensferry. Brodie parks in the car park he often uses on his frequent visits, beside the church, whose architecture has always reminded him of medieval churches in Italy.

He strolls along the high street that, at times, can be thronging with visitors, bikers and the myriad tourists from the cruise ships that occasionally berth in the River Forth. Today, there are no cruise ships and the craft shops, boutiques, coffee shops and bars are pleasantly tranquil and welcoming. He passes 'The Little Bakery' and Cote Lane with its view of the harbour and a slice of the River Forth, and the Forth Rail Bridge in the foreground. He knows the area well. He has often wandered past with Jasper by his side.

He finds the address above a hairdresser and looks searchingly at the white window frames. Brodie presumes these are flats, several of them with commanding views of the bridges and beyond, in the background, the undulating skyline of Fife.

Not for the first time, a level of doubt invades him, and he wrestles with the thought that this is a mistake. Yet, there is something inside him that emanates a conviction; it settles on his shoulders and he is reluctant to let it go. He is doing this for Isaac, even though they only spoke for a few minutes. He remembers their encounter that day on the bridge; he had felt shaken, alarmed and the stirring of adrenaline. These have now been supplemented by the need to know that Cheryl and her son are safe. He has no idea what he will do or say, but he hopes, maybe, just seeing her will be enough.

He lights a cigarette and wanders over to a bench, keeping the view of the building in his sights. He can see an opening that runs alongside the hairdressers. Has he thought this through? All his ponderings concerned the need to be here, to see for himself that the woman and child were here, settled. Beyond that, he hasn't applied much thought.

He turns and finds it extraordinary that he never tires of looking at The Forth Rail Bridge, which today is perfectly mirrored in the reflected water.

He regrets not bringing Jasper. With a dog, he would have had the benefit of some camouflage, blending into his surroundings. He tries not to look too conspicuous, just a man sitting on a bench enjoying the view. He decides against a further stroll; instead, he crosses the narrow street and buys The Guardian newspaper and a coffee to take away.

He doesn't know what Cheryl looks like. However, if a youthful woman emerges from the opening with a toddler, he reassures himself, it must be her. He sits on the bench again. This time several people are taking selfies with the bridges in the background. A man with silver hair and beard asks Brodie if he could take a picture of his wife and him together. Brodie obliges and fires off several. When the couple inspects them, they thank Brodie with grateful smiles and wander off, arms interlocked.

Brodie watches as they disappear into a shop. Heather enters his thoughts and the hole now left in his life feels enormous. He takes a deep intake of breath, that part of his life is irretrievably lost.

He looks across the street in the direction of the flats. A woman is struggling with a buggy on the steps in front of the hairdressers. It's her. It must be. Brodie crosses the street and takes the steps two at a time.

'Let me help you.' He takes the weight of the buggy and cautiously descends the steps. The infant stares at him, expressionless, and Brodie can see it is a boy.

'I didn't think it would be that heavy.' Brodie smiles, but inside it is taking every effort of restraint to project a casual manner.

'Thank you so much.'

'It's no bother. I saw you were struggling.' To Brodie's relief, her accent is undeniably that of a Londoner. Several carrier bags are strapped to the buggy. Taking a toddler out is like a mini-expedition, Brodie thinks.

'The steps are a killer when you've got to get this lot down them.'

'Why are you using them then?'

'I've just moved into a flat up there. I've no option.'

Brodie is aware she has not mentioned anyone else. She is on her own.

'I didn't think you were from around here. That accent gives you away.'

She gives a nervous smile.

'Sorry. I didn't mean to pry.' Brodie assures her.

She flicks her hair from her face and gives the slightest shake of her head. 'You're not. It's me. I've moved up from London, me and the little chap.'

She has a pretty face and crinkly blonde hair and Brodie's manner helps her to relax.

'It's a lovely town. I wouldn't mind living here myself.'

'You're not local?' Cheryl asks.

'No. I'm from Edinburgh.'

'I've never been but I'd love to go there.'

'It's only ten minutes away by train.'

'Really? This is my first time in Scotland. Getting away from London has been a good choice, especially for the little one. The air is so much cleaner up here.'

'How long have you been staying?'

'This is just my second week. I need to get registered at a GP's, get this one to a playgroup and, if I'm lucky, a little job would help.'

'Well, good luck to you. I hope it all works out.'

'Thank you.'

Brodie bends towards the boy. 'I'd better let you and your mum get on your way. It was nice meeting you.'

'Likewise, and thanks for your help.'

He watches her walk away from him, a surge of satisfaction seeping through him. He is glad he has met her. It relieves him that he likes her. She has a friendly and gentle nature, which appeals to him and, because of this, he feels sorry for her. He contemplates why this may be. It is guilt; he knows that now. The sight of her struggling with the pushchair gave him the perfect opportunity to introduce himself. It was a deception of a kind which is not sitting easily with him. He knows nothing of her life, only the circumstances that have led her to this small town. And there it is. She knows nothing of this. Brodie was the last person the man she loved spoke to before he died. If she knew this, what would her reaction be?

As he strolls along the high street with these thoughts, the satisfaction he felt is drifting from him.

The experience on the bridge was unexpected, inexplicable even and, until now, Brodie has failed to understand just how much it has transformed him. Despite his best intentions, he can't just walk away from her. Although they have only shared a few words, he finds himself enamoured by her. And like the immediate lucidity that comes with clearing fog, he now feels it an obligation; his conscience weds him to this young woman's welfare.

Chapter 1

The Idea of Finding Elora

On Comely Bank Road, the sun breaks through a bank of clouds, casting elongated shadows outside a café. Brodie sits reading a copy of The Guardian, sipping a black coffee and indulging himself in a slice of raspberry cheesecake. Jasper, curled at his feet, lifts his head expectantly and then, with the deepest whine, sinks his head between his outstretched paws and shuts his eyes.

Brodie glances at Jasper, whose paw is twitching, seizure like, but he knows he is only dreaming, probably chasing squirrels or cats, a staple activity that his ageing legs, defiantly, can still accommodate.

A couple slip into the chairs at a table next to him. The woman smiles at Jasper and removes a scarf from her neck. She places her hand over the man's hand which rests flat on the table, a gesture, Brodie thinks, they will often repeat many times between them. Brodie can sense a natural affection; it sits easily in their posture.

Though he has become used to his own company since his wife died, he has missed such moments, however fleeting, that now feel momentous. The ache is unexpected, and he gasps at it.

Jasper lifts his head, sniffs the air and yawns, smacking his lips.

'We'll be going soon, Jasper.' Brodie scratches Jasper's ear.

As he turns the page, a headline snags Brodie's attention. He has been thinking of attending one or two of the events at this year's Edinburgh Book Festival, and the article is a commentary on several authors who will be attending. As he reads, a name catches his attention. His eyes widen. It can't be, can it? He reads it again, *Elora Alanis, Best*

Selling Author, and the memory the name evokes takes him to another place, another life.

Brodie reaches for his mobile phone and types her name into Google search. He takes a long breath. Suddenly he thinks he is being ridiculous. He taps on a link and there she is, smiling at him. It electrifies him. Amazingly, she has changed little. Did he think she would have? He tries to recall her younger face, the only one he knows. He can't believe her face is before him.

He realises he has been holding his breath. He looks at her photograph determinedly, examining her image more closely. He can see faint lines spread from her eyes and at the edges of her lips. He wants to absorb every detail.

Since his wife died, he has tossed and turned the idea of finding Elora, but always with a hesitation. He never thought such a moment would ever present itself. Not now, after all these years.

And here she is, back in Edinburgh. He can't believe it. He pictures himself meeting her. It runs in his mind. He knows nothing of Elora's life. She won't be the same person he knew all those years ago; he isn't. He wonders if she is still living in Greece. She's probably married with a family. She is an author and a successful one at that. He is suddenly seized with a desire to meet with her. He must see her at the book festival. He'll need to buy a ticket. He'll want to meet her afterwards. It will be like old friends catching up, peeling back the years that have layered an expanse of time before them.

Brodie has a feeling of plummeting.

What if she's disappointed in me? I'm not the young man I was when she knew me.

He lights a cigarette. His hand is shaking. He wonders if this reaction will ever stop and if so, when? He has tried to forget, but it hasn't worked. In the ebb and flow of his life, there has been an impression of separation from the only time he was ever truly happy.

He has masked this estrangement by becoming a husband, a lover, a father... he has embraced them all, the passing of the years has conditioned him.

He has been busy with the business of living, moments of intimacy, times of joy and passages of grief. He has played his role flawlessly, but always, interwoven in his thoughts, she surfaced, and he was torn between the memories, and the desires, and his determination to keep his family together. He loves his wife explicitly. He loves his son and daughter.

Sometimes, he cannot hide from the treachery he feels. It is the representation of his reality. How can he have lived a lie if that's what it has been? Because it illuminates the truth. He knows that now. It has never been a question of choice. The solace he seeks never comes, life continues to nudge him and quietly, he submits.

Brodie sucks on his cigarette and inhales deeply.

'Hello, Brodie.'

He turns his head, squinting up at the figure silhouetted against the sun. He need not see the face; he knows her voice. It is as familiar to him as is the geography of his face reflected in a mirror.

'Hana, what a nice surprise. I thought you'd still be in London.'

'Me too. The project ended sooner than expected, so I thought I'd come home for a few days. Thanks for keeping an eye on the house.' Hana sits opposite Brodie.

'Not a problem. I've left your mail on the kitchen table.'

'Probably just bills. That's all the post brings these days.'

'And the cat hasn't lost weight. I remembered to feed him every day... well, almost every day... only kidding.'

Hana smiles. 'I hope he wasn't too much trouble. I know you're not keen on cats.'

'We got along just fine. I told him if he didn't behave himself, he'd have Jasper to answer too.'

'What! Jasper would lick him to death. He's the most affectionate dog I know.'

Brodie pats Jasper's head. 'Do you hear that Jasper? Hana thinks you're a wimp.'

'And a lovely one at that.'

'Oh, there was a parcel from Amazon. It looked like a book.'

'Oh, good. I've been looking forward to reading it.'

'Anyone I know?'

'I shouldn't think so. His readers are mainly woman as far as I know.'

'Who is the author? I might know him. I've maybe even read one of his books.'

'I shouldn't think so. I don't think they'd be your type.'

'Go on then, tell me. I might surprise you.'

'Nick Alexander.'

Brodie looks at her blankly. He doesn't know who Nick Alexander is.

'See, I told you.'

'Is he any good?'

'Well, I wouldn't be buying his books if he wasn't.'

'No, I suppose not. Is he appearing at the book festival?'

'I shouldn't think so, he's independently published.'

'So, he's not a real author then. Anyone can self-publish.'

'That's such a narrow-minded and…' Hana stumbles trying to find the word. '… and condescending, no, even worse, snobbish attitude to have. Do you know that, as well as writing the book, the authors have total control of their brand? They develop the cover ideas, hire editors, then there are the advanced readers, the proofreading, the marketing, the advertising, they do it all. It's a business. And most importantly,' she sighs in exasperation. 'A lot of these independent authors often sell more books than your traditional authors. So, don't give me that high and mighty attitude.'

'Sorry. I just thought most people thought about it like me.'

'Well, they don't, and if they do, they need to get thrown from their ivory towers.'

'I never knew you felt so passionately about it.'

'He's a bloody good author, and he's not the only one.'

'Okay, okay. I get the picture. So, what are you going to do now you have a few unexpected days off?'

'Not much. I'll be glad of the rest. It was intense. The client was a stickler for detail, never off our backs. I even worked on weekends.'

'It doesn't sound worth it.'

'No. That part of the job can get to you. The financial rewards… well, that makes it all worthwhile.'

'It comes at a price though.'

Hana glances at her hands.

'I'm sorry. I shouldn't have said that.'

'No. You shouldn't have.'

'I'm sorry.'

'I know, you've just apologised twice.'

He offers her his cigarette pack. 'A peace offering.'

She pulls one from it and lights it with Brodie's lighter.

'I thought you were giving up,' she says, blowing a plume of smoke towards him.

'Willpower was never my fortitude.'

'Nor is your tact, it would seem.'

'No… I'm…'

'And don't say you're sorry again.'

'I won't. Forgiven?'

'I'll think about it,' Hana says with a good humoured grin.

Brodie smiles. He has known Hana for a long time. She was a friend of his wife, Heather, and when Heather died, Hana had been there for him. She had been his shoulder to cry on and he relied on her more and more as the months slipped past. She often spent long periods working away from home. She worked in management consultancy, but Brodie could never get his head around it. It wasn't his thing. All he knew was it came with a good salary, but it was not always conducive to a stress-free life. It had cost Hana her marriage and put a strain on her relationship with her teenage children who had taken their father's side.

'So, what have you been up to since I've been away?'

'Not much. Oh, I went to a reunion night out.'

'You did?'

Brodie nods. 'I did.'

'What kind of reunion?'

'From my days at university, history and politics, the class of 1995.'

'Really?'

'Does that surprise you?'

'Well, it does. I've never really heard you speak about your university days.'

Brodie moves in his chair. 'It was a long time ago.'

'How did you find out about it?'

'I didn't. They found me. Twitter.'

'Ah, I see. Well, how did it go? I bet it was weird meeting everyone again and hearing what they've done with their lives.'

'Kind of, I suppose. Some people didn't show up and a few have died.'

'That's only to be expected. After all, it was, let me see… nearly twenty-five years ago. You would have been twenty then, just a young pup.'

'God, that was a quarter of a century ago.'

'Does it matter?'

'Sometimes.'

'What do you mean?' Hana asks, surprised.

'Since I went to the reunion, certain things have been… well, on my mind.'

'Like what?'

'Oh, you know,' he says. 'It just got me thinking about that time and how quickly life seems to have passed and how people change and what if things had turned out differently.'

'What things? Are you talking about regret? About you, Brodie?' Hana studies him.

'I was just being silly. Caught up in the moment, meeting everyone again. You know, seeing older versions of the faces I'd had in my head for all these years. In my mind, that time has stood still, almost as if it has been paused when, in fact, it doesn't exist. We have all moved on, gotten older, had new experiences and lived lives that define who we are now, who we have become.'

'It sounds like you've been preoccupied with it… or with someone?' Hana meets Brodie's eyes. He looks away.

'Is there something you want to tell me, Brodie? Was it someone you met?'

'No… maybe. I mean no, it wasn't someone I met.'

'Was it someone you had hoped to meet? Someone who didn't go… who wasn't there?'

Sensing that Hana wasn't about to give up, he moves in his chair and says, 'Something like that.'

'So, she goes back a long way then?'

'I never said it was a she.'

'No, that's right, you didn't.' Hana comments noting Brodie's sudden diminishing eye contact. 'But I'm right, aren't I?'

He nods a confirmation. 'The truth is, I don't know what I was expecting. Right up until the last minute I wasn't even going to go,' he admits.

'But you did. She must have meant a lot to you?'

Brodie hesitates a moment. 'She did.'

'It looks like she still does.'

'It was a long time ago, before Heather.'

'I'm not judging you, Brodie.'

Brodie is suddenly aware this is the first time he has ever spoken about Elora to another.

'What's her name?' Hana asks curiously.

Edinburgh 1995

The Beginning

It wasn't her confidence that attracted him. The moment she tilted her head and smiled, her face lit up and it caught Brodie in her glow. There was an urge inside him so strong, all he wanted to do was absorb her.

He learnt from a fellow student that her name was Elora. It was unfamiliar to him. He loved the way it rolled off his tongue. He spent several days reciting her name out loud and in his head. She wasn't part of the close-knit community he surrounded himself with at the university.

She was in the year above him. He thought she might be Spanish or even Italian. It was difficult to tell. It didn't matter.

Days went past. Walking to the university, in a lecture or the company of others, he found the image of her was a constant presence on his mind. His response surprised him. He had tried to decipher it, this feeling. He compared it to reading a book and within the story, there is a continuous theme that persistently introduces itself within the narrative. Elora was his theme.

He resolved he needed to meet her, so he embarked on a bold plan to manufacture an encounter. He intended that his introduction to Elora would unfold unexpectedly and in pursuing his plan, he presumed it was foolproof. He had meticulously gone over each possibility in his mind and he noted, with satisfaction, the outcome was as reliable as the sun rising each morning. Once set in motion, the momentum would speed him towards the conclusion that, in his mind's eye at least, depicted them as destined to be together.

Unfortunately, real-life has developed a habit of intruding upon the best set plans with the distraction of unwelcomed realities. For a week, Elora seemed to have disappeared. So, Brodie bemoaned his naivety and his failure. He knew where she drank her morning coffee, which lecture theatre she attended, and he often saw the group of friends she was seen with. Although she was always a palpable presence in his thoughts, still she eluded him.

Faced with his self-humiliation, eventually, he spent a night out with friends, with one thing on his mind, to drink as much as he could during the infamous '*happy hour.*'

It was during this indulgent self-drowning, Brodie heard Elora had taken ill with suspected appendicitis and was rushed to Edinburgh Royal the week before. This revelation started a round of interrogation where Brodie, through a haze of Peroni and shots, felt relief and then subsequently concern for Elora's wellbeing.

The light returned to his eyes; he still had a chance.

Chapter 2

Infused with Expectation

A steady light rain follows Brodie's progress along George Street. He glances at Charles Tyrwhitt's window display, a shop whose clothes he has admired and worn for years. He remembers the pop-up umbrella he once bought and never used; the irony is not lost on him. The rain hasn't deterred the throng of pedestrians that etch their way to numerous shops, bars and restaurants. He crosses Castle Street, and a break in the cloud allows the sun to warm his back. As he makes his way towards Charlotte Square, the familiar white tents that house the book festival send warmth through him. She is near.

He settles into a chair in the back row and glances around the room. He wasn't expecting so many people. The place is busy with breathless anticipation. He estimates there are around a hundred people in the audience with only a few empty chairs available. The intimate stage is illuminated by a single spotlight. In the centre of the stage, there is a small table with a jug of water and two glasses. A brown leather chair sits on each side of the table.

A woman in a flowing skirt, blue-rimmed spectacles and with silver-streaked hair strides onto the stage. She is carrying a tablet and a microphone. She introduces herself and thanks the audience for coming. There follows a brief introduction and Elora receives an enthusiastic welcome onto the stage by the expectant audience.

He has thought about this moment for half his life and now that it is here Brodie feels a knot of unease in his stomach. He feels unable to breathe; his palms are sweating and, from the moment she appears, his eyes fix on her. He feels a wild and desperate urge to go to her, but untangles himself from such an unthinkable impulse.

As Elora sits down, she straightens her skirt, crosses her legs and folds her hands in her lap with an air of calm assurance. Her eyes widen as she acknowledges the audience's warm welcome.

Brodie sinks into his chair. Elora's hair is still as thick and wavy as he remembers it. Brodie wonders if she dyes her hair or is it just the advancement of time that makes her hair lighter? Time has been kind to her.

The interviewer leans towards Elora and, off the microphone, says something that makes Elora grin, the white of her teeth glimmering. Her look is natural, and Brodie remembers she always wore the minimum of makeup.

He wonders what she would make of him now, after all these years?

The interviewer asks Elora, since it is her first time at the Edinburgh Book Festival, is this her first visit to Edinburgh?

Has she done any research at all on Elora's past? Brodie resists an urge to laugh. Instead, he slides further into his chair.

Elora's lips curl into a smile. 'It was a long time ago, but no, this is not my first visit. I went to Edinburgh University when I was younger.'

From the corner of his mind, he too remembers. Unravelling memories, he gasps with happiness. He fingers his wedding ring, and the feeling is instantaneous like it always is, and he does what he always does, he buries the rapture.

He listens intently as Elora answers the interviewer's questions. He learns that her latest book is her tenth and seventh New York Times bestseller. He is astounded at this. He finds it incredulous that before now he had not heard of her books. Then again, why would he? Although he is not an avid reader, he likes the occasional thriller.

This did not stop him buying her latest book and reading it in one sitting.

Elora speaks about her influences, what motivates her to write, how she constructs her initial ideas and plans her plots. There is a questions and answer session, where a man roams around the audience with a microphone. A woman sitting two seats from Brodie asks Elora, what character in her books, if any, is like Elora and why? Elora gives a short laugh and says it is a great question. She combs her hand through her hair and considers her reply. She has barely spoken when momentarily something distracts her flow. Brodie shifts in his seat as a look of astonishment steals over Elora. A prolonged hesitation grabs her. With an effort, she collects herself and continues to talk.

Elora adjusts her reading glasses. She reads an extract from her novel. Brodie thinks her tone to be magisterial.

Around him it is that quiet, Brodie can almost hear the blood flowing in his veins. The audience is hanging on to her every word.

Her voice tickles his skin. He watches her mouth and imagines kissing her again. He remembers the feel of her mouth; he has never forgotten. He is mapping out the years in his head, a vast sea of time lying between them. He worries she might not want to see him, and an initial burst of nerves comes over him.

Brodie jumps at the wave of applause that suddenly erupts. It takes a moment to comprehend the talk is over. Elora is standing, smiling, acknowledging the warmth of appreciation from the audience. And then she leaves the stage.

Brodie is one of the last to leave the auditorium. He has sat in his chair wrestling with the thought this might be all a mistake. Eventually, he stands, and the thought enters his mind again. He has waited half of his life for this moment.

Brodie examines the room. She is sitting at a table, a tower of books beside her. A line of people clutching her novel snaking towards her. She signs each book and casually chats to every reader.

Brodie is standing beside an array of bookshelves where people are browsing and chatting. Absently, he takes a book and flicks through its pages. It is just a decoy. He glances up. He wonders, briefly, if he should just wait his turn. There is a hesitancy about him. No, that would be too public. With a surge of decisiveness, he waits until she's finished.

Elora obliges each request for a photograph. Brodie is struck by her composure, and how she makes time for each of her readers. He hears a trill of laughter coming from her table. A brash American couple, cameras dangling from their necks, have bought a copy of every novel Elora has published and as she signs each one, they take it in turns to crouch beside her while the other takes a photograph. Before they leave, they ask the woman next in line to take a photograph of them both with Elora. The woman smiles, a thin smile, she takes the camera and Brodie thinks, for a moment, she will throw it across the room, but she doesn't and to Brodie's surprise, he feels a nagging disappointment.

Eventually, the book signing ends. Suddenly, and to Brodie's astonishment, a man, thirty something, wearing a slim fit dark blue suit, and white opened neck shirt embraces Elora. There is specific ease about them, a casualness that slams into Brodie. Elora is smiling. As they part, his hand rests on her arm.

There is a definite closeness, an intimacy about their gestures, and an over friendliness that bores into Brodie. It feels like a physical assault.

They are talking. Brodie feels ridiculous, stupid even. His heart pounds his chest. He fidgets with the book still in his hand. He looks down at it and reads the title, The Vanishing Act of Esme Lennox by Maggie O'Farrell.

Brodie sighs, the irony is not lost on him, for at this moment, all he wants to do is vanish too. He needs fresh air. He needs a cigarette.

Outside, the rain has stopped. The air is muggy, under a low and heavy sky, still promising the likelihood of more rain. Brodie lights a cigarette and inhales deeply, savouring the burn in his throat.

'Brodie. It really is you.'

He turns. She is looking at him astonished.

'Elora.' His voice cracks.

'It is you. You were in the auditorium. I saw you. I can't believe it.'

'I had to come.'

She walks towards him, smiling. 'Were you leaving without seeing me?'

'I thought it was for the best.'

'What do you mean?'

In all the years he had imagined this meeting, he never thought seeing her again would feel so awkward.

'I saw you with him.'

'Who?'

'The guy in the suit.'

'Alex?'

'Yes… Alex. I presumed you'd want to be alone with him.'

'Whatever for? Ah, I see now. Alex works for my publisher. I've known him for years.'

Brodie feels foolish and simultaneously relieved.

'I thought… '

'He's a good friend, that's all.'

Brodie smiles and his heart leaps. 'I feel silly now.'

'Don't be. I would have thought the same.'

He doesn't believe her, but he is grateful all the same.

She shakes her head. 'My God. How long has it been? Over twenty-four years. You haven't changed. I knew it was you.'

Brodie's eye falls on one poster of Elora advertising her presence at the book festival. 'And neither have you.'

'I've got wrinkles now and I dye my hair,' she says self mockingly, but her face is lighting up.

'I never thought I'd ever see you again.'

'And here I am.'

'Yes, you are.'

There is an agonising silence. 'Do you have time for a coffee?'

Elora smiles. 'Yes, I'd like that.'

There is a fluttering in his stomach. 'I know a nice place not far from here.'

They walk the short distance to Contini. In the sun's scrutiny, Brodie thinks his face will show its age. Lately, he has become sensitive to the furrowed lines around his eyes and lips. As they arrive, the waitress escorts them to a small booth. Brodie gestures for Elora to sit first and, as she slides into her seat, her skirt rises above her knees and Brodie can't help but glance at her legs. They order coffees and, as the waiter leaves them, Elora takes in her surroundings and compliments the décor.

'It used to be a bank,' Brodie tells her. 'All the banks on George Street were architecturally quite grandiose. Now they're all restaurants and bars.'

As he settles next to her, he looks at her and he is astonished. He has imagined this moment, never thinking for once it would transpire. Her eyes are a vivid brown, he remembers them well. How could he forget?

'Are you staying in Edinburgh long?'

'I've a meeting with my publisher in London tomorrow and then on Monday I'm going back home. I've spent two weeks in the U.K. promoting my new book, before that I was in Germany and France.'

'It sounds fun.'

'It's work.'

'I suppose so. I didn't think of it like that. And where is home, now?'

'Corfu. I lived in Paris for nearly twenty years, but each time I went back to Corfu to visit family, that feeling of returning home just grew stronger and I knew I had to stay. What about you, where do you live?'

'Here, in Edinburgh. I've never left.'

'And why would you? It's a beautiful city.'

A waiter arrives with their coffee. Brodie takes his cup and drinks from it. The taste is strong and bitter, and he recalls Elora likes strong coffee.

He considers the outline of her face, the curve of her chin and the shape of her lips. When she raises her cup to her mouth, Brodie catches the detail of her hand and he remembers her touch, the soft brushing of her fingers. It sends a charge through him. She is not the woman he knew. She looks similar but older, and now she is a stranger to him as he must be to her.

'Are you married?' she asks, placing her cup on its saucer.

His hesitation surprises him. 'I was. My wife passed away two years ago.'

'Brodie, that's dreadful. I'm so sorry to hear that.'

'She'd been ill for some time. It was a relief in the end.'

He is glad she doesn't enquire further. 'I've got a son, Tom and a daughter, Jessica. They both live in London. Tom's married. What about you?'

'I was married, not now. It wasn't the best decision I ever made. It was a long time ago. We made each other… let's just say, unhappy.'

'Have you any children?'

'No. It just never happened.'

He can hear a spasm of regret in her voice.

He takes a breath. 'I still have a photograph of you. The one I took in The Meadows. One of my biggest regrets is I didn't have a photograph of us together. I know some were taken, but I don't know what happened to them or who had them.'

'I don't have one of you.'

'It's not like today, is it? Things seem so trivial now that I've been told people take photographs of what they had for their dinner and post it on social media for everyone to see. Why would you do such a thing? And who cares what you had for your dinner, anyway?'

'It was different when we were young, when we met.'

He thinks for a moment as if something of importance has just occurred to him. 'I didn't even think of looking to see if you were on social media, I suppose you are?'

'I am. I have to be, really. I have an author page and a personal page on Facebook. And you?'

Brodie shrugs. 'Twitter. Facebook is not for me.'

She smiles at him. 'What did you do after university?'

It is a cautious beginning as they feel their way around each other. There are things he is not prepared to disclose, for now. He must think about this. 'I went through a tough time,' he says slowly. 'But then, I met Heather. I got a job at The Bank of Scotland. It offered financial security, a pension, and we could put a deposit down on a house. What about you? Have you always been an author?'

Elora looks up from her cup and smiles. 'Not always.' She tilts her head and Brodie lets his eyes wander over her face. 'I worked in publishing in Paris, writing seemed like the natural course to take.'

'I can't remember you ever talking about writing. Did you always want to be an author?'

'I've always written. Even as a child, I'd write these little stories that nobody saw, and I kept locked away in a drawer.'

'So, were you still writing stories at university?'

'I'd written my first novel by then.'

'You never told me.'

'I didn't tell anyone.'

'Why not?'

'I was afraid people would think the writing was terrible. I'd never write again if they did so, to continue doing what I loved, I kept it to myself.'

'That obviously changed. I didn't realise your books were so popular.'

'I'm a long way off giving J. K. Rowling a run for her money.'

'But you make a living at it.'

'I do, and a good one, more than I did when I worked in publishing.'

Brodie nods towards Elora's cup. 'Would you like another one, or something stronger, perhaps?'

'No. I'm fine. What about you, what do you do now, Brodie?'

'I'm a free spirit. I took voluntary severance. The bank was offering it, and to tell you the truth, I couldn't refuse. Heather needed me. I didn't have to be asked twice. By then, her health was failing rapidly, and I wanted to spend as much time with her as I could before...' He swallows hard. 'Before there was nothing left of the real Heather.'

She looks at him and his eyes remain fixed on her. 'I can't imagine your pain. You must have loved her so much.'

He draws a breath.

'Do you ever think about that time? I mean, us. Do you remember it, all of it?'

Her question surprises him. He hesitates, but his voice is steady. 'The strangest thing about all of this, meeting you again and being here now, it's... well, it's like the times you wake in the morning and there's a particular song in your head that keeps playing, over and over in a loop and no matter how hard you try it won't stop playing. You have always been on my mind and in my thoughts like that. It's astonishing, I know, but it's the truth.'

This startles Elora. It soaks her in perplexity; his words swivel in her head and she is not expecting such honesty.

'I didn't mean to alarm you, I'm sorry.'

'No. I am. I'm sorry for leaving the way I did. It was unforgivable of me.'

Brodie gives her a half-smile. 'Did you have a choice? It was a long time ago. We were young.'

'Sometimes, I wish I was still that young woman.'

'You do?'

She nods.

'Why?

'Because, now, life has taught me to be cautious, to be reticent, to be restrained, to inhibit my true feelings, to be pensive when getting to know someone. That way, your sensibilities don't get hurt... that kind of thing.'

He doesn't know what to think, what to say next.

She sighs. 'I know I hurt you, and I'm sorry, truly I am.'

'As I said, it was a long time ago.'

She smiles and to his surprise, it is a relief to him.

His stomach is doing acrobatic leaps.

Brodie looks at her and it astonishes him how intricately speckled her brown eyes are. How has he forgotten this detail?

'Do you come here often?'

Brodie looks thoughtful as he meets her eyes. 'Sometimes. The food is excellent, authentically Italian. By that I mean the chefs are Italian.'

Elora smiles. 'I was in London recently and went for dinner at a Greek restaurant recommended to me. I ordered my meal in Greek and the waiter couldn't understand a single word I said.' She laughs. 'It turned out he was Turkish. I couldn't believe it.'

'Do you want to stay and have something to eat?'

Her gaze meets his. 'I can't. I mean, I'd like that, but I must get going soon. I'm expected.'

'More interviews and readings?'

'A meeting, actually.'

'Oh.'

'With my publisher over lunch. So, you see, it's not that I don't want to, but two lunches in one day wouldn't help with the diet.'

'You're on a diet. Whatever for? you've looked after yourself, I can tell. I mean, you look good.'

Elora grinned. 'I wouldn't say that. This is not natural. It takes a lot of self-control and determination. If I don't watch what I eat, I daren't think about how I'd look.'

'Well, I must be delusional because you look good for…'

'A woman of my age?'

'I didn't mean it like that.'

Elora smiles. 'Don't worry. I'll take it as a compliment.'

He looks at her and Elora's expression is serious, and he can't help feeling he has contributed towards it.

'Are you alright?' he says sympathetically.

She shakes her head gently. 'The way things turned out between us has been my biggest regret in life. I'm the one who should take the blame, not you. You must have hated me for what I did. I haven't been able to forget that. Even after all these years it still haunts me.'

He chooses his words carefully. 'If it makes you feel any better, I didn't blame you. I still don't. It was years ago, and it never defined us… what we had together. I remind myself of that all the time.'

'You still do?'

He takes a deep breath. 'I never stopped.'

Elora looks away from him, she doesn't know what to say.

'Earlier, when you spoke about your writing, you seem contented.'

'I suppose I am when I'm talking about my work.'

He feels her gaze on him.

'Are you content with life, Brodie?'

'That depends.'

'On what?'

'On what part of my life you're referring to. My children have made lives for themselves. They both have good jobs, they are financially secure, they have partners, they are loved. So, yes, there is spreading contentment when I think of my children.'

'I detect that this contentment only spreads so far.' She tilts her head as if to say, am I right?'

His eyes fall to her hands, resting on the table. A vague memory of their touch passes over him, like a shifting shadow.

He feels the spike of betrayal. Heather's death brought relief and insufferable pain. Their life together was not always perfect, but he needed her as much as she needed him. Through all their years together, he never once told Heather about Elora and how she constantly lurked on the surface of his consciousness. How could he tell her that for each day they were together, there had been a cavernous echo of Elora's absence in his life? And now, here she is sitting opposite him. It is hard to believe. If he is honest with himself, he never really thought he would see her again. She would be just a memory from his past. And people change, don't they?

He tried; he really tried to leave her in his past. His contemplations urged him to unburden himself from the memories of a time that didn't exist anymore, it was only real in his thoughts and his persistent poring over of their time together.

He often forced himself to contemplate how fortunate he was. When he considers everything, he had a happy life overall: a wife, children, a job, a home. Life was rich, he had his family; it bonded him to their happiness, it moulded his heart around his family. It has all changed. Heather is dead and his son and daughter have their own lives now in London. He no longer feels needed. It's a strange feeling he cannot get used to.

'I actually liked your book.'

'You read it. Oh. I didn't think it would have been your genre.'

'I wanted to. It was good. I really enjoyed it.'

'What did you like about it?'

'It kept building a feeling of suspense. There was always the anticipation that it was moving towards something big, a defining moment.'

'Did you see the end coming?"

'That's another thing I liked, the twists and turns kept me reading. The ending was a surprise.'

Elora sighs in relief. 'I'm glad you like it. It means a lot to me.'

'Really? But why? Why should you care? You've sold a lot of books.'

'That's not the point. I'm never fully aware if my readers like the way I've ended a book.'

'Surely you read the reviews?'

'I used too, but not now.'

'Why not?'

'I haven't been able to develop a thick skin, even after all this time.'

'They can't be all bad, surely?'

'They're not. In fact, the majority are five stars. It's always the ones that aren't complimentary that I remember. Sometimes, I wonder if they even read the books.'

'If they're in the minority, why bother with them?'

Brodie notices a moment of hesitation. 'I know. I can't help it.'

He looks at her, trying to detach the young Elora he once knew from the woman sitting before him.

Her cheeks colour. 'It's sad, I know. What does that say about me? I'm a bestseller, for God's sake.' She permits herself a slight smile.

They talk about their interests, their opinions, their families.

Elora looks at her watch.

'You need to go, now?' Brodie asks.

'I do. I've stayed later than I should have. I need to get going. I'm late.'

Now he has found her again it is unimaginable to let her go.

'Can I see you again?'

'I'm staying at The Kimpton Hotel, it's close by, just around the corner.'

'I know it well.'

'If you have nothing on tonight, I'll meet you in the bar at seven.'

'Even if I did, I'd cancel it. Seven will be fine.'

Elora stands up and collects her handbag. Brodie pushes his chair back and stands beside her. He feels her hand press gently against his arm. 'I'm so glad we met, Brodie.' She leans into him and kisses his cheek. The softness of her lips feels blissful. As she pulls away, he catches the sweet fragrance of her perfume. As he indulges himself in it, he knows it will be a scent that will stay with him until he sees her again.

Back home, Brodie feeds Jasper and inspects the inside of the fridge in search of something to eat. When nothing catches his eye, he decides he's not hungry after all and, instead, makes himself a cup of coffee.

In the living room, he settles on the sofa and reaches for the TV remote but then thinks better of it. All he ever watches these days is the news on Sky, and he isn't ready to hear of the world's troubles at this precise moment. He has other things on his mind.

He was tempted to tell her. He almost did but pulled back. He's relieved about that. She need not know about that time; it was over twenty years ago now. A long time ago. No, she need not know. And anyway, after tonight, he might never see her again. This thought succumbs him to a despondency that takes his breath away. She has slipped under his skin.

He can hear the padding of paws on the kitchen floor and knows that, within a few seconds, Jasper will bark to get out into the garden to do his business.

In the garden, Brodie watches Jasper prowl around, his nose skimming blades of grass, seeking the desired spot. The sun has uncharacteristically escaped the cloud cover as Brodie steps onto the decking and lowers himself into one of the rattan lounge seats he recently bought. Around him, an aromatic trace of jasmine fused with lavender populates the air. The grass dispels a deep green that is interspersed by a stone cladding path that curves towards a bedding of white and red roses and a large oak tree that has grown to dominate and shade the bottom of the garden.

The heaviness of time lifts from his shoulders. There is something lighter within him and immediately a swell of profound contentment washes over him.

Meeting Elora has felt like a wonderful dream, the kind that he doesn't want to wake up from. It has also burdened him with questions. Perhaps it is too late for them? He thinks about this carefully. Too late for what? He has convinced himself he can't let her go. Over the years, he has loved her in her absence; he has never stopped.

There is an uneasiness about him. He has felt it tug at him and it has darkened his exultant mood. Brodie can make sense of it now. After all this time, has it been the young Elora of his past and the memories of her he has been in love with? And now that time no longer binds them, he can be sure of one thing. When he saw her again, it filled him with a rapture that was so unexpected, it confirmed what he has always known, what he has always understood. With immediate clarity, he knows what he must do. It infuses him with expectation.

Chapter 3

Reunion

Wandering the length of Rose Street and after hovering on the steps of the Kimpton hotel, trying not to breathe the bluish-grey haze of a group of smokers, finally, with a deep breath, Brodie pushes open the door and enters the hotel.

He negotiates a path through the reception where a party of Americans are checking in. Brodie hears one of them, a large man with a Southern drawl, describe an unfortunate incident on a previous visit to Edinburgh that ended in a trip to the Accident and Emergency Department of The Royal. In a brash and loud voice, he bemoaned the treatment he received by the medical staff, even though, before this, he had referred to how busy and run off their feet the nurses had been. The receptionist, a young woman, her hair immaculately woven into a perfect bun on her head, offers an apologetic, yet weak smile.

Brodie thinks of the palliative care Heather received and the gratitude he could never adequately express. How could mere words capture the compassion and support of the nursing staff, whose selfless approach made the worst days of his life as bearable as they could be, allowing him to have moments he will always treasure when Heather was lucid and her pain controlled. These thoughts of Heather spear him with guilt and contriteness. In their marriage, Brodie never spoke of Elora, simply because he never told Heather about her. It was a betrayal of their life together and he lived with it every day, then as he does now.

With each word, the American's voice increases in volume and beyond the reception, Brodie's relief is palpable when he catches sight of the bar.

There are only a few people, either hushed in conversation or drinking alone. Brodie is thankful for the quiet ambience and agreeable interior; it means he can talk to Elora without distraction. His throat feels stretched inside him and he is doubtful he will utter a single word of sense.

Brodie glances around. Elora has not yet arrived. He is disappointed and relieved. It is a contradiction that uneases him.

He settles into a chair and is about to take some nuts from a bowl when he stops, for at that precise moment, from the corner of his eye, he can see her.

She is wearing a white blouse, open at the neck and a dark blue skirt that falls to her knees. Her hair waves against her shoulders as she moves into the room. He takes all this in instantaneously. Elora doesn't notice him and as she presses the front of her skirt, Brodie thinks it to be a distraction. She looks just as he feels. Brodie waves his hand and, recognising him with a nervous smile, Elora walks towards his table. Brodie can feel his heart pound in his chest as he stands to greet her. Should he kiss her cheek or gently hug her? The unspoken rules suddenly feel awkward.

'You came.'

He can hear the tangible relief in her voice.

'I had to,' he replies.

She slides into the chair opposite him, an action that dispels Brodie's indecision on how to greet her, replaced by a burdensome sense of regret that he conceals.

'Have you ordered a drink?' Elora asks.

'No. What would you like?'

'A wine. You don't need to go to the bar, the waiter is coming over.'

They order their drinks, a vodka for Brodie and, once again, Elora presses her skirt with the palm of her hand before resting it on her crossed leg.

He's not sure if it is the soft light. It is an odd sensation that comes over him. He has often imagined this. He has pictured it in his mind's eye. Absorbed every detail, the intimacy of it stretching his breath. The feeling is wonderful, seducing, and always, it leaves him spellbound.

'Have you eaten?' Brodie asks.

'I had something earlier and you?'

'I'm fine.'

'Well, this is strange. We haven't seen each other in nearly twenty years, and this is the second time I've seen you today,' Elora says, smiling.

'I know. It feels like this isn't real.' He studies her face.

He can't take his eyes from her face. Even with age, her features are so familiar to him. He had forgotten how her voice sounded, but the moment she spoke, earlier in the day, it was immediately recognisable to him.

'Do you believe we're different now? Has life changed us?'

He takes a moment to consider this. 'Does it matter?'

'I'm not sure.'

'Life has brought us together again. Full circle. Who would have thought it possible? Yet here we are, where it all started. I believe these things happen for a reason.'

'And what would that be?'

'I don't know. Maybe we'll find out. Have you ever wondered what might have happened if things had turned out, well… differently?'

'Do you mean what I think you mean?'

'A life together. I've thought of it often.'

'I'm not easy to live with. So, I'm not so sure. The past should be just that, it has passed. There's nothing we can do about it. There's no point in worrying about it. What good would that do? It's now that matters.'

'Yes. I suppose you're right.'

'I know I am.'

'You seem so sure of yourself. Have you always been like that?'

She takes a moment to consider this. 'Not always. I have my insecurities, you know.'

'We all do.'

'It's what makes us interesting, after all. In life, strange things can happen. It's normal. It's part of the human condition.'

Brodie admires her optimism, although he has always thought of such things as more of a weakness, a curse even.

Their drinks arrive, and they clink each other's glasses.

Elora smiles. 'To unexpected reunions.'

'To us.'

'Yes,' she agrees.

He looks at her over the top of his glass. Would it be a mistake to tell her? He is certain, at this point, it would be. They have just met again. There is so much to say, and yet, so much more he can't say. It makes him ache.

She regards him, her head tilts in a way that Brodie expects a probing question. 'Has life been good to you? Are you happy, Brodie? I sense a sadness about you. Losing your wife. It must have been difficult.'

He shifts in his seat. 'It was and still is… difficult. You know, trying to adjust to being on my own. Sometimes, the house feels so quiet and still, it unnerves me. It felt like emotional grenades struck me every time a place in the house reminded me of her. It took me a long time to let go of her possessions, you know, things like her clothes, brushes that still had her hair in them, her makeup, books, jewellery, although I kept some of her jewellery I just couldn't let go of. These were the things that meant a lot to her, and she was the person who I had shared my life with. It felt like I was taking her life apart, bit by bit, as if she had never existed. I tried to detach myself from it, but how can you hide from emotions, from memories?'

'I can't imagine how difficult that must have been.'

'I often go for a walk into town or I'd probably never see or talk to anyone for days on end. My social circle has shrunk too, mostly it's just Jasper and me these days. I know it's not good for me, but the effort of having to go out of my way and speak to people fills me with dread. I was never like that before. It's weird. I can't explain why I feel this way or how it started. All I know is that, for whatever reason, I get anxious, not a panic attack, but a desire to be on my own. I've often avoided people; it's easier that way. I know it's strange and not like me at all, but there you are. I've said it.'

'Have you tried to get help?'

'The GP! No. All they'll give me is medication and probably a referral for some cognitive behavioural therapy thing. I don't want to talk to a stranger about it. I don't think I could.'

'You're talking to me.'

'That's different.'

'I don't see how it can be. We haven't seen each other for a very long time. I'm almost a stranger to you.'

'Is that what you think? Is that how you see me, as someone you don't know, anymore?'

'I only know what we shared when we were younger. Who you were then? I know nothing of your life from when we left university until now, as you know nothing of mine.'

'I've read about you. I know what you've achieved, what you've done with your life.'

'Those things are just words, printed on paper or a screen. It's like looking at a photograph of someone. It doesn't give you an insight into who that person is, what they think and feel, or the things that are important to them.'

Brodie isn't entirely sure what Elora is trying to say. Does she think by stating that time has made them invisible to each other, they could almost be like pedestrians passing in the street? Is it easier for her to think of him in this way as this would imply there is no longer an emotional attachment, and therefore, less heart rending to say goodbye when that time comes?

Brodie can feel his mood dip. He should feel happy just being with her, and now he realises how fragile such things can be. 'I don't know about you, but I don't want to see a photograph of you. I want to see your face. I want to hear what you think and what you feel. I want to feel a fascination, feel impulsive. I don't want to regret not saying the things that matter. We can make the time, can't we?'

'I don't have that luxury. I only have tonight. I have a schedule that restricts me. Tomorrow I'll be in London. It's work. I wish it could be different, Brodie.'

Brodie's heart pounds. He looks at her intently and then the realisation dawns on him, now that he has found her, this time, he can't lose her, he can't let her go.

'What would life be without complications?' she says, trying to make light of their situation.

'Boring?'

'Precisely,' she assures him. However, despite her smile, he can see the sorrow in her eyes.

Elora swallows. 'It's my grandmother's birthday today. She died years ago. Every birthday since then, no matter where I am, I have always lit a candle for her in a church.'

'That's a special thing to do.'

'Only, today I haven't. I thought I'd have time, but I don't know where the day has gone. It wouldn't feel right not doing it. I need to find a church.'

'Does it have to be an orthodox one?'

She shrugs. 'It hasn't always been. Do you have somewhere in mind?'

'I do. It's only a ten minute walk from here.'

As they head along Alva Street, Elora admires the townhouses. 'I love these buildings. Are they still used as family homes?'

'Some are, but as you can imagine, they're worth a small fortune. Although, I think most are used for business. The Russian embassy is just around the corner.'

'Where do you live, Brodie?'

'Not here, that's for sure. Comely Bank Road. It's in the Stockbridge area. It was where the kids were brought up. It's too big for me now. I don't need three bedrooms anymore.'

Shortly, they turn onto Manor Place, Elora gasps.

St. Mary's, an Episcopal church, is an imposing structure that dominates the evening sky, with spires that can be seen across the River Forth and into Fife.

'You remember?'

She smiles. 'I do.'

'Jessica's wedding.'

'It was a glorious day and what a magnificent church to get married in. I'm so glad you brought me here.'

'I'll wait outside the church.'

'Do you have an aversion to churches?' Elora says with a vague smile.

'No. I just thought you might like to be alone.'

She holds out her hand. It is shaking. 'I'd like you to come with me.'

He holds her hand. Her skin is soft, her fingers warm as they wrap around him. Such closeness feels miraculous. His heart jumps in his chest as the weight of a lifetime dissipates before him.

The candle flickers like a miniature lantern as Elora secures its base into the fine layer of sand. She crosses herself three times as is the orthodox manner and, head bowed, whispers a prayer.

Brodie stands a respectable distance and waits until she is finished.

'Thank you for bringing me here. It means a lot.'

'I can see that. The last time we were here, we were so young, although it didn't feel like it at the time. We thought we could do anything we wanted to. Our naivety shielded us from life's intrusions. Life was simple then.'

'And here we are, older, maybe not always wiser, but we've lived, we've loved, made mistakes, had careers, you have your children and me, well… I have memories and each day; I make new ones. It doesn't matter what we've done in life, what counts is who we are, what we've become.'

Brodie grins.

'What?'

'I still can't believe you're here. I know it's a cliché, but I feel like I'm dreaming.'

'We're both having the same dream then.'

'I don't want to wake up.'

A couple enters the church and Brodie glances sideways in their direction. There is a stilted exchange of pleasantries.

'The church is bigger than I remember. I can't recall it being so spacious.' Elora tilts her head and takes in the vast ceiling.

'There were a lot of people in here that day. The wedding was a big affair. Two of Edinburgh's most important families coming together. It was…'

'Lavish,' Elora says. 'I'd never seen a wedding reception like it.'

'I wonder if they're still married?'

'Did you keep in touch with everyone once we'd all left university?'

'Not really. You know how it is. Did you?' He feels a deep twinge in his chest and a rise in his throat. He pushes it back. It's a question he wishes he could retract; it incites an impending feeling of fear. A menacing possibility that her answer could bring. He can feel his cheeks burn. What if she already knows? Would it change them? Would she think differently of him? At least he could unburden himself from keeping *it* from her. Elora cocks her head. He swallows, his throat dry and tight.

'No… I…' Elora considers and then says, frankly, 'When I left Edinburgh, it was… it was difficult. It confused me. I was hurting. I made a mess of everything. I've lived with regret ever since that night. What I did, well… It was wrong of me. I betrayed you. I shouldn't have gone back to Greece without seeing you first. What I did was unforgivable. I'm sorry, Brodie. You must have hated me?'

He takes a breath. His relief is tangible. 'We were young. What did we know about these things?'

She seems to consider this. 'Oh, I knew. I knew what I was doing.'

They gazed at each other for a moment.

'It was a long time ago, Elora. You can't feel responsible for what happened between us. Not now. And anyway, look at us, a lot has happened since then.' He doesn't tell her more than that. As they walk along Charlotte Square towards the hotel, Brodie looks at her.

'What is it?' Elora asks.

'Now that I've seen you, I'm not ready to let you go.' Brodie remembers the last time she left him. It seems another world, another life. He furrows his brow. Not seeing Elora ever again troubles him greatly. Nothing is obvious, no answer, no option offers itself.

'What time do you leave tomorrow?' Brodie asks.

'My flight's at one.'

They fall silent.

As they cross the street, Brodie muses over the obstacles in front of him. He looks at her intently and he can see she too is contemplating a decision.

'I need a drink. We can go to the hotel bar. It's still early. That is… if you want to?'

He smiles. 'Only if you let me pay?'

She returns the smile. 'I've no choice then.'

Elora reapplies her lipstick as the waiter sets their drinks on the table. Brodie watches her outline the curve of her lips and, not for the first time that night, he feels the rush of wanting to kiss her. He raises his glass to his mouth, a distraction he hopes will quench such thoughts, for the moment, at least.

'I know nothing of your life.'

'What would you like to know?'

'Everything.'

She smiles. 'I don't think we've got time for that.'

'What happened after you left Edinburgh?'

She speaks about struggling with her course, falling behind with her studies. The ending of their relationship and the frailty of her mind and her long absence from her family had become too much to bear.

'I fell apart. I lost my mind.'

'I never knew it was that bad.'

'No one did. I became quite an expert at hiding what I was really feeling. You can mask a lot with just a smile and laughter. Once I was home, I felt a protective warmth. It felt like a warm blanket wrapped around me. I felt cared for. I felt for the first time in months I was secure. I was happy doing very little; just breathing the scented air and feeling the sun on my face lifted my mood. It helped to have my family around me once more. I didn't realise how much I'd missed them.'

'Earlier tonight you mentioned you lived in Paris.'

'When I left Edinburgh, the one thing I did when I went back to Corfu was I continued to write. I let one of my friends read what I had written, and she encouraged me to send it to publishers. I didn't of course, not for a long time.'

'But you did?'

'Eventually. What I was doing was using my writing to put a plaster over something else.'

'What was that?'

'You. I was still hurting. I suppose, deep down, I knew I'd made a terrible mistake.' She taps her fingertips together; he remembers she used to do this when overwrought with deliberating. She shakes her head slowly and rubs the back of her head.

'Are you all right?' Brodie asks.

'Just a dull pain in my head. I've got some tablets in my bag.'

'I'll get you water.' Brodie says and slides from his chair and crosses the room towards the bar.

When he returns, Elora is speaking in Greek to someone on her mobile phone. Brodie places a glass on the table and Elora mouths a thank you.

A moment later, she places the mobile in her handbag, takes a pill and swallows it with the water. Brodie watches her, the elegant jaw, the movement of her throat, the curve of her head. He could never forget her and knowing now that she, too, had felt something, makes his thoughts churn with expectation.

'So, obviously, you sent your book to publishers.'

She smiles. 'Obviously, I did. Lots of publishers. I could have decorated the walls of my parents' house with the rejections I received.'

'That must have been disheartening.'

'It was.'

'So, what happened?'

'I'd almost given up. I'd stopped approaching publishers when I received an email from a publisher asking for the full manuscript and, as they say, the rest is history.'

'That must have been a brilliant feeling?'

'It was.'

'So, how did you end up in Paris?'

'I initially went there to do some research on a book I was writing. I fell in love with it. By then, both my parents had passed away. Nothing was keeping me in Corfu, so I made Paris my home.'

'Is that where you met your husband?'

She nods an acknowledgement.

'You haven't told me his name.'

'I haven't?'

'No.'

'Rafal.'

'He was French, then?'

'Belgian, actually.'

'What did he do'

'He was a partner in a law firm. He spent most of his time working, even when he came home. To compensate, I became obsessive about my writing. I needed to be dedicated to it. I am where I am in publishing today because of it, although it cost me my marriage.'

'How long were you married?'

'Nearly five years. For two of those, our marriage hung like a thread. Twenty-five is a silver wedding anniversary and of course, fifty is gold, do you know what a fifth wedding anniversary is?'

'No.'

'Wood. Which was quite ironic. You see, Rafal was having an affair with one of his clients, very unprofessional of him. Anyway, this client had made a fortune when she sold her company. Guess what her company was?'

Brodie shrugs. 'I don't know.'

'It specialised in wooden furniture. Wood! The coincidence never struck me until the very day that would have been our fifth wedding anniversary. I don't think I ever loved him, not really.'

Brodie leans forward. 'You've lived in my head, most of my life.'

Brodie is not sure if it is the words he has said or the way he imparted them, but something has changed in Elora.

'You were always with me,' she replies.

Brodie reaches over the table and takes her hand. When he feels her skin, every cell in his body tingles.

'Are you sure this is what you want?'

'I think I've been waiting for you. I've been waiting for this, ever since…'

He places his finger on her lips. 'Let's not talk about the past anymore, not here, not now.'

'What now?' Elora asks.

'If this was a novel, then this would be the part where you'd invite me to your room.'

'I'd never let my female characters get motivated by sex in such a way.'

Brodie laughs. Then he says seriously, 'I should get back. Jasper has been on his own all night. He could have been up to anything.'

She looks at him. 'Jasper?'

'My dog.'

'Oh. I see. You should go then.'

He can hear the disappointment in her voice. He doesn't want to go. He doesn't want her to go, but he knows she will. If he could, he would suspend time and never leave her. He tries to muster a smile. 'I'll come back in the morning. I've heard they do an impressive English. It would be a shame not to try one.'

As his mind claws towards the inevitable, a chill runs through him. He takes a breath. 'Will we see each other tomorrow before you leave? I mean… if that's what you want?'

Her eyes find his eyes, and she takes a moment to consider this. It is a pause that finds his mood wavers between happiness and despair.

'It is.' Elora assures him.

Chapter 4

Decisions

It was only temporary. There is no other way to refrain it. He realises, in the weeks and months to come, the intimacy and desire he shared with Elora will be a cruel and ceaseless reminder of her absence in his life.

He has tried not to make a comparison between Heather and Elora. He has always been disconcertingly familiar with how they both parallel his life.

If there is one connection that is indispensable, it is he has genuinely loved them both. They have defined his life, both for different reasons. He feels relief and he is grateful for that.

Elora is a contradiction to him. She used to glow unflinching confidence, self-assured and effervescent energy, but now, that prodigious and visceral intensity has waned with age, replaced by languorous intelligence that reveals another Elora. She is an accomplished author whose reputation seems to know no limits. As a woman, Elora undermines this image. She is poised and self-contained, yet fragile in her confidence, self-conscious about her looks, scared to venture outside her comfort zone.

He wonders what she is doing now. What is she thinking? What is she feeling? Does he cross her mind? Does she think of that night? Is the silence between them the passage of her regret?

He feels trapped between what he has and does not want and what he wants but does not have.

Elora returned to Greece. They swapped phone numbers and promised to keep in touch. She has returned to the life she had before their impromptu meeting, before that night, where now, the images and memories seem surreal to him.

Edinburgh 1995

S'agapo

'What do you think of the band?' Brodie asked, leaning close to her ear.

'They're good, I like them, but it's loud and hot.'

'Do you want to go upstairs and get a drink?'

Elora nodded and they weaved their way through the crowd, trying not to knock into hands clutching drinks, and simultaneously avoiding the vigorous dancing of drunk and spirited students.

They ascended a widening stairwell flanked on each side by posters of bands that had played in Négociants, a student bar and cafe popular amongst students in Lothian Street, Edinburgh. Once they secured their drinks, they sat outside at a small table and enjoyed the evening summer air.

This had become their favoured place for snatched evenings and weekends. During the day, in between tutorials and lectures, they often drank a coffee and ate cake, people watching, seeing in a language of images.

Elora wound her hair around a finger with an enigmatic smile on her face.

'What is it?' Brodie asked, lighting a cigarette.

She continued to smile, and for a moment, Brodie felt uneasy, concerned even. *Is she pregnant? No. She wouldn't be smiling, but maybe she would. She had always said she wanted babies.* He looked at her with intense dread, as if he were standing on a cliff edge, wavering.

'What is it, Elora?' he repeated, this time a little wary and a little anxious.

She's pregnant, I know she is. The phrase kept singing through his head.

'I think we should move in together. Celia is moving out next week; she's moving back to her parents. What do you think? The rent would be a lot less than what you're paying now.'

Brodie felt a rush of intense relief.

'Well, say something,' she prompted.

'It's a great idea.'

She leaned over the table and kissed him. 'Are you sure? I don't want to pressure you.'

'Do I look pressured?'

She studied him and flicked a strand of hair from her face, sending copious amounts shivering down her back.

'Mmm…' Elora took her time to respond. 'I'm undecided.' She smiled at him and her nose creased.

Brodie sat back and folded his arms across his chest.

'Really?'

'What do you think your mum will say?'

'She'll tell me it's ungodly and a man and woman should be married in the eyes of God before they can even hold hands.' He laughed at this exaggeration.

'I'm serious, Brodie. You know how she is.'

'She'll just have to get used to it, that's all. We're adults and we're not living in Victorian times.'

'She will just hate me even more if that is possible.'

'She doesn't hate you, Elora.'

'Well, you know what I mean. She'd much prefer if I was a polite middle-class Edinburgh girl. Remember when we first met, I knew what she thought of me even then. She called Greeks lazy and tax dodgers. I remember her saying, if it wasn't for tourism, Greece would be a third world country.'

'Did she say that? I can't remember, although it sounds like her.'

'She did, and she said it with a smile on her face.'

'You mean you caught her smiling.' There was humour in his voice and his wry smile toppled Elora's defences.

'Just once.' Elora rolled her eyes. 'Why does she have that effect on me, like I'm never going to be good enough?'

'Don't take it personally. Look at my dad, he hasn't. They've been together twenty-five years. She'll never change, it's just who she is.'

'Well, I don't want to be in the same room when you tell her.' She gave a half-smile.

Suddenly, he felt galvanised. 'Well, she'll just have to get used to it.'

'So, it's a good idea?'

'It's not like I haven't stayed with you before, only this time, it will be longer than just a weekend, and just the two of us.'

'There's one more thing. I've been waiting for the right moment.'

'What is it?'

Elora leaned over the table, and found his mouth, and whispered, 'S'agapo.' (I love you).

Chapter 5

Setting His Mind

That Saturday, Brodie wakes, showers and changes into chinos and a shirt. Downstairs, he makes breakfast: toast with banana and coffee. While eating, he can see the sun splay across the bottom of the garden in silky light. He takes in a prolonged, deep breath and lets it out slowly.

He glances at the screen of the mobile phone humming on the table surface. It must have switched to silent; he's always inadvertently nudging the tiny silver switch. How many calls has he missed because of it?

He reaches over and snatches it. 'Hello, Tom. Everything all right?'

'Hi, Dad. We've just landed. We've just got hand luggage, so we won't be too long.'

'I could have picked you up, it would have been no trouble.'

'It's fine, honest. Anyway, Lisa wants to ride on the tram. She's never been on one before, so it's a bit of a novelty. I hope you haven't gone to any trouble, not like the last time I was up. Remember, we're taking you out for lunch this time.'

'Yep, I know. Just clean sheets and towels in your room, that's all.'

'Good.'

'How was your flight?'

'It was fine. It was great to see the new Queensferry Crossing Bridge from the air as we passed over the Forth.'

'You got a good day for it.'

'We certainly did.'

'Seemingly, it's still not cured the traffic congestion. The road bridge is only open to buses and taxis, seems a waste of an iconic bridge if you ask me. Anyway, I'll see you soon. Say hello to Lisa for me.'

'I will. Bye, Dad.'

He finishes the last of his coffee and deposits the cup and plate into the dishwasher. As he straightens himself, his eyes shift towards the garden. He should have cut the grass, and then he remembers, he gave Tom pocket money for mowing the lawn when he was, how old would Tom have been? About fifteen or sixteen. It scares him now, how time slips by so quickly, so effortlessly.

And then, he remembers Heather had always insisted, even when she was suffering her worst, it was better to embrace the business of living rather than worrying about it. He can still hear her humour and see her wry smile.

It wasn't cancer that dimmed the light in her eyes; it was the chemotherapy and its aftermath. Every day he watched her slip from him, the colour fading a little more from his life. Even now, he can't forget that feeling of being so helpless and utterly consumed by emptiness.

He has just got enough time to take Jasper for a short walk. It amazes him how Jasper seems to be telepathic because as he steps into the kitchen, Jasper is staring at the lead hanging from a hook.

'That's right, Jasper. Time for your walk.'

He has frequently tolerated loneliness. It arrives on any day of the week, at any time of day. Is it possible to be angry with Heather? He feels aggrievement when the darkness falls around him, engulfing him like fog. How can he be angry with her when she is not here, when it is not her fault? But that's just it, he needs someone or something to blame.

She left him and he can't imagine how that must have felt, knowing she was dying, knowing she would never see those that were close to her and those that she loved. She kept those feelings from him. Was she trying to protect him? He will never know now.

Heather wanted to make sure she had planned for and prepared for her death. She organised her funeral to the smallest detail, considering every possible scenario.

There was to be no money spent on flowers, there were enough of them in her garden, she had joked. Instead, people were asked to donate to a charity of their choice. She wrote her eulogy, and even the most hardened of mourners wiped tears from their eyes.

In the early days, after Heather died, Brodie wished there had been a grave he could visit, where he could speak to her, be close to her, share his thoughts and worries.

This presumed Heather had left him for somewhere else, somewhere better, a place some people called heaven, but he knew she had not.

And anyway, what if he could have stood by her graveside, what purpose would it have served? Self-gratification? Would it have soothed away his loneliness, just for a while?

Just as there was no Heather, there was also no grave or headstone with words of endearment carved in marble.

Heather wanted her ashes scattered in a corner of the garden by the stone wall. Brodie planted a rosebush on the same spot. He had the crazy idea that Heather would help it grow, after all, she loved gardening; it was her passion.

And now, the rosebush has colonised the stone wall and, in the summer, its colour is breath-taking and, in this, Brodie finds comfort and joy.

On their return from the walk, Brodie towel dries Jasper who took great pleasure, as dogs do, in rolling in the only solitary puddle in the park.

Once Jasper is dried and fed, Brodie fills the kettle and pulls three mugs from the cupboard, lining them up on the worktop. He is looking forward to Tom and Lisa's visit. It's been a while since he has seen them, and he was glad when Tom phoned to ask if they could visit and stay for a few days.

He hears the front door open and then the unmistakable tone of Tom's voice, 'Hello, Dad, it's just us.'

'I'm in the kitchen. The kettles' on.'

'Great. I could murder a cuppa.'

As they enter the kitchen, Tom drops their bags at his feet and hugs Brodie, who then leans over and kisses Lisa on the cheek. 'I've got your favourite biscuits, *Oreo*. Sit down, I'll pour some tea.'

Once they've settled into their seats, Brodie asks, 'Did you enjoy the tram ride?'

Lisa smiles. 'I did. It beats taking a taxi any day. I thought they were meant to go all the way to Leith?'

'They were. That was the plan, anyway. They ran out of money, but I think that's still the intention.'

'Where's Jasper?' Tom asks.

'In the garden, we're just back from a walk.' Brodie gestures towards the biscuits. 'Have a biscuit.'

Tom takes one and bites it in half. 'Oh, these are good.'

'Aren't you having one?' Brodie asks Lisa.

Lisa shakes her head. 'I'm watching my weight. I've put a bit on recently.'

'If you say so,' Brodie says doubtfully, 'but, Lisa, there's nothing of you,' he adds, taking a biscuit for himself.

'How are things going, Dad?' Tom interrupts.

'Fine.'

'What have you been up to, anything interesting?'

'Not really.' Brodie wonders if he sounds convincing. 'Just the usual.'

'And what's that these days?'

Brodie rubs his brow. 'Oh, you know. Walking Jasper, the odd round of golf. Not much, really.'

Tom laughs. 'You're embracing middle-age with ease. It's all downhill from now on.'

For once, Brodie doesn't mind the association, it plays to his advantage. He pulls a face. 'It comes to us all, remember.'

Tom shrugs. 'But I've got time on my side.'

Lisa winks at Tom, who clears his throat. 'Dad, Lisa and I have something to tell you.'

'Ah, and here was I thinking, you're visiting because you've missed me.' Another thought enters his head. 'I hope it's not bad news. Is everything all right, Tom?'

'No. It's not. It's quite the opposite.'

'Well then, don't keep me in suspense.'

Tom takes Lisa's hand. They are both grinning.

'I think I can guess.'

'You're going to be a grandad.'

'At forty-five years old!'

'I know and we're sorry about that, but there's not much we can do about it now.'

'No, there's not. Come here, both of you. I'm so pleased for you both.' Brodie kisses Lisa on the cheek and asks, 'How many weeks are you?'

'Twelve. We wanted to make sure everything was all right before we made it public,' Lisa says.

'Of course, that's sensible. Does anyone else know?'

'Just my mum and dad.'

He embraces Tom. Both know they are thinking the same thing.

'Mum would have been so happy.'

'I know. She would be popping the bubbly by now.'

'I think of her every day.' Tom's words course through Brodie to his core.

'I'm sure she knows.'

'I thought you didn't believe in all that stuff, life after death?'

'It's at times like this that I'd love to be wrong.'

Tom studies his father. 'Is everything all right, Dad?' His face falling into a puzzled frown.

'Of course,' Brodie responds. 'You've just told me the most wonderful news. It's just… well, it's times like this, I wish I could have shared with your mum.'

Tom embraces him. 'I know Dad. I know.'

Lisa looks uncomfortable and smiles sympathetically, her only contribution to the conversation. Although there is some truth to Brodie's words, he knows now he can't tell Tom of his feelings for Elora or even of her existence.

'I booked a table for one o'clock, I hope that's not too early for you?' Tom says to change the mood.

'That'll do just fine. We've got something to celebrate now, maybe I'll buy some bubbly.'

'That would be nice, and Mum would approve.'

'I'm sure she would.'

They are sitting in Gaucho, just off St. Andrews Square. The Saturday lunch crowd make it noisier than Brodie would like. It's Tom's treat, so he grins and bears it.

'Do you know if the baby's a boy or a girl?'

'No. We decided against it. Although it was tempting,' Lisa says.

'A good choice. I'm not sure if I agree with the whole knowing what sex it is and telling everyone.'

'Oh. And why is that?' Lisa asks.

'I suppose it's because… it's tempting fate, maybe. It's things like that, I suppose.' Brodie shifts in his seat. 'You really don't know, do you?' He looks at them worriedly.

Lisa is smiling. 'We don't,' she assures him.

'Oh, good. For a second, I thought I might have put my foot in it. Have you decided on names?'

'We may have.' Lisa says guardedly.

'But you're not going to tell.'

'Correct.' Tom adds.

'Oh well. It was worth a try,' Brodie says as he spears a floret of broccoli.

'Will you still manage to get away this year?'

'Luckily, we hadn't book anywhere abroad. We were thinking about Portugal when Lisa found out she was pregnant, so instead, we've booked a little cottage in the Lake District for a week.'

'Sounds lovely.'

'You're welcome to visit and stay a few days if you want Dad.'

'No. I wouldn't dream of it. It'll be the last holiday you'll have that is just for the two of you. Once the baby arrives, life changes.'

'We don't mind, do we Lisa?'

'Not at all. We don't get to see a lot of you now we're in London.'

'Thanks for the offer, but honestly, I'd much prefer you enjoyed your holiday on your own.'

'Well, the offer will still be there if you do change your mind,' Tom points out.

'I'm sure I won't, but thanks anyway.'

'You haven't been away anywhere since Mum… since you've been on your own.'

'No. I haven't.'

'What's stopping you, dad?'

'I'm not sure Jasper would cope with going into a kennel.'

'He'd be fine. He's a dog. As long as he could go out on a walk every day and eat, he'd be happy.'

'You're probably right. It's just the thought of it, I suppose. It's funny, you should ask, as I've been pondering going to Greece.'

This impresses Lisa. 'Greece. That's great.'

'Yes. Once I get over the kennel thing.'

Lisa smiles with enthusiasm. 'What made you think about Greece?'

He takes a moment to consider this.

Tom's eyebrows rise. 'Would you be going on your own?'

'I see where this is going. Definitely on my own.'

'Will you be okay?' Tom eyes him warily and then adds. 'You haven't been away anywhere on your own, not on holiday, anyway.'

'Thank you for the vote of confidence.'

'I think it's a great idea, Brodie,' Lisa counters. 'Where in Greece are you thinking of going?'

'I thought Corfu would be nice.'

Tom stirs food around his plate. 'And when are you thinking about going?'

'My passport is still in date, so the sooner the better, I suppose.'

'I'd love to feel the warm Greek sun, especially on an island. Lucky you, Brodie.'

'Well, I'm glad someone is pleased for me.' Brodie points out.

Tom's eyes narrow. 'I am, Dad, it's just, you said nothing about it, that's all. It came as a surprise.'

'Well, I'm telling you now.'

'What about, you know, what if…'

'I can't wrap myself up in cotton wool, Tom.'

'Look, dad. If it makes you happy, then I'm happy for you. Okay,'

'Anyway, I still need to check out flights and find somewhere where to stay.'

'If you can go anytime, you have a better chance of getting a good deal,' Lisa advises.

'I'm not doing a package holiday. I'm thinking of staying in an Airbnb.'

'How long are you going for, a week?' Tom asks.

'A few at least. I know it's short notice, so I might be struggling. I've seen a few options online that I like the look of, but I've not enquired about their availability yet.'

'You'll struggle to get Jasper into a kennel at such short notice,' Tom says.

There's a momentary silence, and then Lisa says, 'There are lots of people who have started businesses looking after dogs, you won't have trouble. In fact, my sister knows someone. They live in her street. Wait a sec.' She looks at her mobile and begins to type. 'Here we are. There's someone in your area that does it to. We can give them a phone if you like.'

'Oh! I'm not sure.' Brodie is unconvinced.

'I'll write down their number and you can give them a call when you like, there's a website as well.'

'I'd much prefer if Jasper was staying in someone's home with people for company rather than staying in a kennel. You hear some dreadful stories.'

'Rumours, more like. You can't tar every kennel with the same brush. That's undeserved.' Tom says adamantly.

'Still, I'm not comfortable with it. I was thinking of asking Hana. Jasper knows her, and she's very fond of him.'

Lisa has written the phone number, and she hands it to Brodie. 'Well, take this just in case you change your mind. Have you been to Greece before?' she asks.

'No. I haven't. If I get Jasper organised, I think I'll enjoy it.'

Lisa smiles. 'What would there not be to enjoy?'

Brodie can feel Tom's eyes on him, and he knows Tom doesn't share Lisa's enthusiasm.

Brodie has been wondering how to explain his sudden interest in Greece, and, although he has been apprehensive about telling them his real motive, deep inside, Brodie feels something ease, as if his apprehension has slipped from the dark folds of his thoughts and moved through another doorway. It is a relief. Lisa is right, he reassures himself. He will go to Greece, with the frame of mind it will be an experience he will enjoy. He will not reveal her name to them, even though it is forever on his lips. It sets his mind.

Chapter 6

Hana's Counsel

'I think you would make a wonderful grandad.'

'You do?'

'Yeah. Grandad material for sure.'

Brodie frowns. 'I'm not sure I'd put it that way.'

'You'd have to go down to London a lot more, it wouldn't be fair expecting Tom and Lisa to travel with a baby.' Hana stubs out her cigarette into the ashtray she has brought with her into the garden.

'What makes you think I would?'

'You're not exactly the visiting type.'

'I visit them.'

'Tom has been up here more than you've been down to London.'

'Heather and I went often.'

'Exactly my point.'

'That's unfair.'

'Talking of going places, Corfu! You're going to do this?'

'Does that surprise you?'

'Mm... I'm not sure. I think it's something you should do. You've carried this around with you for so long. You've now been given an opportunity out of the blue. Jesus, Brodie. You'd be crazy to pass it up. You don't want it to turn into poison.'

'I'm worried.'

'About?'

'How I'd cope if this all goes wrong. There's a lot of years between us and things that need to be said.'

'You haven't told her?'

Brodie hesitates. 'No. I wanted to tell her. We had so little time together. I wasn't prepared to jeopardise that. Do you think that was a mistake?'

Hana shrugs. 'Possibly. It's too late now. Will you tell her?'

'We can't move forward if I don't. Anyway, it wouldn't feel right. I've waited a long time for this. I want Elora to know everything, but the moment has to be right.'

'And when's your flight?'

'One o'clock tomorrow.'

'Well then, I hope it goes well for you, Brodie. I really do.'

'Thanks, Hana. That means a lot.'

'Just promise me one thing.'

'What's that?'

'If it all goes tits up, for fuck's sake, get on with the rest of your life and forget her. Okay?'

'Straight to the point, as usual.'

'I don't know any other way. You should know that by now. I won't give you pretty compliments and tell you what you want to hear, I'll tell you how it is. That might not make me the most popular person to be around, but I am who I am.'

Brodie smiles. 'And that's why we've been friends all these years. I wouldn't have you any other way.'

'You'll need to give me Jasper's bowl and lead. Don't worry about his food, I'll buy that.'

'You're a lifesaver, Hana, I don't know what I'd have done without you these past few years.'

'Don't get all sentimental on me now.'

'Afraid I'll crack your hard exterior? I know how soft it is on the inside.'

She smiles. 'If you know what is good for you, you'll keep that to yourself.'

'Scouts honour.' He salutes her.

'You were never in the Scouts.'

'I was… for a few weeks. I hated learning to tie those bloody knots. If there was a form of dyslexia for knot tying, I had it.'

Hana shakes her head 'So, you're all packed and ready to go?'

'Nearly. I've just got a few things still to pack.'

'You should make a list. That way, you won't forget anything. And put your passport at the top of the list.'

'Heather used to do all the packing, you know. All I had to do was turn up.'

Hana squeezes his hand and with a smile says affectionately, 'You're a big boy now.' Without saying another word, she kisses him on the cheek. 'Taking everything into consideration, I'd say, if you didn't do this, you'd become pretty fucked up.'

'I might already be.'

He thinks about the short time he and Elora have had together, and the memories it has left him with, it is entirely possible, he realises, they might be all he ends up with.

Chapter 7

*An Unexpected Appearance in Corfu and Other
Curiosities*

Brodie has never been to Greece; this is his first time. He
has visited France, Spain and even Italy over the years with
Heather, but never Greece. It was not as if Heather didn't
want to go; it was Brodie who was reluctant, blaming the
plumbing and anything else he could think of. These were
not the real reason, Elora was. It would have been
unthinkable. He knew the chances of seeing her were
negligible, that was not the issue. His reluctance was born
out of the certainty that Elora would be ever-present, in his
thoughts and conscience. The guilt he still feels hammers in
his head.

   He should have agreed to go, he knew he should. Heather
said nothing, and Brodie has always wondered if she ever
suspected something. Even now, as he sits at a table outside
the Mikro café on Themistokleous Kotardou in Corfu
Town, nursing a dark coffee accompanied by a glass of
water and a small cheese and prosciutto plate, the thought
knots his stomach.

   He has rented an apartment just around the corner; it is
small, but clean, with a kitchen and air conditioning. This is
his second day, and he is learning the geography of the
narrow lanes and streets of the old town. Tomorrow, he has
decided, he will venture further.

   Around Brodie, tables draw his attention, filling with
young people, chatting and laughing; others looking serious
as they stare at their mobile phones, oblivious to the world
around them.

   Brodie drinks the last of his coffee. What is it he is
looking for? When he reminisces about their time in
Edinburgh, their night together, the last time he saw Elora,

his lungs ache, like he is holding his breath underwater. He wonders what she thought when she disappeared from his life for a second time.

He had to do something. Their encounter was so unexpected and inexplicable. Has Elora not grasped what it has meant to him? He cannot accept that. They were both infused with a feeling that he has difficulty putting a name to, but which has never left him.

The silence between them has been suffocating for him. In Elora's defence, it must have been a shock to see him after all these years, but he is sure he has convinced her of his feelings. He has thought carefully about this, as he has about coming here. He is painfully aware Elora's silence maybe her way of dealing with this, and being in Corfu may exacerbate the situation. It is a kind of madness, but one he is prepared to go through with. He has alternated between spells of despair and happiness. He arrived under his own dark cloud. Now that he is here, he has swept aside his doubt. A profound contentment has settled over him, a burst of certainty that he is doing what feels right. He must see her again.

He spends the evening wandering the labyrinth of lanes and squares, with a guidebook in hand, learning and familiarizing himself with the geography and buildings around him. Underfoot, stone slabs are smooth and burnished, almost polished in appearance. Sometimes, he is fortunate to glimpse the inside of a door, and once, a dark interior where white lace draped a table and an old couple sat sipping coffee, listening to a radio; on an otherwise impoverished wall, an icon of Christ looked divinely upon them. He cranes his neck to view small courtyards with blossoming flowers and miniature fountains. He thinks of these discoveries as wondrous, as petite gardens, secrets that can be discovered but not always seen.

Above him, timeworn and terraced Venetian facades lean into one another, with peeling masonry, sun-bleached shutters and a slice of the sky. His eye is drawn to each shopfront, café and bar. Around every corner, he meets another flavour, other characters, from the pristine to the ramshackle, to the grandiose and slight. It surrounds him with gratifying and complementary contradictions, from the modern and cosmopolitan to the historical and ruinous. Never far, the sight of the sea and ancient walls, where stone seeps with the history of conquerors and empires, dictators and ideology, all long faded, but if he tries hard enough, Brodie can sense them in the air and in the stone around him.

That night, he eats under a canopy of stars and the twinkling yellow light of candles. The food is delicious, along with the accompanying bottle of wine the waiter has recommended. It is a flicker of joy.

As he wanders back to his apartment, the magnitude of his decision to come to Corfu and find Elora sinks into him. It is the effect of the wine or the feelings he is experiencing that find him questioning the rationale of what he is about to do.

The memory of their time together in Edinburgh is like switching on a light in his mind; the clarity has never left him. The visual, the sensual and the intimacy is everything to him. He wants to absorb every word, every sentence she speaks, every look and gaze, every smile and gesture; nothing less will satisfy him.

Is she waiting for him?

He feels a rush of panic.

Is the silence her intent?

His heart pounds at this thought. It would be easier to leave.

Why am I here at all?

What should I reveal and what should I conceal?

Do I fear rejection and the possibility of being rejected and the embarrassment that would follow?

Have I just been romanticising our time together?

Is that all life has ever been… self-deception?

He wonders if it will be possible for them to forgive the betrayals and deceptions. As a thought, it seems so simple, but he knows he can't move forward until they have faced these complications.

She will have questions, as he does too. How will he answer them? With honesty. He can't ever imagine lying to her. He can't predict, with any accuracy, if she will feel the same.

He feels it then, the realisation that Elora has made time fold in on itself. She makes him happy. It is as simple as that. And, to his relief, he smiles to himself. It is a new dimension. She makes it possible that life can become a beautiful thing again.

He realises he struggles to remember ever telling Heather she was beautiful, even though, he knows he did. It is like a blow to his abdomen.

He loved Heather and she loved him. He knows he did not love her like this. This has always been different. He is glad he never told Heather. It would have been a violation; the cruellest sacrilege and he could never have done that to her. It would have been unforgivable.

To Brodie's disbelief, the flow of water suddenly reduces to a cold and painstaking trickle. He sighs. How is he supposed to wash? What kind of plumbing is this? It feels like a biblical drought has descended upon him. Then, just as he is about to fiddle with the showerhead, with a spurt and a whoosh, the shower bursts into life. 'Ouch! Too hot!' Adjusting the temperature and satisfied he is safe from another scalding, Brodie applies a generous amount of lather onto a sponge and hastily washes and rinses the soap from his body before an additional scarcity of water threatens to try his nerves.

That morning when Brodie is eating breakfast, to prepare himself for the visit to meet with Elora, he considers possible strategies and tries to play out the options in his head.

How will he explain his sudden appearance? How should he react if Elora finds his presence an intrusion and refuses to see him? He finds this scenario ridiculous. He needs to tackle all possibilities. However, he is sure this will not be an eventuality. Even so, he must give it due consideration. There would have to be a compromise, a meeting on neutral ground. He stops. Beyond this, there is a resistance to probe further. Some things are complex by nature. 'We can make sense of this. It will be alright,' he thinks out loud, assuring himself.

Something else is troubling him. He feels a surge of guilt as he aimlessly stirs his breakfast around its plate. He drops his fork onto the plate, *Jasper will be wondering where I've gone. He'll think he's done something wrong. Even worse, he'll think he's being punished.* Brodie remembers reading that dogs can feel these things. He hopes Jasper is not sad. Brodie knows he is humanising an animal, but he can't help it; his heart is soft when it comes to his dog. He has heard stories of dogs shunning their owners for days after a separation. He has never left Jasper before. Since he was a puppy, they have spent every day together. Jasper is such a timid creature; he needs human company. Brodie hopes Jasper is resilient. He thinks of phoning Hana, just to put his mind at ease, to make sure Jasper has settled. But that would be pathetic. No, he'll wait a few days.

He assures himself it's a comfort Jasper is being looked after in Hana's home and not in a kennel, and he is confident his contrition will recede with each passing day.

Recently, every flaw he has is at the forefront of his mind. He's just feeling fragile, that's all. It's understandable, he is more self-aware than normal, now that he is so close to seeing Elora again.

***

'It feels as surreal to me too. I wasn't expecting your house to be so big.'

'It's too big, really. After all, it's just me.'

'The garden must take up a lot of your time?'

'I enjoy it.'

Once in the house, they enter a sizeable reception area. Around them, on white walls are paintings of landscapes and villages that Brodie assumes are Corfu. Moving through the house where most of the walls are white, they enter a large living area, airy and luminous, with a glass exterior wall. There is a lot of glass, Brodie thinks but he can see the philosophy of the design, a hybrid of domesticity, openness and light.

'It's just down here,' Elora gestures.

A massive island unit dominates the kitchen. Grateful for the air conditioning that cools his skin, Brodie watches Elora stem the bleeding under a cold running tap and apply a plaster to her finger.

'Your house is lovely. I wasn't expecting this. You must have sold a lot of books.' Brodie smiles.

It pleases Elora he likes her house. 'I've sold one or two.' She reaches over to a mug rack and lifts a cup. 'Tea, coffee?' Elora raises an eyebrow. 'Or something stronger, perhaps?'

'Not for me. I want to keep a clear head. I suppose I should give you an explanation about why I'm here.'

Elora tilts her head. 'It would be a start. We'd better sit down.'

'The last few weeks have been, well, weird. I don't know how the planets are lining up, and I don't normally believe in that kind of stuff, but I'm willing to think there might be something in it. Some time ago, before I came to see you at the book festival, I witnessed a young man take his own life. His name was Isaac, and at the time, I had no idea how my life was about to change... on many levels.

'You see, Isaac… well, if the truth is known, he'd done some unpleasant things, but that doesn't mean he was a bad person. He had a woman he loved, and they had a child, a lovely little boy, Zak. Isaac had got himself mixed up with people who live a kind of life most of us will never see or know about. Isaac owed them money, a lot of money, and he knew even if he paid this debt, the real debt would be paid with his life. He needed to protect his family…'

Brodie tells Elora about the contents of the envelope he found, the responsibility he felt towards Isaac, meeting Chloe and Zak and satisfying himself that they were safe in South Queensferry.

'Why didn't you tell me about this when I was with you in Edinburgh?'

Brodie can see the concern in her eyes. God, he has missed her. 'I don't know. I suppose, at the time, I didn't want to burden you with my problems. I had found you after what seemed a lifetime. I wanted nothing to interfere with the limited time I knew we had together.'

'You should have told me.'

'I know that now. Believe me, I wish I had. But I'm here now because of them. I realised just what Chloe had lost, and what she would have given if she could have made things different. To still have Isaac in her life, for Zak to still have his father. These things tormented me.

'I thought about Heather and my kids. I thought about us, and I just couldn't let it end without seeing you again because, unlike Chloe, I had a choice, but that was not enough. I had to exercise that choice and do something about it. I realised I couldn't let Isaac's death be in vain. It had to mean something. I felt bound to Isaac like it was cutting into my skin. If it wasn't for him…' Brodie catches his breath, 'If it wasn't for Isaac, I might not even be here.'

Elora reaches over the table and places her hand on Brodie's forearm. 'I wasn't expecting that. Are you sure you wouldn't like a drink? I think you need it; I know I do.'

Elora brings a bottle of wine and two glasses out onto the terrace where Brodie is sitting. She sets them on the table and, opening the bottle, she pours a generous amount into the glasses. She settles into her seat and asks, 'Where are you staying?'

The thought of telling her had never crossed his mind. 'In Corfu Town. It's a small apartment. It's clean and comfortable.'

'How long do you intend to stay?'

'I've got it for three weeks. I was lucky. It was a last-minute cancellation. I just happened to enquire about it at the right time.' He takes a sip of wine.

'Do you like it?'

'Very nice.'

'It's Greek wine.'

'Really?'

'Does that surprise you?'

'Now that I think about it, it shouldn't. After all, you've got the perfect climate here.'

'In the summer, not so much in the winter. It does get cold, you know.' She brings the glass to her mouth and looking over the rim says, 'I'm glad to see you.'

'Are you really?'

'Why shouldn't I be?'

'Well, after we last met, I thought you might have regrets.'

She shakes her head. 'I don't... and you?'

'How could I? Not regret. No, not that. Guilt, maybe.'

There is a pause and then Elora says, 'That's a strong word... Do you mean, Heather?'

He nods.

'Has there been anyone else?

'No.'

Elora smiles. 'Then I'm in good company. It doesn't mean that you don't love her. You can't stop living.'

'I don't want to, but it doesn't make it any easier. At least, I've got the consolation that such complexities of the heart cannot be resolved easily.' He empties his glass.

'Another?'

'Why not?'

As Elora fills his glass, there is a strange weirdness about sitting with her, in her garden and on her terrace. It is an odd sensation. Dreamlike.

'This place is beautiful,' he says, trying to pull himself from the garden, the trees that fall gently away from the house, and the cobalt sea that seems to melt into the horizon. He swirls the wine in his glass and admires its deep tannic red. 'How long have you lived here?'

'Let me think, seven years next month. It was built by a British couple, they were Scottish, actually. They stayed here in the 70s. Seemingly, he was a famous author. How weird is that? There was a rumour his wife had an affair and a baby. Anyway, the husband died, the wife stayed here with her daughter. I think at some point the house lay empty for quite some time and then the daughter, who by now was married, stayed in the summer months with her husband and son. Then, one year, she arrived with her son and a tutor.'

'A tutor?'

'Yes. The son was autistic and was being schooled by the tutor who, it seemed, stayed in the house as well. He became a well-known face in the village.'

'He?' Brodie looks at her, thinking he knows what is coming next.

Elora nods and smiles. 'The story goes, the husband was involved in some heavy crime thing, drugs, I think. Anyway, he wasn't around a lot and well, you can imagine.'

'The tutor and the wife had an affair?'

'It seems they did.'

'Wow, this house has seen a lot.'

'It doesn't end there.'

'It doesn't?'

'The husband, as well as being involved with some nasty people was also handy with his fists.'

'You mean…'

'Yes. Their marriage wasn't a loving one.'

Brodie shakes his head.

'The story does have a happy ending.'

'Good. The husband got what he deserved, and the wife and tutor lived happily ever after.' He raises an eyebrow.

'Something like that. Actually, she was a lovely person.'

'You met her?'

'Yes. They stayed on living here for some years before moving back to Scotland. He was nice looking too.'

'The tutor?'

'Uh, huh. I had often admired the house. They did a lot of work to it, as you can see today. When I saw it was up for sale, I bought it. I offered way over the asking price, but it was worth it.'

'I can see why you were attracted to it; the views alone would sell it.'

'I'll never sell this house. I plan to grow old in it.'

Brodie looks towards the sea. 'I can see why.'

There is a silence between them.

'I often wonder what would have happened to us if I hadn't returned to Greece. I probably wouldn't have become an author and enjoyed this comfortable life I have.'

'I would've taken you back… and made it work. Who knows what would have happened to us?' Something shifts inside him.

'I used to think about that a lot when I first left. I wished it could have been different. The truth is, I couldn't go back to Edinburgh. Things changed. I changed. I lost a sense of who I was. I see things differently now. Back then, I couldn't put anything into perspective. It was a mess. I was a mess.'

'Why didn't you confide in me? Had it got that bad, you couldn't speak to me?'

'I was young, we were young. It seemed the easiest option. I did it for reasons that were, well… selfish. I knew I had hurt you. I made a mistake, and I wish I could change that, but I can't. He was your best friend.'

'He was. Look, I don't want to get into this, not right now. It's enough that I'm here, you're here. We need to talk about it, I know, but for now, I just want us to get to know each other again.'

She shifts in her chair. 'You're right. We've got time.'

'My son and his partner are having a baby.'

'That's wonderful.'

He can sense her thinking.

'You're going to be a grandad. Is that what you want to be called?'

He has thought about this. 'I'm not quite sure. I've still not come to terms with the whole thing. Not the baby, I'm delighted about that. I've got this incredible feeling inside me every time I think about the baby. No. It's me… a grandad? In my head, you've to be a certain age to carry that title and I'm just not ready to accept it. I can't seem to get past it.'

Elora grins.

'What?'

'You!' She giggles lusciously.

'What about me?'

'You're scared of growing old. It's not how you see yourself. You can't identify with it. You'll change. It's common now… being a younger granddad. Once the little one arrives, you won't care. Trust me. It will all be about the baby.'

'I'm being stupid, I know. I've got time to get used to it.'

'That's true, you have. It's something we didn't have, was it?'

'No. When I think about what happened after you, what became the rest of my life, our time spent together seems miniscule in comparison.'

'I know. I feel the same. We've become different people. Which is only natural, I suppose? Life changes us, we adapt to those changes, but deep down, some things stay the same.' Elora watches Brodie think about this.

'How would you know that these *somethings* have not changed inside you?'

'Because, when you confront them or meet them, the confirmation that unfolds hits you like a train. I've never regretted us.' Elora's voice strains. 'Never.'

Brodie feels a twinge of something: Delight? Expectation? Possibility? Maybe all three? A complex symphony of emotions grows in his chest.

'I still remember what you were like when we first met,' Elora says warmly, swirling her wine in her glass. 'You were reserved, secretive, pensive, quiet at times. You could be detached but very focused. As you Scots would say, you were like a bottomless loch. Believe it or not, it was your ambiguity that attracted me to you in the first place. I could see you were the type of person who didn't leave their footprint in the sand. I was curious about you, as I still am today. Take now, as an example of my curiosity; what if you hadn't come to see me at the book festival? What if, when you saw my name in the paper, it didn't infuse you with a desire to see me? You went, didn't you? You came to see me, and we spent time together, for the first time, as mature adults, with our different life experiences… didn't we? Then, as it has always been between us, life got in the way. But now, here you are, far from Edinburgh, from your home and your family. You're here, in my home, on my terrace, drinking my wine.' She meets his eyes over the table and wonders if this is the beginning of something. This curiosity, what will it lead to? Or are we already there, wherever *there* is?

'Some things can't go unsaid. I need to explain why I'm here. I haven't been able to forget seeing you in Edinburgh. In my wildest dreams, I never imagined I'd spend an hour with you, never mind a day. It sounds crazy, I know, but it felt almost spiritual. It was a reunion that had been waiting to happen.' Brodie looks away and fixes his eyes on the garden. 'You have always been present in my life, Elora. Even marriage couldn't stop the images of you that frequented my thoughts. I loved Heather, but she wasn't you. I hate myself for that. I'm the one who must live with it.' Brodie takes a deep breath. His heart thuds as he looks at Elora. 'I suppose, the reason I'm here is to find out, if instead of just being a thought or a memory, there is the chance that this could be the beginning of something we both want, something that is real.' Brodie drinks the remaining remnants of wine from his glass. He isn't expecting the relief that his words have produced. It is wonderful, astonishing, as if he has released a great burden. It seems extraordinary to think of spending uninterrupted time with Elora.

'What are you thinking?' Brodie asks quietly, hoping her reply will confirm this beginning for them.

'I'm sorry.'

Brodie's stomach sinks. He thought there was a chance, even just a sliver of a chance. Has he imagined her fondness? He has been craving something unattainable. His hope has turned liquescent, diminishing from him.

Elora sees the slope of his shoulders and the anguish on his face. 'I'm sorry I left you when we were students. I'm sorry we didn't keep in touch. I'm sorry for the times I thought about getting in touch, but never did. Most of all, I'm glad that we've met again and have this time together.'

Brodie looks up towards the unbroken arc of blue that polarises the sky. He feels an immense surge of gratitude. Something can happen between them. Something with heightened significance.

When he looks at her, a sensual feeling begins to slide through him. His eyes track Elora's elongated neck where her lavish and dark auburn hair falls and, as she brushes away one long tendril of hair from her face, Brodie finds the curve of her arm exquisite.

'It has always been important to me to resolve the past, our past. When we met at the book festival, I just wanted to absorb every second I had with you. All that mattered was being with you. I'd visualised that moment for years, never thinking it would ever happen.' He has tried but failed to dislodge the images from his mind.

Elora smiles affectionately; it encourages Brodie. 'It left me overwhelmed. I asked myself, was it possible that we could be together, after all this time? We promised to keep in touch, and I felt guilty about that. I thought your silence was your intent to forget what had happened. Now, I know I was a coward. I doubted you. I couldn't face the truth, whatever that was.' His brow frowns in concern.

'I'm just as much to blame. When I left, my mind was troubled. I thought, what good could it do to drag up the past, drag up things that have lain undisturbed, or worse, pretending it never happened? The longer I didn't hear from you, I thought you felt the same.' Behind her smile, Brodie thinks he senses an avoidance of sorts; in truth, he is not sure.

She smiles. 'You gave me such a fright when I opened the gate and you were standing there.'

'I didn't mean to. I was considering scaling the garden wall. But, seriously, I should've phoned to warn you I was here. I was worried you wouldn't want to see me. It was a calculated gamble.'

'I didn't think you were the gambling type.'

'I'm not, normally. This was an exception.'

'It worked.'

'It seems to have.' Brodie leans back against his chair.

'You live here all on your own?'

'I do.'

'Isn't the house too big for one person?'

'I have people that stay from time to time and, I have a cleaner that comes once a week.'

'That's not exactly a crowd.'

'No. It's how I like it. Didn't you know most writers are introverts? It helps to get the words on the page. My book is with the editor, so I'm not doing much writing at the moment.'

'So, you're not looking for inspiration?'

'Maybe I've found it,' laughs Elora.

'What! You mean me… or us?'

She raises her eyebrows. 'Both, maybe? Characters in a novel should never feel like characters in a novel. If they do, they're not reflecting real life, they're just ink on paper. Before I wrote this current novel, I'd been struggling to write anything I was happy with. For the first time, the ideas didn't flow. I began to panic.'

'What did you do?'

'I decided the story would find me; all I had to do was be patient. It took about a month, but gradually, it started to appear in my mind, in my dreams, and I found new confidence in words, in my characters. I rediscovered my flair for narrative, a sense of drama and rhythm of a sentence.'

'That must have come as a relief.'

'It did. To me, writing is slightly less important than breathing.' Her eyes illuminating at this satisfying thought.

'And so it should be,' Brodie smiled warmly. 'When will it be published?'

'Next year. They're looking at a spring release.'

He nods approvingly. 'Do you get excited, or are you apprehensive when a book is published?'

'A bit of both, really. I'm never confident that it's going to sell well. Authors have a responsibility to their readers. When people hold a book in their hands, that book can change their lives; the written word has tremendous power. On the other hand, you can do the most wonderful creative things in your life and people will still remember you for your supposed transgressions. It's unfortunate, but that's just the way it is,' she says somewhat wearily. 'I've been criticised in the Greek press and by so-called feminist commentators for my views on gender equality. Woman should not expect that it's their given right that we're represented equally in business, politics and the arts. We need to earn that right for it to mean something. Otherwise, it has little substance, it's just lip service. In some quarters, that didn't go down too well.'

'Did that worry you?'

'No. Not really. When I lived in Paris, I was inspired by a novelist called Annie Ernaux, who is thought of as being one of France's greatest living writers. She said that it's the work of the novelist to tell the truth. Sometimes, she didn't know what truth she was looking for, but it was always a truth she was seeking. That resonated with me and, even to this day, those sentiments inspire my writing.'

Before he came to Corfu, if Brodie had been asked how he hoped he would feel once he met Elora again, it would have been this. There is still an inkling of doubt around him, but generally, he is happy. Yes, that is what it is called. For the first time in as long as he can remember, he is finally pleased with himself. His mood is changing, his spirits lifting, reaching towards the sky.

'Don't take this the wrong way, but we're virtually strangers now. We're not twenty-one anymore.'

'Actually, I was twenty, you were twenty-one.' Brodie smiles. 'I suppose we're like ships without a sail.'

'Like ships without a sail. I like the sound of that.' Elora smiles into her glass before swallowing the last of its contents. 'Another?' She raises the glass.

'Isn't it a bit early to be drinking almost a bottle between us?'

'I'm celebrating finishing my novel; you'll have to join me.'

'Another one won't hurt.'

'I don't want you tipsy,' Elora says apologetically whilst pouring wine into their glasses. 'This is definitely our last one. I'll get some water; we don't want to dehydrate.'

She returns carrying a tray, a large jug of water with slices of lemon floating on the surface, and two glasses.

'This has been in the fridge. It's perfect for a day like this.'

Brodie fills their glasses and takes a drink. 'Very refreshing.'

For the first time since he arrived, there is a long silence between them. The sun's rays have dispersed their shade and Elora covers her eyes with sunglasses. Brodie can see his reflection and he finds it slightly disconcerting that her eyes are lost to him.

'Are you hungry?' Elora asks.'

'I wouldn't want you to go to any trouble.'

'We can always eat out. I'll take you to my favourite place to eat, if you'd like. It's not too far. It's my habit to walk at least once a day. I normally go for a walk in the late afternoon when it's not hot, but for you, I can make an exception.' She smiles and Brodie imagines her eyes sparkling.

They've walked for about ten minutes and Elora announces that it is not far now. The combination of sun and wine spreads a dull ache across Brodie's forehead, and he rubs the irritation with a forefinger and thumb.

'Are you alright?' Elora's voice is warm with concern.

'Just the start of a headache. I'll be fine.'

'I've got some paracetamol if you want?' Elora says, retrieving the tablets from her bag. 'I never go anywhere without them… migraines. I don't get them often, but when

I do and feel the start of one brewing, I try to catch it early. Here.' She hands him a silver foil packet.

'Thanks.'

'You'll need water. We'll get a bottle at the restaurant.'

'It's fine. I can take them on their own.' Brodie pops a tablet from its wrapper, places it in his mouth and swallows.

'I don't know how you can do that,' Elora says.

'It's easy. I just swallow it with some saliva,' he says with a shrug of his shoulder.

Elora is a regular visitor to Taverna Limani, as the waiters greet them with welcoming smiles and direct them towards a table with an unobstructed view of the sea. A roof of vines above them offers a welcome shade, and the aroma of cooking infuses the air around them. Most of the tables are taken, and a soft breeze brings a light relief from the heat of the day.

A waiter hands them both a menu. 'Your usual?' he asks in Greek.

'Yes, thank you.' Elora smiles.

'And your friend?'

'What would you like to drink?' Elora asks Brodie.

'Just water.'

The waiter nods and leaves.

'A prime position.' Brodie gestures towards the sea.

'It's not just the view that's the attraction, the food is delicious.'

Tearing his eyes from her, Brodie scans the menu, his eyes travelling the Greek lettering, and then, with relief, the English subtitles. 'What would you recommend?'

'For starters, we should share some olives, bread and a tzatziki dip.' She leans over and points to a dish on the menu. 'This one here, it has aubergine, tomato and feta in a mouth-watering sauce. You'll love it,' She assures him.

Throughout lunch, Brodie can't stop himself smiling. Elora orders another red wine and Brodie sticks to water, his headache thankfully subsiding.

Elora sips her drink. 'I've often thought about our little flat, I still sometimes dream about it, after all this time. Although, usually, they're weird and make no sense at all.'

'After you left, I went back to live with my mum for a while. I heard the flat didn't stay empty long; other students moved in.'

'How is your mum?'

'She passed away.'

'I'm sorry. I really liked her, even though she didn't like me.'

'She was fond of you, in her own way,' Brodie assures her. 'She wasn't one for… showing her emotions.'

'She showed me several!' Elora replies, laughing.

Brodie nods. 'She wasn't slow in speaking her mind. She had no filter, unfortunately.'

'Remember that Sunday, she invited us for lunch. It was the first and the last. Do you remember?'

'How could I forget? She criticized the way you dressed, your accent and your hair. I was mortified.'

'Eventually, I won her round by saying her cooking was just as good as my mothers, if not better.'

'She softened then, thank goodness. Did you mean it, I can't remember?'

'No. I lied.' Elora confesses with a wry smile.

'Wow. You must have been pretty convincing to melt my mother's ice.'

'It was risky, but it worked, although she never invited me over again.'

'It seems a long time ago.'

'It was.'

Brodie tries not to be overcome by the realisation of just how long ago it has been. Maybe he hasn't really dealt with it, has he avoided it, even? He can't help but feel that such time is overawing.

Elora drinks some more wine. 'I've just realised, you haven't smoked a cigarette yet.'

'I'm trying to quit. It's been a long time coming. I should have done it years ago.'

'How long have you stopped?'

'Nine days and…' Brodie checks his watch. 'Six hours.'

'Oh! That precise. How's it going?'

'So, so. I have my moments, especially after a meal, that's when the real craving starts. It's not until you stop that you realise you're addicted to them.'

Elora begins to raise her glass. She pauses, before taking a tentative sip. 'It's a battle, but *you* can win it.'

After lunch, Brodie asks Elora when she last walked in the sea? She looks at him as if to say something, changes her mind and says brightly, 'Not recently.'

Their feet are bare as they stand, side by side, before the clear crystal water, their toes gently sinking into the wet sand.

'I haven't done this for years,' Brodie tells her. He can sense her hand by his side, so close, they almost touch.

'How does it feel?' she asks.

Tentatively, his hand inches towards the light touch of her skin. The expectancy of it pounds in his chest. Then, ever so delicately, his fingers finally curl and fold around hers, a faint pressure that is immediately reciprocated.

'Like I'm twenty again,' he softly says, as the Ionian laps against his feet.

After they visit the beach, they return to the house. Elora brings a bottle of red wine onto the terrace and fills two glasses.

She leans back in her chair. 'When I woke this morning, I thought I had another lonely day in front of me.'

'I thought you said you weren't lonely.'

'Who doesn't get lonely? Whoever says they don't, they're lying. I've been in rooms full of people I know, colleagues and friends, and I've still felt lonely.'

'Has there been anyone else since your divorce?'

Elora bites her lip, a listless sensation coming over her. Brodie can see this and feels the first twinges of regret.

'I'm sorry,' he says. 'I wasn't thinking.'

'His name was Lars.' She tells him in a steady voice. 'We had the kind of relationship that was common amongst writers. We met up at literary festivals, book signings, that kind of thing. We'd go out, have dinner and a few drinks and discuss the subjects that interested us. It was mainly writing we spoke about, ours and other authors were the common currency of our conversations.

'We both believed in words. He existed in a sea of language. He wanted his words, his stories, his novels to be his epitaph. He wanted to take the reader with him, into the story, as if they were there in the first place. Every author wants that, their novel to become a shared thing.

'Ours was a long-distance affair. He lived in Stockholm. He had two young children but was separated from his wife. He wanted to live near them, to see them, have them over at weekends. He wanted to be a presence in their lives. He still wanted to be their father.'

'He would visit me here at my home, between our respective writing schedules and book tours. I never went to Stockholm. He felt uncomfortable about having to introduce me to his children.'

'Did you ever see them?'

'Photographs, I only ever saw photographs. They were gorgeous kids. Two girls.'

'How long did you see each other?' To his surprise, Brodie feels a surge of what he can only describe as jealousy.

'Nearly two years.'

'What happened.'

'I was going to have a baby.'

This unexpected statement, for a moment, threatens to knock him off balance. 'I don't understand, wasn't he happy?'

'It was because I was pregnant that we never saw each other again.'

'I see,' he says, but he doesn't.

'He gave me an ultimatum, either I got rid of the baby, or we were finished.'

'Why?'

'He couldn't do that to his little girls. He couldn't have a baby with another woman who wasn't their mother.'

Brodie raises his eyebrow. 'It happens all the time.'

'But, not to him. I saw then what kind of man he was. He didn't love me; he was in love with the idea of being the perfect father.'

'And the baby?'

'I had a miscarriage.'

'I'm sorry, Elora.'

She says nothing. Finally, she raises her eyes to his. 'It wasn't my first. I've never been able to go full term. That's why I've never had children.'

Brodie tries to process the intensity of this, her loss, and, although he has known the taste and weight of his grief, this seems more intricate than he can imagine. 'Did he know?'

She retains her poise. 'No. And after what he said to me, I wasn't going to tell him, either. He didn't deserve me.'

There is a moment's silence

'I was going to ask you earlier, but it slipped my mind, how did you find me?'

'Google maps.'

'Of course.'

'The taxi driver was reluctant to go any further because of the state of the road. He dropped me off just outside the village. I had to do some detective work. I couldn't get access to every little lane and dirt track on Google. You were quite hard to find. I almost gave up.'

'Really?'

'Yes. If it wasn't for this guy who stopped his car and asked if I was lost, I'd be on my way back to Edinburgh by now. Luckily, he knew exactly where you were. I was only a five-minute walk away.'

'Did you get his name?'

'No. But his English was good. Why?'

She realised with a little shock the significance of this. 'Imagine if he hadn't stopped and just drove straight past you, you wouldn't be sitting here now. We have him to thank for that. He's brought us together.'

'You're right. I never thought about it like that. A little act of kindness really goes go a long way.'

She lifts her glass. 'To the stranger and his sense of direction.'

Brodie tilts his glass in her direction.

Elora takes a drink and puts her glass down. 'I knew you'd come. Deep down, I just knew you would.'

He looks surprised. 'You sound so sure. Even I didn't know if I would, not for some time, anyway. There were days, entire days, I'd think about it.'

'Well, you're here now.'

'Yes, I am.'

'How did your son and daughter react? I'm sure they must have had some objection to you coming here.'

He hesitates. 'Actually, they don't know I'm seeing you. They think I'm here on holiday. It seemed the best thing to do, at the time. Only Hana, an old friend, knows about you.'

'So, you haven't told them about me, about us?'

Brodie takes a sharp intake of breath. 'No.' He reaches over and touches her arm. 'I'm sorry. It's not that I didn't want to. I didn't even know if I'd find you, or for that matter, if you'd want to see me.'

After a moment Elora says, 'It's all right, Brodie. I understand.'

'You do?'

'Of course. You were protecting them. What father wouldn't?'

To his relief, Elora is smiling.

'I would have done the same.'

'It's worried me. I knew at some point you would want to know.'

'I've been your secret for half your life.'

It seems to Brodie that she enjoys saying this.

'One day, you'll tell them about me.' She smiles with an air of confidence, 'Do you have any photographs of them? I'd love to see your children.'

'Sure.' He finds them on his mobile and hands it to her.

'Your son looks like you. He has your smile and your eyes. Your daughter is different, I don't see a lot of you in her. Does she look like Heather?'

The mention of her name on Elora's lips feels physical, a reaction that, for a moment, unbalances his thoughts. 'She always has done. Would you like to see a photograph of Heather?' It seems the natural thing to say.

Elora hands the mobile back to him.   2

'I've got a few. Do you want to see them all?'

'You pick. Show me your favourite one.'

Brodie looks at each photograph on his mobile phone and even though he has scanned them in detail a thousand times and knows each one he likes, Brodie wants to be sure, the photograph will be a true representation of Heather. He finds the one he has in mind. Her hair is shining in the sun, as it unfurls and rests on her shoulders, and she is smiling.

Brodie recalls it was a sweltering day, a weekend away in London, a posh hotel and a show, *Les Misérables*. He took the photograph after a visit to Shoreditch. They just emerged from a tube station and were walking back to their hotel. He recalls how happy Heather was. It was her birthday; he remembers now.

He hesitates, finger poised above the photograph.

Heather, meet Elora. Elora, this is Heather, my wife. With a tap of his finger, the photograph enlarges, and he shows it to Elora. She places her hand upon his, to steady the image, or to feel close to him? He is undecided. Brodie studies Elora's face. At first, she does not speak and it unease's him. After what seems like an eternity, Elora looks up from the screen. She pushes her hair behind her ear.

'It's strange seeing her, the woman you spent most of your life with. She's not what I expected. I had this image in my mind, but she's different.'

'In what way?'

'She has an infectious smile, and that tells a lot about her personality, who she was. She's not beautiful, she's pretty. I can see why you were attracted to her, why you loved her. She wore a cross?' Her tone of voice is more a question than an observation.

'It was a gift from her mother on our wedding day.'

'Was she religious?' There is a reproachful timbre to her voice that puts Brodie on the defensive.

'If she was, it was before I met her. No, she wasn't into religion. The thing about Heather was, she believed in the goodness she saw in the human spirit. That was her. I suppose you could say that was her faith.'

Brodie looks at the photograph before closing the screen.

She reaches over and touches his arm. 'I didn't mean to make you feel... awkward. I'm just curious, that's all.'

'I'm not. It's fine. At times, we had our difficulties, but we continued to love each other in the simplest and easiest of ways.'

'I can tell you love her, and so you should.'

'But I feel so much guilt. I've been betraying her all these years. Even when I was with her, there were times I'd be thinking of you. I'd be wondering where you were, what you'd be doing. I never told her about you, or how I felt about you and how you were always with me, in my thoughts, every day. What does that make me?'

'Oh, Brodie. Don't do this to yourself. What good would it have done to tell her such things? Sometimes, it's better not to know. You were protecting her…'

'From the truth,' Brodie interrupts.

'No. From the hurt and pain you would have caused her. What good would have come out of that?'

'I kept things from her… secrets.'

'We all have our secrets, Brodie. Even I have my secrets.'

Edinburgh 1995

Green Shoots

Brodie was standing outside Elora's flat on Forrest Road. There was a chill in the air and, as he glanced skywards, the watery sun and autumnal light lifted his spirits as the ill effects of a hangover receded from him.

As Elora approached, he unwrapped a stick of chewing gum and popped it between his teeth, hoping it would dispel the acid taste in his mouth.

She smiled at him. 'I managed to get brown bread. The price was reduced… today's date.'

'Once it's toasted you won't know the difference.'

She pushed open the door to the stairwell and, as they climbed the steps together, she said, 'Did you have a good time last night?'

'I would have preferred spending it with you.'

'It's not every day you have a twenty-first birthday.'

'That's why I should have been with you.'

They reached the landing. 'I've got a present for you.' She turned the key in the lock and looked at him mischievously as the door opened to a narrow hallway.

'You shouldn't have. You should be spending your money on other things, not me.'

'Oh, it didn't cost me anything.' As they let themselves into the flat, Elora took his hand and, dropping her bag, she led him to the bedroom.

Brodie sat at the kitchen table, spreading butter onto a slice of toast. He could feel a warmth behind him. Elora wrapped her arms around his chest and snuggled into his neck, her breath tickling his skin.

'Did you like your present?' she whispered.

'It was the best I've ever had.'

She reached over and took a slice of toast. 'Good. Have you any plans for today?'

'No. I just need to hand some books into the library, that's all.'

'I thought we could go for a drink, maybe something to eat, later tonight?'

'I'd like that.'

'My treat.'

He was about to protest when she placed a finger on his lips. 'I made a lot of tips last night.'

Brodie stroked her arm. 'Where do you have in mind?'

'There's a new place opened up on Lothian Road. Fiona and Martin went there the other night and were impressed. It's Lebanese.'

'I've never tried Lebanese.'

'It's similar to Greek food.'

Brodie turned his head and kissed her neck. 'Well, if it tastes anything like you, I'll be in heaven.'

'Good. I've already booked a table.'

'You have?'

Elora nodded enthusiastically. 'For seven.'

'Do you have any more surprises?'

Elora smiled at him. 'No. Is that coffee I smell?' She walked around him and poured the steaming coffee from a cafetière. She sat opposite him, cradling her cup. He watched her and, in such moments, it was unthinkable that one day she may leave him and return home to Greece.

'What is it?' Elora asked.

'Do you miss home?'

'Sometimes. Why?'

'I'm not sure I could move to another country, study and work… I've never really thought about you like that. It says a lot about you. It also means that someday you might go back.'

She shook her head. 'That's not an option.'

'It's not?' Brodie felt a sudden relief.

'I was always going to have to leave home, my options were on the mainland. I had offers from universities in Athens and Thessaloniki. I was about to accept the offer I had for the Aristotle University in Thessaloniki when Edinburgh accepted me as well.'

'What made you chose Edinburgh?'

She blew across the top of her cup and Brodie was aware the pause felt awkward.

'I was not only going to university, I wanted to get away as far as I could.'

It was not the answer Brodie was expecting. It was his turn to hesitate. 'Oh. Really?'

'You see… oh shit, this is hard.'

'You don't have to tell me. I can see you're uncomfortable. I didn't mean to put you on the spot. You don't have to tell me, honest. It's no big deal.'

She has been avoiding his eyes, but Brodie's dismissal strikes her like a bolt of lightning to her chest. Her eyes are now glued to him. 'But it was… a big deal. That's the point.'

'I'm sorry. I didn't mean it like that.'

She stared at him and then her eyes softened. 'I know you didn't. How could you? It's me that should be apologising. You must think I'm deranged?' she smiled apologetically.

Brodie reached over the table and took her hand.

'I've thought about this a lot.' Elora dropped her head and peered at her cup. 'I really thought coming here would somehow help me forget or at least I could learn to live with it.' The words escaped in a resentful, small laugh. She gulped some air.

Brodie squeezed her hand. 'Take your time.'

'It's like time stopped. There are days I feel I'm still back there. There had been fires in the hills and we heard that some villages had been evacuated. No one thought the fire would come close to us, but that day the winds changed. There was no evacuation, no warning system. We woke that morning with the sound of flames, explosions, houses and trees on fire. When I looked out of the window everything was black with smoke.

'In the house, there was me, my sister, my mother and grandmother. We grabbed what we could and ran out of the house. My grandmother was eighty years old. She walked with a stick, so I stayed with her as the others headed for the beach and the sea. It wasn't the flames I could feel, but heat. The heat burned our skin. Lots of people were heading towards the sea, our neighbours and friends. People were shouting and screaming, panicking. As we made our way down the street, I looked back, and the sky was black. Eventually, I don't know how, it must have been the adrenalin, but I was never so relieved to feel sand under my shoes. It was then my grandmother collapsed. Two of our neighbours helped me and we managed to get her to the sea.

'We were all standing waist-deep in our clothes. It was raining ash, red hot ash. I could feel it in my hair and on my skin. I tried to wash it off with water. I've never seen so many people crying hysterically and frightened. When I looked at where the houses should have been it looked like a version of hell. The noise was enormous. It never stopped. We were in the water for hours, our legs freezing and the parts of our bodies above the water burning in the scorching heat... and then the boats came.

Tears ran down Elora's face. She wiped them with the back of her hand. 'Lots of people we knew, neighbours and friends, lost everything, their houses were gutted; everything inside their houses and everything they owned obliterated in minutes.'

Brodie tried to imagine how Elora must have felt but how could he, he had never experienced anything like it.

'Elora,' Brodie said gently. 'I don't know what to say. You must have been devastated?'

'We were the lucky ones. Our house was hardly touched. That didn't make it any easier. In fact, it felt worse in a way. It wasn't just the fire that was extinguished. All around us, everywhere we looked, we were constantly reminded that people's lives and memories had been extinguished too. Trees were dark jagged shapes, everything was charred. Shells of cars blackened and twisted. I had nightmares. I could still feel, hear and smell the flames. Some nights, I could hardly breathe. I was too scared to go to sleep.

'After the funerals, and over the next couple of weeks, the earth was still black but, in some places, green shoots began to push out of the ground. From all the destruction and loss, life was gradually beginning to emerge, conquering death in a way.

'So, to answer your question, why did I decide to study in Edinburgh? I saw it as my green shoots. It was my opportunity to erase the memories of that day by being as far away as I possibly could be.'

'Time's a great healer.'

'Do you really believe that?'

He looked at her and suddenly realised he wasn't so sure anymore. 'I think it might depend on the person and their coping mechanisms, to be fair.'

Wrestling her mind back from the flames and blackness, Elora managed a smile. 'Meeting you has helped. I know now, I can't manage this on my own. Without you, I think I might have fallen apart.'

Brodie, still holding her hand, raised it to his lips and softly kissed each finger. 'Then, I'll be your glue.

Chapter 8

Dimitra

The next morning, Brodie hires a car. Now, he won't need to depend on taxis, which in his naivety, he has discovered to be an expensive luxury. Yesterday, it took the taxi a good thirty minutes to reach Elora's house, the time of the journey he hadn't appreciated. Also, it was late last night when he returned by taxi to his apartment in Corfu Town. There was always public transport which he has been told is reliant and cheap, but it would not give him the freedom that he will now enjoy.

Brodie drives parallel with the coast, passing through Dassia and Ipsos. Now and then, he steers the car around a bend and the sight of a horseshoe bay, or a tumble of roofs and the tranquil sea where boats bob in turquoise waters, meet him.

As he keeps his attention to the road, over the sea, a haze of receding hills often draws his eye. He knows this to be the coastline of Albania. He hasn't expected it would be so close and, to his surprise, he can even make out the occasional village.

On a whim, he turns off the main road and, with every twist and bend, the road coils like a snake as he climbs higher alongside olive groves bordered by stone walls. Nestled at the ends of gated driveways, houses of every size border the road at generous intervals where salmon and tangerine stuccoed walls support tiled roofs, sprinkling the pine-clad hills in terracotta patches.

Brodie feels a slight apprehension. He has strayed quite far from the coastal road and it is only the sight of the landscape and sea below that urges him to continue his climb. He is sure he has travelled several miles and he must have rounded thirty bends in the road by now, maybe more.

When he guides the car around yet another, immediately he pulls to a stop. He hasn't seen another vehicle on the road, so he feels confident in leaving the car.

He walks to a low wall at the edge of the road and scans the view that unrolls for miles below him. He is astounded. The tree-covered hills slope towards the coastline, stretching for miles into a molten haze. It's almost as if he can see the entire east coast from here. He knows it is not, but he doesn't care, he is caught up in the moment, transfixed by the cobalt and azure, colours that tint the sea and sky and blend into a haze of receding hills. He takes several photographs and, invigorated by the view; he moves the car out into the road to face another bend.

With light relief, the houses he passes are becoming more frequent. Brodie realises the village he has just entered has no trinket shop or bar offering happy hour, Spartilas is an authentic Corfiot village. The road shrinks into almost a lane and a car coming in the opposite direction squeezes passed, almost clipping Brodie's hand mirror.

He stops at a small supermarket and buys bottled water, a bouquet, cheese, some olives and a bottle of wine. The fresh smell of cooked bread draws his attention to a small bakery. He purchases a loaf of bread and Koulourakia (Greek butter biscuits). He orders a coffee at a small café and sits outside. As he savours the strong bitter taste, his mind wanders.

Usually at home, if he was out walking Jasper, they would spend time in Inverleith Park. Then, he would sit in his favourite coffee shop, the dog friendly Artisan Roast on Raeburn Street, with Jasper nodding off and curled at his feet.

He wonders what Heather would have made of his decision to come in search of a woman he hasn't seen since his days at university… 1995. He reaches for his mobile phone and scrolls through the photographs until he finds

Heather. A slight smile breaks across his mouth and he can feel her approval wash over him. He lifts his head and gulps the warm air around him. His throat aches and his eyes fill with tears. These moments are scarce now but always felt like a hole has been bored through his chest.

That morning, Brodie had initially intended to drive along the coast and head north. Now, this is not a possibility as he is some distance from the coast, and he would have to turn back on himself. He checks the map on his mobile phone and from his current location he traces the route he would have to take to arrive at Elora's house. He has gone off track, heading in the wrong direction. It would be best to do this kind of thing with Elora, he tells himself. At least she would know where she was going.

He checks his watch, it's eleven-thirty, he could be there by lunchtime. He pays for his coffee and returns to the car. He puts Elora's address into the Sat Nav and heads inland.

Brodie is aware that the houses he now passes are becoming fewer and farther in between. As the Sat Nav instructs him to take a left turning, Brodie can see a road sign that tells him in 2 kilometres he will be approaching Zygos.

As far as the eye can see, the land around him and the hills are swathed in distinctive shades of emerald, from pine to the cypress tree and many more that are unknown to him. He comes across a newly built house with a 'For Sale' sign displayed prominently by the side of the road. Brodie tries to imagine why anyone is attracted to living in such isolation. Further on, and to his surprise, an impressive and newly built villa comes into view. There must be a market for living in seclusion, Brodie considers. For most of the journey, he has been alone, seeing only a few cars pass on the opposite side.

The road is now but a single lane as he passes through Zygos and Sokraki. He drops into third gear as the gradient climbs higher again, and then the road descends over the other side of the hill and the landscape opens into a vast plain, ridged by imposing hills. Skirting the environs of Doukades, Brodie begins to relax his grip on the steering wheel, and he is aware of a pressure that has built up in his lower back. Life has returned beyond his windscreen and the single lane is now a double lane, olive groves spread out before him and it seems as if the world has expanded around him with wide-open spaces, houses and farmland.

The Sat Nav instructs him to turn right towards Liapades. He repeats the name and likes the way it rolls off his tongue; he can sense Elora is getting close.

Then, in an instant, everything changes. Brodie recognises familiar landmarks he remembers from yesterday; the sea is in view and soon he has pulled into the tree-covered lane that leads to Elora's house.

He peels himself from the car into the stillness and the heat. Bird song accompanies him as he presses the intercom at the gate and waits. Then a movement catches his eye.

Elora is walking towards him. She is wearing a Baku straw hat with a wide brim and a lemon-coloured dress that flails around her knees as she walks. She is smiling, as is Brodie's heart.

'Brodie, it is you. I was beginning to think you had changed your mind. Are those for me?'

Brodie hands her the flowers. 'I hope you like them?'

She lifts them to her nose. 'They're lovely, thank you.'

'I've brought lunch.' He gestures to the plastic bag in his other hand. 'I hope you're hungry?'

'I'm starving. I didn't see a taxi.'

'I've hired a car. That's why I'm late. I did some exploring and saw the real Corfu.'

'Well then, you can tell me all about it over lunch.'

Elora prepares a salad, and some humous while Brodie plates up the olives, cheese and bread. He cuts the cheese and bread into generous slices and when Elora comes out onto the terrace, Brodie opens the bottle of wine and pours two glasses, one smaller than the other. He takes the small one.

'I better be careful if I'm driving.'

'There's a zero-tolerance policy here.'

'Maybe I'll pass on the wine then.'

'A few sips should be alright. This looks lovely,' Elora says as she sits.

Brodie reaches over and takes some bread and cheese.

Elora smiles. 'This bread is delicious.'

'It was made this morning or so the lady in the bakers said.'

'Which bakers?'

Brodie thinks out loud. 'What was the village called again? I want to say, Spartacus, it's not that, obviously, but it sounds like it.'

'Spartilas.' Elora corrects him.

'That's it, Spartilas.'

'What were you doing away over there?'

'I was a bit over-enthusiastic. I was heading up the coast and, on a whim, I turned inland. I was going to turn back but the view was amazing, so I kept going. Those roads were hairy. My arms were aching, I've never seen so many bends on the one road before.'

Elora laughs. 'Well. At least you got to see another side of Corfu.'

'I'm glad I did. I'd like to see more of the island and now I've got a car, there's nothing stopping me. I was thinking you should show me around. Take me to your favourite places.'

'I'd like that,' Elora says with a mouthful of cheese and bread.

'You're right,'

'About what?' Elora asks.

'I saw a different Corfu and I prefer that one to the purpose-built resorts along the coast.'

'It's a difficult balancing act. I was just reading the other day; Greece is now one of the most popular destinations in the world and, despite the global economic uncertainty, thirty-three million tourists will visit this year. Can you imagine that? I thought it was a misprint, there are only eleven million people in Greece, and the tourist industry grew nearly seven percent last year, which is almost three and a half times faster than the wider economy. Although, we might think some of the resorts are tacky and lack character, the jobs they provide are twenty-five percent of Greece's labour market. And, if I can remember this correctly, people visiting Greece last year spent eighteen and a half billion Euros.'

'Wow, that's a lot of money.'

'And with that comes responsibility. Locals and tourists need to be happy. There needs to be a massive investment in public infrastructure, roads, airports and, as you will have seen, waste disposal. Services need to be improved; ports need to be fit for purpose. Tourism might be Greece's jewel, but it won't continue to sparkle without investment.'

'What about the debt Greece has, austerity and the impact of the last ten years?'

'It has been hard, but every day, the sun has always risen and set. People will always come to Greece for the weather, the natural beauty and the quality of life, and that can only be good for the economy. I read the other day that Greece sees its future in becoming the Florida of Europe, and by that, I mean, attracting other nationalities to come here and make Greece their home.'

'That worries you?'

'It does. It just doesn't sit right with me. I'm not against people settling in Greece if they stay here and contribute to the local economy. I'd be very suspicious of people who would buy properties but only use them as holiday homes. Like Spain, for example.'

Brodie nods. 'I can see your point. We get that back home. City people buying houses in picturesque coastal villages and only using them at weekends and bank holidays. I can't ever see myself leaving Edinburgh. I've never stayed anywhere else. Is that sad?'

'It's not as if you haven't seen anything of the world, is it?'

'No. But it was always good to come home.'

Elora smiles. 'I know what you mean.'

'It's not just my memories that keep me connected to the place, it's more than that.' Brodie smiles warily.

'I know. I can't imagine what it must have been like, to lose Heather as you did.'

'It was difficult for us both, especially to watch how it affected the kids. Even as adults, they're still your children.'

Elora looks at the ground, her fingers twitch. 'It's unimaginable.'

'I'm sorry.'

'For what?'

'I've upset you. I'm an idiot. I didn't think.'

'Don't be silly. It was never meant to be. I was never meant to be a mother.'

'You would have been a wonderful mother.'

'Do you think so? I'm not so sure. My books are my children.' She paused. 'Did she suffer?'

'She wanted to be at home when her time came. She could not bear the thought of being in a hospital bed. She wanted her family around her. It gave her a lot of comfort; in a strange way, it helped her face it.

'On a good day, when she was up for it, I'd take her out for walks in her wheelchair. She loved the feeling of the sun on her face. She often said it would be one of the things she'd really miss.

'On a bad day, the outside world was sealed firmly behind a closed door. I'd read to her, play radio four, but mostly, I'd talk to her. Even when she didn't have the strength to say a single word back to me. It made me feel helpful when mostly, I felt devastatingly helpless and useless. In a sense, it was a distraction from my grief.

'It was emotionally exhausting, but we'll do anything when the unimaginable happens to the ones we love.'

They sit silently for a while.

'In a strange way, Heather's illness brought us closer. I don't know if on my part, it was guilt or because, for that time, nothing else mattered.' Brodie hesitates. 'Then, after Heather died,' he says. 'I felt the world's injustice, it's judgement. Socialising was exhausting and draining, not that I did much of that. You see, the friends I thought were part of our life, faded away. Without Heather, I wasn't part of a couple anymore.

'Heather made me a better version of myself. When she died, everything I thought was fixed and permanent suddenly vanished from my life. That heartache, like love, is non-transferable, the only way to ever escape the pain it brings is to never love again.'

'Is that how you feel now?'

'No, it's not!' Brodie says. 'That's how I felt for a very long time, but it was before I met you again. I think you're worth taking a gamble on.'

'I'm not sure if that should make me feel special or insulted?'

'You know what I mean.'

Elora smiles. 'I do.'

'I realise now, I've been lonely for a long time.' Brodie looks at Elora. 'I'm sorry. Listen to me wallowing.'

'Nonsense, and anyway, I can sympathise with you.'

'You can?'

'Sure. When I came to Edinburgh as that young woman to study, for months, I was entirely alone. I missed my family and my friends. I missed the sun. I'd never seen the sky look so low. It made me miserable. All I had to look forward to was my weekly phone calls to my family, especially my grandmother.'

'Your grandmother?'

'My grandmother partly brought me up. In Greece, grandparents often live in the family home. She was a wonderful influence on me, she was independent and authoritarian. She spoke perfect Italian and English. It was she who taught me to speak English.

'I always wondered about that. When we first met, I was really impressed by your English. How did your grandmother learn to speak English?'

'She married an Englishman. His name was Joshua Brown. He was an engineer and was working for a British company who had contracts with the Greek government at the time. They met and fell in love. They had to keep their affair secret because, if my grandmother's family knew about it, they would have stopped them seeing each other.'

'So, what happened?'

'My grandmother's best friend became jealous and she exposed their relationship. They weren't allowed to see each other.'

'They obviously did.'

'Joshua's time in Corfu was coming to an end, and he was to return to England. It didn't take much persuasion for my grandmother to go with him. She left her family and everything she knew for the man she loved.'

'That's a real love story. It must have taken a lot of courage to do that in those days.'

'She went to another country with just a suitcase and a heart full of love. She was a very determined woman. She always told me that if you believed in something, then nothing was impossible.'

'I'm beginning to like her already.'

'When they arrived in London, Joshua's family was very supportive. She always spoke fondly of them, especially Joshua's sister, Edith, who was just a few years older.

'Eventually, Joshua and my grandmother married and, a year later, my mother was born. By then, they were living in a house of their own. They were happy, they had built a life together, they were a family. My grandmother often told me they were the best days of her life. She loved living in London. Joshua had moved to a different company by then, it was a promotion, more money and he didn't have to travel away from home. Her life in London was a world away from her life in Corfu.'

'What was her name?'

'Dimitra.'

Brodie nodded approvingly. 'It's a strong sounding name. Just like the women she was, going by your description of her life.'

'Her name day is on the same day as my birthday.'

He looks at her quizzically. 'What's a name day?'

'In Greece, nearly every day of the year is dedicated to a saint or martyr and if someone shares the name of a saint, then that day becomes their name day. It's a big deal, like birthdays. Family and friends visit and bring presents, so we always celebrated my birthday and her name day together. She always told me it was a blessing we shared that date.'

'I can tell she meant a lot to you.'

'She was a big part of my life. I loved her so much. I miss her every day.'

'So, she moved to London, got married, had a family but, later in life, she is back living in Corfu. What happened?'

'Joshua was conscripted into the army. World War Two broke out. As an engineer, his skills were invaluable. He joined The Royal Engineers and, after his training, he was gone. Then, several months later, the army informed her, Joshua had been captured by the Germans and was presumed to be in a prisoner of war camp. That was all they could tell her.' Elora said sorrowfully.

'That must have been awful.'

'That's not the end of it.'

'What do you mean?'

'The Germans were bombing London on a nightly basis, houses and streets demolished in an instant. The war had visited them from the skies.'

'The blitz.'

'Yes. My grandmother told me stories of sheltering from the bombing in the underground stations. After emerging into the morning light after another night of constant bombs, she returned to her street to find her house had been hit during the night. She spent hours trying to recover what she could from the rubble, which wasn't much. She was taken in by Joshua's family, but it was difficult for her and them. She did the best she could. At one point, there were eight of them living in a small terraced house with an outside toilet and no bath.

'She managed to find work in the local hospital, assisting the nurses and doctors with the injured and dying. She really enjoyed that kind of work and hoped to train as a nurse after the war had ended. During this time, my mother who was still a toddler was looked after by Joshua's elderly parents while grandmother helped at the hospital. Everyone had to do their bit for the war effort. It helped to boost everyone's morale and hopes that, one day soon, it would be all over.'

'She told me that she could never give up hope. She worked many hours a day at the hospital and the thought of Joshua being incarcerated in a prison camp, not knowing what had happened to his wife and child, trying to survive the brutality of the Nazis kept her living from day to day. She could never give up on the hope that each new day would mean another day closer to when they would eventually be together again.'

'How old was she during this time?' Brodie asks.

'She was only twenty years old but had lived a life many would never experience. She was strong and indomitable.

She knew her mind, but she was not ignorant of the world around her. She was a foreigner in a country at war, luckily Greece and Britain were on the same side or it could have been a lot more difficult for her. However, she knew she was vulnerable. She had no home; it was still a mound of rubble. The only money she had was the small amount Joshua had prudently saved, and she was mindful that she would need it to begin over again, to rebuild a life, a future for herself, Joshua and her daughter once their hell was over.'

'How do you know all of this in such detail?'

'Because, unlike most people who bury these kinds of things inside them, she was determined the past would be just that, it would not influence her future. She would never forget those times, but it would never define who she was or who she could be. She told me all of this. We had many discussions about it when I was young and as an adult.'

'I'd loved to have met her.'

Elora stands. 'Well. I can give you the next best thing.'

She disappears into the house. A few moments later, Elora appears holding a photo frame. She hands it to Brodie. In the photograph, Elora is standing next to an older woman. Dimitra is taller than Elora. Her hair, even though it is flecked with streaks of silver, is mostly dark and tied in a large bun. She is wearing a blouse and a skirt. She is smiling to the camera and, next to her, Elora's head is slightly turned, and she is smiling at Dimitra.

'I wanted another photograph taken with me looking at the camera. I was quite insistent. I thought I'd ruined it. My grandmother was having none of it. She said it would be priceless because it was natural, it captured a moment in time and she was right, it's my favourite photograph of us together.'

'When was it taken?'

'A few years ago, now. I think it was when I'd returned from Paris.'

Elora pours more wine. 'One day, I remember it distinctly. I was only eight years old. I told her I wanted to go to university, maybe Oxford or Cambridge. I wanted to visit London as she had done. I wanted to get a job and live in an apartment overlooking The Thames. She never belittled me, she said, '*Elora, if you want all of these things, how are you going to achieve them?*' And I replied in my eight-year-old way that I'd do well at school and pass all my exams and buy a plane ticket that would take me to England. I remember she looked at me admiringly, nodding her head in approval. I felt so proud of myself. I was going to go to university in England, and then she asked, '*So, does everyone in England speak Greek?*' I looked at her as if my grandmother had lost her mind. '*No, they speak English, of course.*' '*They do?*' she asked. '*Yes. Of course, they do.*' '*Then, how can you go to England? You only speak Greek.*' And that's how I began to learn English. She taught me. She said that you can only ever truly learn to speak a language once you live in that country and live amongst its people. That's how she learnt.

'So, certain parts of the day, we would speak only in English. It was the second-best thing. By the time I was ten years old I was able to have conversations with her in English. As I got older, I taught myself to read and write in English.'

Brodie looks at the photograph. 'So, what happened after the war?'

Elora sighs. 'It was difficult for her. Joshua didn't return. After the war, there was so much confusion and the documentation the Nazis had was either destroyed or lost. Joshua just seemed to vanish. There was no trace of him. She didn't know if he was alive or dead. The official line was that he was missing, presumed dead. Some of the prisoners managed to escape, just before the end of the war, when Germany knew the allies were advancing at a steady pace. Those that survived the camp said that a group of men had escaped, but they were caught and brought back to the camp. They were shot and their bodies lined up and they lay for days in the open air. There was a rumour that a few managed to hide in an animal transportation train and were never caught. If they ever resurfaced after the end of the war, my grandmother never knew about it. She held on to the slimmest of chances that one day Joshua would find his way back to her.'

'Did he?'

'Oh, he did.'

'He did?'

'Yes. Two years later.'

Brodie looked at her in astonishment. 'Two years? How is that possible?'

'One day, he just turned up at her door like a ghost. Well, you can imagine her shock… she was heavily pregnant.'

'Wow! That must have been some reunion, after all those years. There's more questions than answers.'

'My mother was only seven years old. Dimitra always told her that her father was a hero and that's all she knew of him. She couldn't remember him. Joshua was a stranger to her. She remembered when Dimitra opened the door, and the sound that came out of her when she saw Joshua standing in the street. It scared my mother so much that she hid behind Dimitra and only peered around Dimitra's skirt when Joshua said my mother's name. My mother remembered being sent to her room, thinking that she was being punished. She had an immediate dislike towards the strange man.'

'How did Dimitra react?'

'They sat in the front room. Dimitra asked Joshua if he would like some tea. She told me, she often thought about that, why she offered him a cup of tea as if Joshua was just an unexpected visitor and she was being polite and hospitable? She put it down to shock.'

'So, they were civil towards each other?'

'At first. Have you heard of the term PTSD?

'Yes. Post-traumatic stress disorder. Why?'

'In those days, just after the war, it wasn't called that, but that's what it was…'

'I never thought I'd see you again. I thought you were dead. There was no word about you, nothing. The army said you were missing, presumed dead.'

'In a way, they were right. I'm not the person you knew. That Joshua is dead.'

'What do you mean? Why are you speaking like this? Joshua, tell me.'

He pulled his fingers through his oily hair, and Dimitra noticed a slight tremor in his hand.

He began by telling Dimitra he was captured by the Germans and sent to a prisoner of war camp. He was incarcerated in the camp for the rest of the war, until, amongst others, and because of his engineering background, he was chosen to be part of a carefully orchestrated plan that involved digging a tunnel under the camp. Joshua spoke of the mixture of elation and fear that accompanied the escapees as they disappeared into the blackness of night.

Dimitra made the odd enquiry, but mostly she listened. 'There were three of us hiding in the train, a foul-smelling carriage full of cattle, piss and shit,' he was saying. 'After what seemed like hours, it eventually stopped. We could hear the carriages behind us being unloaded. We didn't have a plan. We knew we were about to be discovered; we had no choice. Through the gaps in the wood, we could see trees, a thick forest about fifty feet away. When the doors were slid open, we ran for it and were almost within touching distance of the first trees when I heard three gun shots crack the air.'

Joshua's eyes closed; his breathing quickened. Damitra thought he was having a panic attack.

'You don't have to tell me, Joshua. It's upsetting you.'

'I have to, don't you see? I need you, of all people, to understand.'

After a moment, he described his friend's head exploding like a melon and splattering his face with shreds of bone, blood and brains. He continued to run as the forest engulfed him. He described it as being swallowed by the forest, becoming invisible. He was running blindly and fell down a ravine into a river. He let the water carry him for miles. He came to a farm, and the family took him in and that's when he learnt they were in the final days of the war; the Germans were defeated.

He told Dimitra that by then; he had lost his mind. The nightmares started, the sweats, images, smells, sounds and constantly reliving the moment his friend was shot and killed. He felt incredible guilt that he survived, and the others didn't.

'I was lucky, I spent several days with the family whose farm I had stumbled upon. They fed me, I was able to wash in hot water in a bath and sleep in a bed. Time to recover. But that was just it, my physical body was mending itself, but my mind wasn't. I was becoming increasingly withdrawn.'

He described it as feeling numb to his surroundings and the family that were caring for him. He was devoid of emotion, staying in his room, not wanting social contact. He wanted to isolate himself from the world around him. He began to forget the details of his past. Gaps in his memory appeared. Just living and breathing was an effort. He felt threatened by those around him, constantly on the edge, until, one day, he exploded and struck the farmer, breaking his nose. He couldn't remember how he came to be in the hospital, but he woke one day and found himself in what would now be a psychiatric ward. Only a few doctors spoke any English.

*'I couldn't sleep, I felt angry and irritable and found it
hard to concentrate, even for short periods. I often thought
about different ways I could kill himself. I felt worthless.'*

*Sitting opposite Joshua in her small front room, Dimitra
felt numb listening to Joshua describe his ordeal: the
prison camp, the deaths, the starvation, the cold and
disease and how he escaped, witnessing the others being
shot and how he came to be a patient in a foreign hospital.
He told her everything, his addiction to alcohol and living
under a bridge, where he protected himself from the
elements by building a rudimentary shelter with wood and
corrugated sheets of iron. He was taken in by a local
church that helped the homeless, and they helped with his
eventual recuperation and return to London.*

*As he spoke, Dimitra looked at him sadly and listened
with a heavy heart. She pushed all thoughts of her hardship
from her mind. When he had finished, she waited on him to
ask about the baby. Bizarrely, it was like he hadn't noticed.*

*It was Joshua, and it was not. He was thinner. It
sharpened his facial features. Once broad, his shoulders
were now rounded, his chest sunken. Mostly, Dimitra was
struck by his eyes, shadowed and hollow and his pallid
complexion which aged him beyond his years. She had so
many questions; they swirled in her head like leaves caught
by the wind. She had to speak.*

'I'm pregnant, Joshua.'

*'I can see that. I didn't expect you to be a nun. Although,
I've been like a priest these past years.'*

*She was unsure if Joshua's remark was meant to chastise
her. His face gave nothing away, it remained pensive.
Dimitra rubbed the swell of her stomach, it had become a
habit of hers, a comforter. Joshua looked around the room.
He seemed detached, and Dimitra suddenly felt uneasy.*

*Joshua lit a cigarette and leaned back against the chair.
He inhaled sharply and exhaled a plume of smoke.*

'I've still got the photograph of us that day we went to Brighton. Look, it's on the sideboard.'

'Who's the father? Do I know him?'

The change in the subject startled Dimitra. Joshua's mouth was straight and hard, not with anger but... an absence of emotion.

'No. I don't think you do.'

Joshua's demeanour was unbalancing for Dimitra. She would prefer anger. Yes, that was a normal reaction, not this. He was talking as if he was casually asking after an old friend. The realisation shocked her.

'Does he live here with you?'

'No.'

'Then where?'

'He's dead.'

'I see. What happened?'

'It was an accident. He was hit by a bus. He died in hospital two days later.'

'It's for the best.'

'Why do you say that?' Dimitra can feel the air around them change.

Joshua was staring at her stomach. 'Because, this is my home, not his. You'll have to get rid of it. Like its father, it is dead to me.'

Brodie winced. 'He was not well, poor man. A part of me can't help feeling his disposition was not entirely due to his state of mind, though. The way you describe him, it's as if he was enjoying saying those things.' Brodie wondered what it must have been like to live with such a man.

'It was an impossible situation Dimitra found herself in. They were, by now, two strangers forced by circumstance to live together. Any love she did have for him evaporated in the months that followed. Dimitra didn't know Joshua, not anymore. She still had an affection for him, the before the war Joshua, but this was not who returned. Rage seemed to always fill him, and Dimitra was the only person he could aim it at.'

'Did he... you know, assault her physically... sexually?'

'No! No. That never happened. If it did, Dimitra never told me. She was just as much a victim of Joshua's illness as he was. She feared for her daughter. My mother witnessed the psychological abuse, the drunken rants, now a daily ritual. Dimitra feared her daughter would become used to it, and believe this was what adults did, this was normal. My mother slept with Dimitra, and Joshua slept in what was my mother's bedroom. Their marriage was in name only.'

'What about the baby?'

'She lost it. A miscarriage. Given her circumstances, it may have been for the best. There was no way of knowing what he would have been capable of. With a new-born in the house, she would have feared Joshua's fierce and uncontrolled anger and her children's safety. Joshua never asked her about the miscarriage, nor did he show her any empathy. She often wondered if Joshua was purposely trying to make her leave him, his sudden outbursts were fuelled with more fury, more hurtful and malicious remarks and anger. It was always her fault that he was like this. The humiliation she received outraged her and the desire to retaliate was so irresistible. Dimitra told me she often came close to it. The only thing that stopped her was Joshua's revenge. Dimitra feared that one day, her daughter would also become the victim. He was already seeing the worst in her little girl, albeit untrue, but it was meant to purposely hurt Dimitra. She wouldn't put her daughter's safety at risk.

'From the outside, Dimitra's life looked like another's dream come true. What was she doing there? She didn't have to put up with it anymore. No one deserved to live like that.

'She knew, every night, Joshua would be intoxicated and fall into bed in an unconscious state. That would be her opportunity to escape unnoticed. So, secretly, she planned to leave him and made the arrangements for a passage back to Corfu. She would no longer be a prisoner in her own home.'

'She returned to Corfu?'

'She did.'

'And what about Joshua? What happened to him?'

'Dimitra kept in touch with Edith, Joshua's sister. They wrote to each other, frequently. She was my mother's auntie, after all.'

'Dimitra never asked about Joshua and Edith never spoke about him. I think she was embarrassed by what happened. She mentioned him only once, and that was to tell Dimitra Joshua had committed suicide. It was about two years after Dimitra left him.'

Brodie felt it then.

A change in the air. He could smell the sea and feel the breeze rise from the water as it shifted across his face and through his hair. He heard the voice first. The anger stunned him, throwing curses across The River Forth, then confused ramblings spilt from the young man's lips. He looked exhausted, swaying and bending on the grey steel beam, staring oblivion in the face, above the seagulls majestically gliding and diving upon invisible currents. A beat of silence. Brodie hesitated, only briefly, a quick breath and anguished words. A sense of losing him rippled through Brodie. He remembers the scream that left the young man's throat, and like the young man's face, it haunts him still.

'Are you all right?' Elora asks. 'You're sweating.'

Brodie doesn't know how to respond.

'It looked like an absence or something like that. What just happened, Brodie? You said a name, *Isaac!* Was that the man on the bridge?' Her eyes also ask the question.

Brodie can feel a sheen of sweat on his forehead. He swallows and coughs. 'It's happened a few times.'

'Have you seen a doctor?'

'No. There's no need for that. I'm fine, honest.' He knows she doesn't believe him.

'Well, if it happens again, you will see a doctor.'

'If it makes you feel better.'

'It's not about me, although you did give me a fright.'

'It hasn't happened that often. I can deal with it. There's no need to worry. If it happens again, I'll see a doctor.'

'Promise?'

'I promise.'

'It's all right saying you'll be fine, but what if it happens when you're back in Corfu Town? You could fall, hit your head, it doesn't bear thinking about.' She thinks out loud. 'You don't have to stay in Corfu Town.'

There is a pause.

His eyes fix on hers.

She smiles.

'I don't think I can keep saying goodbye.'

'Then stay.' There is an expectant air to her words.

'Do you mean that?'

'Yes. I've room here. More than enough, as you can see.' Elora eyes him cautiously.

'I'd like to. I would.'

'I sense a *but* coming.'

'It's just… I don't want you to feel obliged to… that it's something you feel you have to ask.'

'No, no, it's fine. I don't, really, I don't.'

He knows that Elora can already predict he wants to, but such a prospect hadn't crossed his mind. 'I never expected an offer to stay, that's why I rented the apartment.'

'It makes sense to me anyway. Think about it.'

'I will.'

She smiles satisfactorily. 'Good.'

Chapter 9

A Reply to an Invitation

Elora spends a lot of her time in the garden. She has told Brodie she finds it clears her head; it helps her to think, it is her therapy. She has tied her hair back with a hairband and wears large gloves that make her hands look out of proportion to the rest of her body. She has on a lilac blouse, white shorts and flip-flops with inserted diamond patterns over the straps. She crouches, prodding the earth with a handheld trowel.

Brodie has been watching her, this woman who has defined most of his adult life, even in her absence. It has been several days now since he first arrived. Each hot day melds into another.

His modest apartment in the Old Town of the capital has catered for his needs; however, he has wanted to spend as much time as he can with Elora. Each second they are together is shared time he thought would never be possible. He knows Elora is comfortable with his presence. After his *little turn*, as he refers to it, Elora would still like him to stay. She has assured him it is what she wants as there is an awkwardness about the current arrangement. Brodie feels it too, it has troubled him, but he can't disown the fact this has made him somewhat apprehensive and is the reason he is still deliberating over his reply to her invitation.

He is sitting in the terrace's shade watching her plant flowers and, once again, he considers the practicalities of Elora's request. The apartment in Corfu Town was a precautionary measure that gave him a place to retreat to just in case Elora did not the warm to his unannounced arrival which would have undoubtedly complicated things.

Brodie is feeling more assured, now that they have grown into each other's presence and their relationship is re-established. The circumstances favour a decision suitable to them both.

He steps from the terrace and feels a thrill of excitement. Sensing his proximity, Elora lifts her head from her work, pleased to see him.

'I've got something to tell you.'

'I thought you had been thinking. You looked all serious and thoughtful hiding in the shadows.' Elora peels the gloves from her hands and stands to her height. She seems delicate and breakable, but Brodie knows behind her seamless demeanour there is a spark of steel.

Elora wipes her brow. 'Well, before you do, let's get out of the sun. I need a drink.'

Brodie pours lemonade from a glass jug freshly plucked from the fridge. Elora settles into her chair and takes a long drink.

'I think you're right.'

'You do?'

'I do.'

'Are you sure? I don't want to pressure you into it.'

'You haven't, honestly. I've been thinking about what you said and you're right, if I were in your shoes, I'd feel the same. If you had come to see me in Edinburgh, I'd feel slightly offended if you stayed in a hotel when you could have stayed with me.'

'You've paid for the apartment in Corfu Town.'

'It's only money, some things are worth more,' Brodie declares.

'Even with all my imperfections?'

'None of us are perfect, especially me. We're all complicated creatures who hide behind our masks. We show the world what we want it to see. At some point, we need to reveal the secrets we've buried inside ourselves.'

'Is that why you've come here?'

'There are things that need to be said.'

'You've got that serious look on your face again.'

'If there is any hope that we have a future, then we need to face the past together.'

Elora sits composed, her face masking her frantic thoughts. She is glad that Brodie has come, but fears what it will inevitably lead them to.

Chapter 10

Something is Happening

Elora looks out into the garden and fingers her bracelet. How quiet the house is, she thinks. She loves this time of morning as the thought of another day stretches out in front of her.

She worries about what might follow in the coming days. She knows Brodie is close to telling her something and that something may not be what she wants to hear. He has been candid with her, and for that she is grateful. She is certain something troubles him and the days that follow will test them; she is sure of it.

Brodie's sudden appearance and recent daily permanence have offset her normal equilibrium. She finds herself in a peculiar state of mind and, because of it, sleep has eluded her. She thinks it will be a relief telling him. After all, he deserves to know.

She tells herself this must happen. She has carried this inside her for far too long. It is always there, menacing and prowling like a wild animal. She knows it intimately. It wears her out. Elora has tried to envisage Brodie's response. The thought of it makes her ache with worry.

Perhaps it is because she is at the mercy of events and not driving them, she feels nervous. She must pull herself back from the edge of her worry. She must shrink this burden.

She is feeling tense and the rumblings of a headache radiate across her forehead.

In the kitchen, she slides open a drawer and finds a packet of paracetamol. She swallows two pills with a glass of water and hopes they will take effect soon. From a cafetiere, Elora empties the remnants of last night's coffee into the sink. She tips three spoonsful of fresh coffee into the cafetiere and pours boiled water from the kettle, inhaling the intense and satisfying aroma that rises towards her as she waits for the coffee to settle.

'Good morning.' Brodie says, crossing the kitchen, his hair still wet from his shower. He is wearing the chinos and a t-shirt he wore the day before.

'Did you sleep well?'

'I did. The mattress is much better than the bed in Corfu Town. I woke with a sore back the first night I slept there.'

'I've just made coffee. Would you like some?'

'I'd love a cup.'

'I'll bring it out onto the terrace.'

They sit opposite each other. The coffee is strong and bitter. The pine trees that line the garden wall give their soft ligneous quiver as their branches stir from a breeze emanating from the Ionian.

'You make lovely coffee,' Brodie comments.

'I never start a day without one.'

Brodie smiles. 'Do you have any plans for today?'

'I've got a few phone calls to make and some emails but, apart from that nothing else.'

'I thought we could drive to Corfu Town and get my things. If you're still okay with me staying?'

'I haven't changed my mind. Yes, I think that's an excellent idea.'

***

The smooth paving stone underfoot shines as if for centuries, someone had polished it daily, reflecting the sky and tangerine facades of terraced and timeworn buildings.

They pass a square where people hover at the entrance to a church. Above them, flora clings to flaking stucco, creeping along salmon facades in an explosion of green and blood red. Even the wires that span the street have yielded to nature's colourful encroachment. Small rectangular balconies have become miniature gardens sprinkled in clay pots that spill with flowers. Every corner reveals another array of wooden shutters: green, blue and white.

As they saunter through the old town, Brodie's thoughts churn with retrospective relief. He is with Elora. After all these years he could never have imagined this. In his thinking, such a possibility was far-fetched to say the least. This has not been the first time and it will not be the last that his mind will be in awe at this. Something is happening, he tells himself with cautious happiness. The prospect exhilarates him.

As they round another corner, Elora asks if Brodie is hungry?

They head down one of the many narrow lanes and take a seat at a table outside a small café bar.

Elora gives an exhalation of pleasure as she surveys the menu. 'Some olives, houmous and tzatziki with pitta bread to share?'

Brodie nods. 'Are you hungry enough to have a main dish?'

'Yes, why not? Mm… I think I'll have the Moshari Kokkinisto.'

Brodie scans the menu until he finds the dish. 'Beef cooked in red wine and a tomato sauce. It sounds nice.'

'I've eaten it here before. I'd recommend it.'

He looks up from the menu. 'Lamb is almost a Greek national dish, isn't it? I might have the Paidakia.'

'An excellent choice. The lamb is good here too. I think you'll like it.'

'The Paidakia it is then.'

Once they have ordered and the waiter brings their drinks, diet coke and lemonade, Elora sits back and grins at Brodie.

'What?' Brodie asks.

'I still can't believe you came all this way.'

Brodie upturned his hands. 'Here I am. I found you.'

She nods. 'I know there are things that need to be said, by both of us. And they will be when it is right to do so. For now, let us enjoy our meal and each other. I'd like to show you around this amazing town and then we can get your things.'

After they have eaten, Elora suggests they visit the old fortress.

'You'll love the views of the town from up there,' she tells Brodie, pointing towards the stone fortress.

They pass through The Liston, an arched stone colonnade where tourists and locals alike are eating in the restaurants and drinking in the coffee shops. They walk along an expansive esplanade and to access the fortress; they cross a bridge, the water underneath leading to the sea and where fishing boats rest.

Elora explains that the fortress was built on two rocky peaks and, like the Old Town, it is now a World Heritage site. She goes on to tell him, as with the buildings and neoclassical houses of the Old Town, the fortress' construction is a blend of Venetian, French and British influence, reflecting the many periods of occupation that have speckled the island's history

Angular and smooth ramparts dominate their approach and Brodie can appreciate why, throughout its history, the fortress was impregnable.

Eventually, they make their way to the highest viewpoint. Brodie marvels at the site of The Old Town spread out like a blanket in front of him and the distant peaks of undulating hills in the hazy background. He insists that he takes a photograph of them both, with the view behind them and the surrounding sea where a flotilla of sailing boats streak white across the deep blue waters of the Ionian.

Elora smiles, a gleam in her eyes. 'What do you think? Didn't I tell you it would be worth it.'

'It's stunning, simply breath taking.'

As they make their way through the narrow lanes and pedestrianised streets of the Old Town once again, Brodie is aware of an increase in the bodily traffic, the shops and café bars are filling with customers and restaurants are busily plying their trade. There is something distinctly different about their surroundings than there was earlier. The ambience has altered, Brodie can feel it. Above the narrow streets, the sky is muted in a soft haze, infused with hints of pastel and dark speckles, swifts he thinks, that acrobatically dart, with purpose it seems, in unison of performance. Something else is different too. There is a shift in light. It coats the walls and shutters in a new layer of colour, like an artist's brush, softer to the eye.

'It's just up here,' Brodie says.

Nicola's Studio is along a narrow lane. Once inside, Brodie packs his clothes and toiletries.

Elora looks around approvingly. 'It's very small, but nicely decorated and clean.'

'I was relieved when I first arrived. I hadn't even seen a photograph of the place. I couldn't find any online. It was a little disconcerting, but I didn't have the luxury of choice.'

'Well then, you were lucky. I love that there's no plaster, just the use of the original brick on the walls and these stone floor tiles are nice too.'

Elora cranes her head inside the tiny bathroom, which is just a shower, basin and toilet. 'Small, but nicely done and modern. It seems a shame to leave it.'

Brodie raises an eyebrow. 'I might have to come back.'

Elora gives him a roguish stare. 'That's true. You might have to.'

Edinburgh 1995

The Elephant in the Room

Friday night and Négociants was crammed with students and twentysomethings, all competing to be heard as the walls breathed with the Beatle-esque melodies of Oasis piping loudly through the cafe bar. Elora was on an evening out with friends, Maria and Lianne. They were sitting at a table and Elora was leaning into Maria, eyes screwed in concentration, her forehead furrowed as she listened with set lips.

'What do you mean by that Maria?' Elora's face was pale with panic.

'It's obvious, Elora. He fancies the pants off you.'

'Rubbish. I would know if he did. He's always in the flat, visiting Brodie.'

'And?'

'And what? He's Brodie's best friend, for God's sake!'

'What's that got to do with it. A hard prick dulls the loyalties.'

'Marie!'

'Well, it's true.'

'How would you know?'

'Believe me, I do. You wouldn't believe what goes on. You've been cocooned in your flat with Brodie for far too long now to notice what the rest of us are getting up to.'

Just then, Lianne appeared with more drinks. 'Get these down you, girls. Where shall we go next?'

'Somewhere a bit quieter,' Elora suggested. 'Lianne, did you know about Chris?' Her accent sounding more pronounced.

Lianne kept her face neutral. 'Know what?' She flashed a look in Marie's direction.

'You did! My God, does everybody know?'

'That depends on what you mean by everybody? Your tutorial class? Yes, most of them do.'

Elora sank into herself. She brought a glass to her lips and drank half of its contents. 'It's not a glass of wine I need. Right now, I could drink a whole bottle.'

Marie put her arm around Elora. 'We'll share one, but I'm not carrying you home.'

They moved on to The Pear Tree, in West Nicolson Street, and sat outside on one of the long benches, where it seemed half the student population of Edinburgh were drinking.

Marie's eyes widened. 'He's here!'

'Who? Brodie?' Lianne asked.

'Chris!' Marie corrected her.

'No!' Elora shrieked, embarrassed and terrified. At that moment, she ached to be invisible.

'It's all right. He hasn't seen you. We can leave if you want?' Marie suggested sympathetically.

Elora shook her head. 'No. That would be silly. Let's just enjoy ourselves.'

'Where is he?'

'Two tables along to the left.'

Lianne gave a sly look. 'So he is.'

'Will you two stop it?'

'He's looking over!' Lianne said. 'What will you do if he sits beside us?'

'Nothing. He's Brodie's friend, that's all.' Inside, Elora's heart was racing.

'He is. Fuck. He's coming over.' Marie slapped the table with her palm.

Chris smiled at the women as he came closer towards their table. Marie swept her hair with a graceful arc of her arm and simultaneously sucked in her stomach.

'Ladies, what a pleasant surprise. The Charlie's Angels of Edinburgh University.'

Marie exaggerated a forced laugh.

Lianne lowered her voice. 'My God. You fancy him.'

Suddenly, Elora felt a burst of longing for Brodie.

'Hello, Elora. Where's Brodie?'

'I'm meeting him here, later,' she lied.

'Cool. What are you ladies drinking? Your glasses are almost empty.'

'We're fine,' Elora stressed.

Marie drains her glass. 'I'll have a red… Merlot.'

Not wanting to come over as prudish, Lianne also asked for wine.

'Elora?' Chris asked expectantly.

'Just water for me.'

'Elora, it's Friday night. Let me buy you a proper drink.'

'Jesus, Elora. Let him buy you a drink.' Marie is insistent.

'Just a small one then, a red.'

'Perfect. Don't go away now.'

'We won't. We're glued to our seats.'

Chris laughed and headed off inside, towards the bar.

'That's was pathetic,' Lianne snapped.

'What!' Marie retorted.

'It's obvious.'

'What is?'

'I'm going to the toilet.' Elora stood up, carefully avoiding her friends' eyes.

When she returned, Chris had settled at their table, drinking from a bottle of lager. He sat opposite her two friends, and Elora felt an obvious reluctance to sit beside him. She wanted to keep on walking into the street. A plausible reason to excuse herself evaded her and as she neared the table, she averted her eyes from him. She slid into the space next to him and placed her handbag on the bench.

She wondered what the rules and regulations were when the elephant in the room was pressing against you. She straightened her back and held herself stiffly.

'We were just telling Chris about the party tonight.'

Elora gulped a mouthful of wine. A trickle of wine ran over her mouth. She lifted her hand and moved a finger over her lips. Chris gave the impression he wasn't looking.

'Do you know Marsha? It's her twenty-first.' Elora said.

Chris turned to look at her, and Elora could see the irises of his eyes, and realised she had never noticed their colour, a striking green.

'I do.' Chris smiled. 'She's in most of my lectures. I told her I'd pop by at some point tonight. There's a band playing too. They're called Jellyhead. I've seen them before. They're good, rock with soul, a bit like The Black Crowes.'

'We're heading over there, after here.' Marie said.

'Some of the guys are going.' Chris nodded towards the table he had been sitting at. 'Is Brodie going?'

Elora could sense the expectation around her. Marie smiled conspiratorially at Elora. There was an apprehensive pause. She smoothed her hair and sat up straight. 'I'm not sure. It's not his thing, really.'

'I know he likes the band. He's seen them before.'

'He likes me better. I suppose you can't blame him.'

She waited for a reaction. Chris smiled but said nothing. She found herself disappointed. God, I'm flirting with him!

'Well, if I don't see him could you tell him I'll call around tomorrow about lunchtime to pick up the book I loaned him. It's due back at the Uni library and I've already had to pay a fine. My third in four months. It would be cheaper buying the books.'

Marie laughed. She knew it sounded pathetic, so she tried to soften her embarrassment with a smile.

Elora cleared her throat. 'Sure. I'll mention it,' she said, not quite meeting his eyes.

'So, I might see you all later. They're getting restless over there. We're heading off to another pub by the looks of things.' Chris finished his drink and stood up.

'Thanks for the drink,' Lianne said. 'It's my shout the next time.'

Chris smiled. 'I'll hold you to it. Maybe later tonight?'

Chapter 11

Confessions

When they return from Corfu Town, Brodie unpacks his suitcase in the bedroom next to Elora's room. As he is doing so, he thinks of phoning his son, and then Elora surfaces in his mind. How strange this all feels, Brodie thinks. He will be sleeping in the room next to her. A quiver runs the length of his spine and it feels like time has collapsed in upon itself.

He hangs his tops, shorts and trousers on coat hangers and puts his socks and underwear in a drawer and, although these tasks are performed mechanically, his thoughts are far from the mundane. He has not been honest with Elora. The absences have been more frequent than he has suggested, and this doesn't sit easy with him. He wonders if he should tell her, but then, he doesn't want to worry her. No. What would be the point in that?

When he finishes unpacking, he descends the stairs and wanders into the kitchen. Elora has her back to him. She is humming a tune whilst chopping an onion. Brodie smiles and his shoulders relax. Elora's contentment is pleasing to him.

'Can I help?'

She looks over her shoulder and smiles. 'Not really, this won't take long. I wasn't sure how this was going to work. Should we eat in or eat out? We can do both, I suppose, but for tonight, I thought, after our day in town, we could just relax here and maybe go out tomorrow night for something to eat?'

Brodie nods. 'That would be nice. I'll set the table then.'

'You'll get the cutlery in that drawer and the plates are over in that cupboard.'

'What are you making?'

'You'll see. There are some candles and matches in that drawer.'

Around them, the air is soft. The sun is setting, melting into the horizon as Brodie and Elora finish eating dinner on the terrace. Brodie marvels at a streak of orange and yellow light where the horizon touches the sea and crimson clouds fire the sky with flames that mirror in the waterline.

'Are all the sunsets like this?'

'Not always,' Elora admits. 'Some are better.' They laugh in unison.

He is attracted to her mouth; he always has been. His eyes slide to the curve of her upper lip and the fullness of the bottom lip whenever he looks upon her face. It has always been like this.

He thought suddenly: *Elora's sister.* 'The other day, you mentioned your sister. I was going to ask you about her, but it must have slipped my mind. When we were students in Edinburgh, I can't remember you ever mentioning her. It came as a surprise.'

Elora shrugs. 'Are you sure?'

'I am. I wouldn't forget something like that.'

'Well, it must be true then.'

Brodie can sense her irritation and wonders where it has come from. 'Does she live in Corfu?'

'No. She lives in London now. Or she did. We don't keep in touch.'

'You haven't visited her when you've been in London?'

'We're not close. We haven't been for a long time,' Elora says flatly.

Brodie's instinct is to enquire further, but he holds back, sensing Elora's unwillingness to add any more. Intrigue gets the better of him and like an itch that he must scratch, he says, 'Has she been back to Corfu?'

'Not that I know of.'

'That's a shame.'

'It would be if I cared at all.' Elora regrets the words, even as they spill from her lips.

'I don't understand.'

Elora turns her head from him. She takes a deep breath. 'Things happened. It was a long time ago.'

'I see,' Brodie says, but he does not.

'We're twins. Not identical but twins, all the same.'

This fresh piece of information amazes Brodie. It is the last thing he expects to hear.

'Her name is Eliana,' she tells him before he asks. 'She was always jealous of me, even as children. I could ride a bike before her, I learnt to swim before her, I could read better than her, boys spoke to me first; as a child, I was unaware of this, but Eliana's resentment began then. My mother was always the referee, breaking up arguments, trying not to take sides. She never treated us differently, rules were rules, and we daren't break them. With them came expectations, chores to be done around the house, our rooms to be kept tidy. I achieved good grades at school and Eliana, well not so much. As young women, we were different. I always had my head in a book, where Eliana would read women's magazines and experiment with make-up and buy the latest fashion in clothes.

'She believed our grandmother liked me better than her and always had done. I told her this was nonsense, but she wouldn't have any of it. She said that our grandmother spent more time with me, she showed more of an interest in me. She taught me to speak English and not Eliana and when I said she never wanted to learn it, she screamed at me that wasn't the point, and she hated grandmother for it. When it came to us, she always came second best and because of this, she hated me too.

'I couldn't believe what I was hearing. Why would she say such things? How can two people with the same upbringing, the same parents, have two different paths like ours? Is it fate, or chance, what can it be?

'Her behaviour became more extreme. She got into a bad crowd, started drinking and staying out late.

'And then, one day she announced she was pregnant, and she was going to stay with the father, someone from the crowd she hung about with. It broke my mother's heart. My father was going to kill her boyfriend for bringing shame on our family. He didn't, obviously.'

'I wouldn't have thought so, although I could imagine his desire to do so.'

'My mother blamed herself. If only she had tried harder to convince Eliana she loved us both equally, that she was special and contributed to everyone's happiness, then she would never have taken that path. Eliana wouldn't have fallen into the wrong crowd, she wouldn't have gotten pregnant and she would have a daughter who wasn't filled with rage and anger and a husband who died of a heart attack, which she believed the shock contributed to. My mother believed she had failed Eliana, and she lived with that right up until the day she died.'

'Oh, Elora. That's tragic.'

Elora runs her fingers through her hair. 'She wasn't content to stop there.'

Brodie leans forward. 'What do you mean?'

Elora closes her eyes. 'She never set foot in our house again. She lived with her boyfriend, had the baby, it was a boy, but she never let any of the family see him.' When she opens her eyes, Brodie can see her tears. 'They left for London not long after he was born. My mother felt that God was punishing her. It broke her and my grandmother.' Elora dabs her eyes. 'I'm sorry. I haven't spoken about this for a long time.'

'I never knew any of this.'

'It's not something you want the world to know,'

'No. I suppose not.'

'I did confront her.'

'You did?'

'Before she left for London. I went to see her. She didn't invite me into the house, and I wasn't expecting her to, so, I never saw the baby. I asked her why she had done this? How could she have done this to her own family? She looked at me and said, because it was the first time in her life, she could do something that I could never do. I was shocked, I couldn't believe what she was saying. This whole tragedy was about me. It was then I realised how much she must have hated me. To be able to contemplate such actions is one thing but to carry them out is abhorrence at its worst. At that moment, the revulsion I felt for her eclipsed any thought of making her see sense or the utter disillusionment she had caused her family. I've never felt such rage before or since. I slapped her across the face as hard as I could, and I turned away from her and left. I never saw her again.'

'Did you ever think about her? How life might have turned out for her and her son. She may have many regrets.'

'I didn't, not for a long time. I banished her from my thoughts. But now, sometimes I do. I blame myself for what happened. It was because of me that my parents and my grandmother were put through so much pain and grief. My mother went through so much heartache. Not only could she not see her daughter, but her only grandchild was also a stranger to her because of me. It took me a long time to see that.'

'How can you say that?'

'If I wasn't who I was when I was younger, none of this would have happened. Throughout her whole life, Eliana was jealous of me, so much so, that it ate away at her until, finally, all she had left was the one thing she could control... to cause her family pain and suffering. She knew what she was doing.'

'You can't mean that. You can't. It's...'

'Why not? Why can't I? If I was different, more like her…'

'She was the one with the problem, not you. Elora listen to yourself. You're not making any sense. Your thought processes are… well, they're not logical.'

'I know what I feel and no matter how hard I've tried, I can't change that. You don't understand. How can you?'

'No, I don't. What you're saying just doesn't make sense to me.'

Elora stands up. 'And I need a drink.'

She returns from the kitchen with a bottle of red wine and two glasses. 'I thought you might need one too.'

She fills both glasses and hands one to Brodie. When she sits, Elora takes a long drink and then places her glass on the table. She closes her eyes and when she opens them, Brodie can see they are filled with tears.

'I'm sorry, Elora. It matters to me…' he doesn't want her to think what he said was a criticism. 'You matter to me. I'm not belittling you or what you feel, I just can't relate to it, that's all,' he says reflectively.

'I'm not expecting you to.'

'I don't want to make a big deal about it.'

'It is to me. I've lived with this all my life, the self-blame, the guilt. When I went to Edinburgh and the university, I thought I was escaping it all. The fire, my sister. You can escape the physical aspect, but not what's in here.' She taps her forehead.

She wants him to know. If she is to mean anything to him, he must know. It has exhausted her; the years hang heavy on her. She has tried to erase the memories. She has tried so hard…

'Sometimes I come out here and watch this.' She gestures with an opened hand towards the sea and hills. 'I don't always see the beauty in it.'

'What do you see?'

'Nothing. All I want is for the world to stop spinning.'

Brodie glances beyond the garden towards the sea and fading light. He looks at Elora. She is smiling. What has come over her?

'A smile can hide a lot of things. What do you think?'

'I suppose it can.' Suddenly Brodie craves a cigarette. He swallows some wine. 'Are you okay, Elora?'

'I just want to tell you, over the years, I've become an expert at hiding behind my smile. If it was an Olympic sport, I'd win a gold medal.'

She takes a deep breath; *It is necessary,* she reminds herself. 'I just click into social mode and put on a veneer. Then, when I'm on my own, it returns, it has just been lurking in the background waiting and, like a mist, it's pervasive, seeping into every aspect of me. It's crippling. I can feel it suck away my personality and who I am and replacing it with... just... emptiness.'

He looks at her. 'I... I don't know what to say.'

'Don't say anything. Not yet.'

She refreshes their glasses. The wine glugging thickly from the bottle.

'It has always been there, even before Eliana left. But after that, at times, I started to feel paranoid. It got worse, and I still do. Everything that personifies me as a writer, as a friend, as an individual, can be lost. It simply melts away. It can leave me feeling an imposter, a fake. It scares me, for I've no control over it, no influencing it. It lurks in the background, waiting for an opportunity to impose itself and spread like a virus through my mind, through every muscle and cell. It doesn't care who you are, how much money you have, how big your house is, the kind of car you drive, what you have achieved in life, it's all irrelevant. It doesn't discriminate.'

Keep going. I can't stop now. She is wary of withholding; she is drained by the constant concealment.

'At its worse, I drink. Believe me, I've tried to stop, I really have. It's like a friend that consoles me, it takes the pain away. The thing is, I regret it in the morning. I really do. It hangs over me all day and I promise myself, I'll never take another drink again. But I do.'

Brodie hears the words *drink* and *regret*. 'I didn't know any of this.'

'I know this has come as a shock to you. It hasn't been easy telling you. I wanted you to know. You don't have to stay; you can just walk away. I wouldn't blame you.'

'You know me better than that.'

'If you're disappointed in me, it's okay. I've got used to the disappointment,' she says defensively.

'I could never be disappointed in you, never.'

'I hate myself. I loathe myself for being weak and not in control.'

'You're not weak. Look at what you've done with your life. People admire you. They buy your books because it was *you* who wrote them. You have touched their lives. They escape into the worlds you create.'

Brodie reaches for her hand, but she distances it from him and instead wipes her tears with a napkin.

She breathes in the soft night air and smiles at him. 'You see, I've become an expert at portraying myself as confident and assertive in the literary world. In that universe, on the outside, I am well-balanced and content and why wouldn't I be. I'm the successful author everyone comes to see and hear talk about her books. They think they know me because they have identified with a character. They have gone through the same experiences, felt the pain and that mirrors their lives. What they don't see is the terrified little girl inside me, who just wants to roll up into a tiny ball and hide from the world.'

As Brodie tries to take this in, Elora continues. 'I've been on medication for years. It doesn't help anymore. I think I'm immune to it. I have good days and I feel normal again… and the bad ones, well, they take me to a dark place. It's a cliché, I know, but it's true.

'Have you tried to get help, counselling maybe?'

She rebuffs this with an inarticulate gesture of the hand. 'I've done all of that. I've tried yoga, meditation, even a weird and whacky retreat in England.' She tosses back her hair. 'I admitted to myself a long time ago my relationship with alcohol is not healthy. That doesn't mean I get drunk every day. I try to have, what I call, free days, where I try not to drink.' She looks away from him. 'I sometimes hate myself. It doesn't mean I'm a bad person… weak, yes, but not bad.'

'To me, you're beautiful inside and out.'

Elora gives a bitter laugh. 'I am who I am. I can't be anyone else.'

'I don't want you to be.'

'Do you still want to be here with me, after this?'

'It's a long way to come for nothing.'

'I'm serious, Brodie. You've no idea how hard this is for me. I've never told anyone. I can't. I just can't.'

He reaches over and this time she doesn't move her hand, he lightly squeezes it. 'I know it is and you've shown tremendous courage, believe me, you have. I'm not going anywhere.'

She stares at him intently. 'You really mean that?'

'It's taken me half my life to find you again. I'm not going to give you up that easily.'

'Sometimes, I don't even know myself. It scares me.'

'You don't have to do this on your own anymore.'

Elora feels tears rising to the surface.

'You can tell me anything, you know that don't you?'

She wipes her eyes. Brodie is snared by her eyelashes, thick and dark.

'All I want to do is sleep. I just want to sleep for now.' she says apologetically.

He holds on to *now*. It suggests an expectation. He too has his secrets to divulge, the responsibility for the tragedy

that has led him here. The realisation is both exhilarating
and horrifying.

Chapter 12

Something to Light the Darkness

Brodie is lying on his bed and staring at the ceiling. Sleep has eluded him. Outside, the moon is so bright it shines like a torch, coating the bedroom walls in a soft lunar light.

Brodie never expected Elora's honesty would make him see her in a new light and alter the person he thought she was. He has tried to comprehend this. He has tried to understand it.

The frankness of her conversation disconcerts him. The details have made it horrendous.

He was not prepared for what she had told him. The damage was done when she was young. Now he knows the sum of it all has ruined her life, in a way he had no idea of. And now that he does, how can he ever come to imagine how she must feel?

Given the fragility of her state of mind, Brodie fears that his intention to tell Elora what he has hidden from her will be intolerable for her to hear. He tries to imagine how she will react. It is impossible to say with any certainty, but is he willing, knowing what he now knows, to find out?

He stands up from the bed and paces the room. He pulls his hand through his hair. What he would give now for a cigarette.

She needs help. I must be there for her. Part of the process in coming to Corfu was to fill the gaps left within us by being honest with one another. Without telling her the truth, there can be no future for us.

He finds the walls of the room oppressive. He craves open space and the night sky.

He quietly moves through the house, past Elora's bedroom, and tentatively places his feet as he descends downstairs. He takes a deep intake of breath as he steps out into the night.

His head is spinning with thoughts, with doubt and with what he has feared most. Has this been a mistake? He glances at his watch, it is nearly midnight, at home, it will be 10.00 p.m. He takes his mobile from his trouser pocket and scrolls through the telephone numbers until he finds the one he wants.

'Hello, Brodie. I wondered when you'd call.'

'Hi, I hope it's not too late?'

'No, I won't be in bed for a few hours yet. What time is it in Corfu?'

'We're two hours ahead.'

'Oh. So, it's late.'

'How's Jasper? Behaving himself, I hope?'

'That dog of yours has got ADHD, he's full of energy.'

'He will settle down, I'm sure. He's just out of his routine, that's all.'

'He is lovely though. He's just a big softy. He wants to be clapped constantly.'

Brodie smiles at this. 'He'll be taking advantage of your good nature.'

'He'd eat all day if I'd let him. Every time I get a biscuit with my cuppa or if I'm making something to eat, he's there behind me, drooling on the floor.' She laughs and Brodie can tell she is already getting attached to Jasper. It is a comfort to him.

'So, are you going to tell me how it's going? You're still there, so I guess Elora was happy to see you.'

'I think I surprised her, but, yes, after the initial shock, she seemed happy to see me.'

'That's good. And how is your apartment, comfy, I hope?'

'It was.'

'What do you mean, it was?'

'I'm staying at Elora's house, now.'

'God, that was quick. So, you're both getting on?'

'We are. It's an arrangement that suits us both. It's easier this way.'

'I imagine you've been talking?'

'We have. A lot. That's why I'm phoning you, really.'

'Oh.' Hana can sense it troubles Brodie.

'She has opened up to me, told me things from her past. Things I had no idea about. They've scarred her, psychologically. I can't tell you more than that. She told me in confidence. I wouldn't betray her trust.'

'No. Of course not. I wouldn't expect you too.'

'How can I tell her now? I don't know what to do, Hana.'

'You'll just have to trust your instincts. Maybe it would be better to wait a while longer, you know. It was always going to be difficult for her to hear. Bide your time. You don't have to rush into it.'

Brodie sighs. 'I know what you're saying, but it just doesn't feel right to wait. It might make it worse. What would you do, Hana?'

'It's your choice Brodie, you have to do what you feel is right. It doesn't matter what I think. You know her better than I do.'

'I thought I did. I'm not so sure now.'

'Don't tell me you're regretting this, Brodie?'

'No. It's nothing like that. I suppose it's just a shock to the system, that's all.'

'Whatever it is, it can't be that bad.'

'Believe me, Hana, it is. It was going to be difficult in the first place, but I never imagined this. It puts a whole new perspective on my intentions. I'm sorry, Hana, for burdening you with this... like this, on the phone.'

'I don't mind, really I don't. I'd rather you were able to speak with me than having to deal with this on your own. Although, there's not much I can do.'

'Just talking to you helps. I've got no one else I can talk to, not about this anyway.'

'Do what you think is right. That's all the advice I can give you. Be true to yourself and Elora.'

'Thank you, Hana. I think I just needed to hear that.' He feels relieved. 'I promised myself to do the right thing. I just didn't realise how hard that was going to be.'

'Well, keep that promise and phone me again soon, okay?'

He takes a deep, shaky breath. 'I will.'

'Even if you phoned every single day, I wouldn't mind.'

'I won't do that.'

'I know you wouldn't, but now you know you can if need to.'

He is feeling more contained now. 'Say hello to Jasper for me.'

'I will.'

'Speak to you soon, Hana.'

'Take care, Brodie.' And then she is gone.

Around him, moonlight covers the garden in silver. He looks towards the night sky. The stars are magnificent, he even thinks he has seen a meteorite. It dawns on him that the stars are still there during the day; because of the light, the naked eye cannot see them, yet they shine in the darkness. Around Brodie, there is a peculiar silence, lying heavily over the garden, and he is aware of it loosening the knots inside him. He raises his head towards the night sky and takes a deep breath. What he needs right now, is something to light his darkness.

Chapter 13

A visit to the Past

The days blend into one another effortlessly. Brodie and Elora have established a pattern of familiarity and routine. When Brodie wakes in the morning, he makes a cafetiere of coffee, a jug of freshly squeezed orange juice, he toasts four slices of bread and boils four eggs. He takes it all out onto the terrace and sets the breakfast on the table. Every morning, he goes into the garden, chooses a flower and picks a single stem which he then places in a small vase in the middle of the table.

He has not mentioned that night, and Elora has volunteered no further discussion, apart from she is grateful for his understanding.

He sees her walking through the garden towards the house; she waves at him and the sight of her fills him with an effervescence that wells up inside him. Elora covers her head with the straw-coloured hat she often wears when out walking, its large brim protecting her from the sun even this early in the morning. Over her shoulder, she is carrying a worn leather bag, which he knows will house her book and notepad.

Each morning, she wakes early and takes a walk down to the beach, a secluded inlet protected by tree-covered hills and cliffs. She will then sit on the flat rock as she has done for years and read a book or jot down notes, ideas and plots that may eventually find their way into one of her novels.

'I need to do some work today. This new book won't write itself,' Elora says, lifting the sunglasses from her eyes and placing them on the table. She takes her hat off and runs her fingers through her hair, letting the strands fall onto her shoulders. He watches as they sway and rest, he can hardly take his eyes from her.

'Do you know what you're going to write? I mean, do you already have characters and a plot?'

'I do.'

'I don't know how you manage to come up with all those ideas and still make it fresh and compelling.'

'Well, really, there is only one thing to say but we have to try to say it as many ways as possible.'

'That's a good way of putting it.'

'I wish I could take the credit for it.' She raises an eyebrow. 'But I can't. It's a T. S. Elliot quote.'

'Well, I'll get out of your way. I might take a walk into the village. Is there anything you need?'

'I don't think so, everything I need is right here.' She reaches over the table and touches his hand. 'Have I told you, you make the most wonderful boiled eggs?'

Brodie laughs. 'No. I don't think you have. Tell me when you're getting sick of them and I'll make you an omelette or scrambled eggs instead.' Brodie grins. 'My culinary expertise, I'm afraid, is rather limited, but as long as we have eggs, I'll still be able to make you breakfast.'

'Thankfully, I like eggs. The irony is, I don't care much for chicken.' Elora smiles at him, and Brodie finds it a relief to see her happy.

Brodie follows the narrow and dusty path that rises steadily, shaded in parts by trees and a quilt of green foliage. In the other direction, he knows, if he were to descend the white stone steps that run the length of Elora's garden wall, it would lead him to the pebbled sands of a sheltered and secluded beach.

He sets his eyes on an olive grove and an orchard of capillary branched trees, where sunlight spears the shadows in silver light. To his left, small boats float on translucent water, as clear as glass, bleached in patches of turquoise and azure. It is a sight that lifts his spirits.

Soon, Brodie sets his sight on an old bell towered church and its cemetery, dotted with headstones and small white crosses. Eventually, he is amongst the labyrinthine lanes of the village, negotiating stone cobbled arteries that climb steadily, amongst salmon and tangerine houses and spilling bougainvillaea that adorns his progress, to his delight.

Finally, he wanders into a square and the thought of a cold drink is appealing as he notices three people sitting outside a café - a couple and a priest. He climbs several steps and walks into the dim light of the interior, in stark contrast to the brightness of the square. As his eyes adjust, he makes out two men sitting at a bar drinking from small cups. One of them is speaking to a heavily set woman on the other side of the bar. The woman, speaking in Greek to her customer, glances towards Brodie and smiles.

'What can I get you, love?'

Brodie is astonished to hear her Brummie accent. 'Eh, a small beer, please.'

'We only have Mythos.'

'That's fine, as long as it's cold.'

'I'll bring it out to you.'

'How much am I due you?'

'You can pay when you're finished. There's no rush.'

Brodie takes a seat outside and gazes around. The square is almost empty. A large tree snatches his eye, it dominates the square, spreading shade from the sun into every corner. There are several smaller cafes with chairs and tables, most unoccupied, and a church with an arched bell tower as an entrance to its grounds.

The woman brings his drink and clears the table where the couple were sitting, who by now are sauntering over to the church, camera at the ready.

Brodie takes a drink and savours the taste. The priest is reading a newspaper and chewing his bottom lip, the silver whiskers of his beard twitching like an involuntary spasm.

Nikolaos Chiotakis is the local priest. Now in his early sixties, he has spent the best part of his life serving the villagers and seeing to their spiritual needs. He lifts his gaze from the newspaper print and smiles at Brodie, nodding a greeting. 'I heard your unmistakable accent,' Nikolaos says.

'It's difficult to hide.'

'Are you on your own?'

Brodie realises it must be an unusual and infrequent occurrence to see a visitor to the village alone and not part of a visiting group or as a couple.

'I am today anyway. I'm staying local.'

'Oh, down by the holiday apartments?'

'No. I'm staying with a friend.'

'There's every chance I'll know them. Everyone knows everyone around here and, if they don't, their face will be familiar.'

'I'm staying with Elora Alanis.'

Nikolaos folds his paper and places it on the table. The name has caught his interest. 'Ah, the author. My wife has read her books.'

'Yes, that's right.'

'She stays in Villa Katrina.'

Brodie shakes his head. 'I've never heard Elora call it that.'

'Ah, I knew the last occupants of the house. That's what it was called back then.'

'Elora told me she bought it from a woman who was originally from Edinburgh.'

'That's right. Georgia and Adam. I still keep in touch with them. They moved back to Edinburgh once they sold the house. Adam and I often played chess sitting in these very seats.' Nikolaos smiles affectionately at the memory.

'That's how we met. Just like you, he wandered in. And a group of us were playing chess, as we always did, Giannis, Thanos, Stamatis, and Mida. We invited Adam to play a game with us. He became a dear friend. That's how I recognised your accent. The sound of it brings back treasured memories.'

'Do you still play chess?'

'Not now. Times change. This place used to be a Kafenion. It was where the men would come to discuss politics and drink coffee and, in our case, play chess. Unfortunately, Giannis and Stamatis are no longer with us.' Nikolaos brushes his beard with a hand dappled in sunspots. 'I baptised Giannis and Stamatis' children. I was the priest who married those children when they grew into adults and, in turn, baptised their children. I also buried my friends, Giannis and Stamatis, such is the joy and pain of being a priest.' He clears his throat. 'I'm Nikolaos, and you?'

'Brodie.'

'Well, it's good to meet you, Brodie.'

'Likewise.'

Nikolaos tilts his head. 'Do you play chess, Brodie?'

'No. I can stretch to the odd game of drafts, but chess, it always seemed a complicated game to me.'

'It's all about strategy.'

'Maybe one day.'

'Are you an author as well?'

'Me? No. Elora and I go back a long way. We met at University.'

'Which one?'

'Edinburgh.'

'That is a place I've heard so much about. I'd love to visit. I keep threatening Adam that I'll just turn up at his place one day.'

'I'm biased, obviously, but if you go, you won't be disappointed.'

'I've always liked the idea of going at New Year. They know how to celebrate and throw a good party.'

'Yes, we do, especially at Hogmanay.'

'What is this word?'

'Hogmanay is the word we use to celebrate the last day of the year.'

'What is that song you sing?'

'Auld Lang Syne. We sing Robert Burns' version.'

'Yes. I've heard of him. He was a poet.'

'He wrote songs as well.'

'And then there's your famous drink.'

'Uisge baugh, the water of life.'

Nikolaos scratches his beard. 'I've never heard this word.'

'Whisky. It means whisky.'

'Ah, yes. I like whisky. Especially Scottish whisky.'

'I've never cared for it much myself. I prefer this.' Brodie holds up his glass of beer. 'Or wine,' he adds.

'Now, that is the water of life,' Nikolaos smiles.

'I'd have to agree with you there.'

Nikolaos looks at his watch and stands. 'I'm afraid I have to go.' He holds out his hand. 'It was nice speaking with you, Brodie.'

Brodie shakes his hand. 'And you too… what should I call you… Father Nikolaos?'

He shakes his head. 'Nikolaos will do, I think.'

'Bye for now.'

Nikolaos cocks his head. 'I like that… *bye for now*. It means we'll meet again. Yes, I like that. Bye for now, Brodie.'

Brodie watches as Nikolaos crosses the square, his black cassock swaying around his polished shoes as he disappears down a narrow lane.

Brodie leans back into his chair, finishes the last remnants of his beer, and gazes around the square. He thinks of Adam, who sat here, playing chess, and drinking strong coffee with Nikolaos and the others. He feels a surge of connection with a man he does not know, but he can see what Adam would have seen: the church, several modest coffee bars, the imposing tree that diffuses the sun's light in its protective shade, and then, there is Nikolaos the priest. Brodie can sense the bond there must have existed between them, and why Adam would have taken so easily to Nikolaos. For there is an infectious warmth that radiates from him, an unrestrained calmness that immediately put Brodie at ease in his company, melting his instinctive inhibitions. Thinking back, Nikolaos had an absolute and compelling presence. There is bewilderment about it all.

Suddenly, Brodie is aware of someone materialising by his side.

'I'll take that if you're finished. Would you like another?'

That distinctive accent again. 'No. Thanks. I'll just pay for this.'

'That's three euros, my love.'

He gives her a five euro note and tells her to keep the change. She expresses her gratitude with a smile that puffs out her round cheeks. 'That's kind of you. You can come back anytime.'

And I just might do that, Brodie thinks to himself.

***

The house is deathly quiet when Brodie returns from the village. He suspects Elora will be in her office and, not wanting to disturb her, he ambles into the kitchen and from the fridge, he pours himself a glass of lemonade. He turns on his heels and knows it is coming. Nausea swirls in his stomach, and he is suddenly sweating, although cold dampness sweeps over his skin. Weightlessness engulfs him; it fogs his mind and stabs behind his eyes. Blurred shadows retreat from him as the nausea grips his throat, and he stumbles into the island, his hand releasing the glass that shatters over the marble surface. He is falling through the darkness like a bird with broken wings. And then, nothing. His world has stopped.

It is the smell of her perfume that draws him to the surface as he feels her fingertips brush his forehead. It takes a gigantic effort; his eyelids are heavy, and flecks of silver light float behind them like a shower of meteorites across the night sky. It obscures her face from him, behind a hazy film of muddled features and concealed detail, but her voice is clear and tapered with alarm.

'Brodie! Brodie! What has happened? My God, your head, it's bleeding.'

Brodie groans and pulls himself to a sitting position. Elora parts his bloodstained hair and, to her relief, she can see the cut is not deep. Brodie's head throbs like the mother of all hangovers. He draws himself up, leaning on the island for support and crunching fragmented glass underfoot.

'I must have slipped. I'll be fine.'

'I think you should see a doctor.'

'It's just a cut.'

'This is the second time this has happened, Brodie. You're lucky it's just a cut. You could have seriously hurt yourself. You need to find out why this is happening. You need to see a doctor.'

'And I will.'

'Well, I'll phone them and take you myself.'

'There's no need for that. Look, you phone the doctor and I'll go on my own. He can speak English, can't he?'

Elora grins at Brodie. 'Yes, quite well, actually.'

'Ah, sorry, I didn't mean it like that,' he says defensively.

'I'll come too.' Elora's sets her face.

'No, no, you don't have too.'

'I will. I won't go in with you, I'll have a coffee and wait until you're finished.'

Brodie knows he will have to give in. He knows how stubborn Elora can be if she has set her mind to it.

'Okay,' he sighs. 'Make the call.'

'I will,' Elora says triumphantly and reaches for her mobile phone.

Edinburgh 1995

A Sense of Betrayal

Elora heard the knock at the door as she was making a sandwich. She wasn't expecting a visitor. She put down the knife and grunted. Elora had skipped breakfast, and now all she craved was the satisfaction of her hunger. She took a quick bite of her sandwich and headed for the door, wiping crumbs from her mouth.

Elora stopped herself just in time from blurting out, 'What are you doing here!' Instead, she wobbled, 'Chris!'

'Hi, Elora. Is Brodie in?'

'No. He's out…' Her brain froze and she struggled to organise a single coherent thought.

'Oh! I've come to get the book I gave him. Remember I told you last night I'd pick it up around lunchtime.'

'You did… that's right. It slipped my mind. What was the title of the book?'

'I can't remember, but I'll know it if I see it.'

'Right. You'd better come in.'

As Chris followed her into the living room, Elora regretted not making an excuse.

'I didn't see you at the party last night,' Chris said.

'I didn't go. I wasn't feeling well.'

'You missed a good night. I hope you're feeling better?'

'I am, thanks.' Elora gestured towards a stack of books sitting on the floor next to the sofa. She had been on at Brodie to move them for ages but now found herself relieved they were still there. 'Hopefully, it's amongst this lot.'

'Let me see.' Chris crouched down and inspected the covers.

Elora stood uneasily. Then, for the first time, she felt a spasm of guilt. Chris had been nothing but civil to her whenever he was in her company. She peered out of the window. She was judging him on what others had told her. With this came a relief. She wanted to apologise to him. Had she always been abrupt with him? Had he noticed her terseness? How unfair of her.

'It's not here,' pointed out Chris. Elora sensed disappointment in his voice, and when he stood up and sighed, she felt mortified at her previous thoughts that had questioned his integrity.

'Well, why don't I make us a coffee and we can wait for Brodie. I'm sure he won't be long; he just went out for milk.'

'Luckily, I like my coffee black.'

Elora met his eyes, and they both laughed.

She felt her muscles loosen. 'Are you hungry? I was making tuna sandwiches, there's enough for two.'

'I wouldn't say no, but what about Brodie?'

'He won't starve.'

'No. He likes his food too much.'

'So, how is the studying going?'

'Okay, I suppose. I've got a dissertation to do that's due in another two weeks. I really need to get my head down. And you?'

'Yeah, it's going fine. Six months to go.'

'It seems to have gone so quickly; don't you think?'

'It has, hasn't it? I can't believe I'll soon no longer be a student.'

'We'll have to find our way in the grown-up world.'

Elora smiled. 'We will. Strangely, it feels frightening, but also liberating.'

'I know what you mean. I think we're at that point now where we are desperate to make our way in the world. Well, maybe not everyone thinks like that, but I do.'

'I think you're right. I feel the same.'

He takes a bite of his sandwich. 'Oh, this is nice. There's lemon in it.'

'There is. Brodie would never have noticed that.'

'I like to cook. I like the creative aspect of it. It's like an artist painting a picture, or an author writing a book. It gives pleasure to others.'

'I've never thought about it like that.'

'The next time you're making a dish, you'll think about it differently. You will.' Chris smiled.

Elora sat back. She was enjoying herself. She was enjoying Chris's company. 'Do you know, I've known you for over a year, and in that time, this is the longest conversation we've had.'

'Is it?'

Elora laughed softly. 'It is,' She confessed to her shame.

'I'm not that scary. Am I?'

Elora tilted her head, 'Of course not.'

'What are your plans for after uni?' Chris asked.

'To get a job, I suppose.'

'Here in Edinburgh or will you be going home?'

'I don't think Brodie would leave,' she said hurriedly.

'And that would make a difference to your choice?'

She considered this. She felt a mild sense of tenseness in her shoulders. A nervousness.

'You've spoken about this. Look, I'm sorry. It's none of my business,' Chris said uncomfortably. 'You don't have to answer.'

'Why shouldn't I?' Elora genuinely felt taken aback by her reaction. 'In fact, it feels good to be able to talk to someone about it.'

Chris regarded her, curiosity tugging at him.

'It's been getting in the way, really. I had hoped that Brodie would at least visit my home.'

'Corfu?'

'Yes.'

'And he doesn't?'

'It's not that he won't. He's happy to go for a week, meet my family and everything, but that's all. He's not going to commit to the possibility of staying longer. I want him to go for a month or two, and then, after living there, he'd be in a better position to make his mind up.'

'It sounds like he already has.'

Just then, they could hear the front door opening. There was an awkward moment of silence. 'That will be Brodie.' To Elora's astonishment, she wanted more time on her own with Chris, and she was frustrated that their time together had ended abruptly. Chris lifted his cup to take a drink and Elora could see that his hand shook slightly. She stood up and cleared their empty plates from the table, depositing them in the sink. Nervous energy. Why was she feeling this way? It caught her by surprise. As she turned to face Brodie, who, by now, was entering the kitchen, she caught the disappointment on Chris's face, and she wondered if her face mirrored his.

'Hello, Chris.' Brodie patted Chris's shoulder and placed a carton of milk on the table. 'That took longer than I thought. The shop on the corner had run out of milk, so I went to the Co-op.

Chris responded immediately, 'I need the book I loaned you. It's due back.'

'It's here.' Brodie smiled knowingly. He went back into the living room and reappeared with the book, handing it to Chris.

'Where was it?' Elora asked.

'Under the sofa.'

'No wonder we couldn't find it.'

Chris stood up and gave a brief nod. 'Well. I'd better get going. Thanks for the sandwich, Elora.' His gaze travelled her face.

Elora could feel his disappointment as much as she could feel her own.

Brodie smiled. 'I'll see you to the door.'

Elora took a breath. What had just happened? She stood up and cleared the table. She could hear Brodie and Chris talking but struggled to comprehend their words. Brodie's tone was cheerful, it helped to ease her concern. He had noticed nothing out of the ordinary. But there was. There was a definite attraction between them. How could she deny it when that was exactly what she was feeling? As Brodie returned to the kitchen, he kissed her on the cheek. 'Fancy a cuppa?' he asked, going to put the kettle on.

'That would be nice,' she replied, as a devastating sense of betrayal consumed her.

Chapter 14

A Delicate Situation

'Mr Lucus. I'm Dr Theodoros but most people call me by my first name, Galanis.'

Galanis extends his hand, and Brodie shakes it. He is in a small airless room, the balminess immediate.

'I'm Brodie.'

'Please, take a seat.' Galanis sits behind his desk and smiles. He is probably in his early thirties, Brodie presumes, clean-shaven with sharp features and a receding hairline that is cropped close to his scalp.

'You are a friend of Elora?'

'I am.'

'A lovely lady. She was insistent that I see you. So, what can I do for you today?'

'I've been having some dizzy spells, that's all. Apart from that, I feel fine.'

'How long have you been experiencing this dizziness?'

'On and off for a few weeks.'

'Are you taking any medication?'

'No.'

'Do you have any medical diagnosis?'

'No.'

'Any fatigue, nausea?'

'As I said, in general, I feel well.'

'And how often do you get these dizzy spells?'

'Not often.'

'Daily? Or every other day?'

Brodie shifts in his chair. Galanis has a soft manner, reassuring, almost soothing. Brodie can see how his patients would feel at ease during a consultation. 'Just a few times, really. To tell you the truth, Elora is more worried about them than I am.'

Galanis rubs his chin. 'Yes, she did mention that you lost consciousness.'

'I think I slipped and banged my head. I smashed a glass as well, and when Elora saw me it looked worse than it actually was.'

Galanis leans back in his chair, his brows furrowed. 'I see. Well then, let's take your blood pressure and pulse.'

Galanis pushes his chair back, stands up and washes his hands in the sink by the window. He shoots Brodie a sideways look and half-smiles. He's not convinced, Brodie can tell.

Galanis wraps the cuff around Brodie's upper arm. 'Just relax now,' he says, lightly pressing the stethoscope's bell over Brodie's brachial artery. He inflates the cuff and releases air from it while listening with the stethoscope and studiously observes the sphygmomanometer.

'Mm. Your systolic reading is low. I'll take another reading just to make sure.' Galanis keeps his gaze concentrated. After a moment he says, 'Still the same. I'll take your pulse.'

When he is finished, Galanis settles himself into his chair. His fingers dance across the keys of his computer and he studies the screen. 'I'd like you to get a thorough examination at the hospital in Corfu Town. I'm limited to what I can do here. I could get you an appointment for next week? Tuesday looks good.'

Brodie stiffens slightly. 'I'll be returning home before then.' Brodie's voice is measured, but he feels the heat rise along his neck. 'I'll make an appointment to see my GP when I get home.'

'Well, I would strongly suggest you do that, if not for yourself, then do it for Elora.' He gives a small, philosophical nod.

Brodie crosses the narrow street and Elora is still sitting where he left her, sipping a coffee under the shade of a parasol.

'Well, what did he say?' Elora holds his gaze.

'I'm fine, I told you so.'

She leans forward. 'And that's it.'

'Yes. I thought you would be happy?'

'I am... of course, I am. So, why have you been passing out?'

'He said I'm dehydrated. I need to drink more fluids, lots of water and try to keep out of the sun, especially when it is at its hottest.' His pretence feels like a wound.

'Well. We'll need to get you a hat.' Her relief is palpable'

'Not like yours, I hope?'

She sweeps her Baku straw hat from the table and holds it close to her chest. 'This hat is my favourite and I'm very attached to it.' She says in feigned insult as she places it on her head.

'It looks nicer on you than it would on me, that's for sure.'

'I'm really glad it's nothing serious.' She touches his arm and his breath catches.

His purpose is not to hurt her. Brodie is certain, for the time being, he has done the right thing. Yet, there is no satisfying recompense. How can there be? When it feels like a knife, sharp and piercing.

Chapter 15

Realisations

Towards the horizon, a faint haze obscures the perfect blue of the sky. Around Brodie, the amplifying sound of cicadas is so strident and yet, he considers, it emanates only from tiny rasping wings. He had forgotten how encompassing the sound was, as the rhythm and constant beat accompany him through the garden.

Elora is spending the morning writing; the new novel is taking shape, and she is enjoying a rich vein of creativity. Brodie has promised Elora he will make a meal tonight, and so he is heading off to the village to shop for ingredients.

When he reaches his car, he opens the door and is accosted by a waft of heat that rises towards him. He eases himself into the seat and flinches as the leather is hot against his back and legs. Even the steering wheel is fiery to touch. He starts the engine. Warm air blows from the vents, and his eyes frantically search the dashboard, until he finds what he wants. He fiddles with the air con and waits for the icy air to wash over him. Already, sweat is dampening his shirt. *Jesus, it's like a furnace,* he tells himself as the electric windows sink halfway into the front doors.

Brodie leans back against the headrest and sucks in his breath.

He wonders how much time they have together. Weeks? Months? And then, as soon as he thinks it, he knows it does not matter. Time has taken on a peculiar dimension.

He is determined not to think; he wants to empty his mind of thoughts and words, of memories and recent revelations. This morning, he just wants to be in the moment.

It is impossible, and though there is a measure of
resistance, Elora floods him in a deluge of images, and he
is struggling to surface.

He aches to slide his fingers over the contours of her face
and gaze into her striking eyes and long, dark lashes. He
has noticed, when she screws her eyes from the sun or
when she smiles, light wrinkles spoke from them. He has
thought of kissing her there. He has always wondered about
the colouring of her hair, that berry-hued auburn so
uncharacteristic of the Greek makeup. He knows now, she
inherits it from her English grandfather, Joshua. It was the
first thing Brodie thought when Elora described Joshua's
complexion and hair colouring.
He remembers watching her in the garden the other day.
Normally, Elora wears her hat to protect her from the sun's
glare, but not on that day. She had tied her hair in a tight
bun. She stood and pressed her hand to the base of her
back; she stretched and then untied the knotted bun. It
astonished him how much hair fell away, covering her
shoulders and back in auburn waves. Sparks like electricity
fluttered in his stomach. He had never marvelled at such an
act, so simple, yet its effect was magnifying, sensual and
seductive.
He feels he has been in a state of hesitation ever since he
arrived. He has thought about nothing else and then
refrained from the one thing he must do. Now that he is
here, its execution will be insufferable.
Perhaps, he thinks, he should tell her tonight? He closes
his eyes.
It is inconceivable to keep her from it. The finality of it
will bring a conclusion. What chance of happiness then?
His stomach curls with the thought. He tries to think
logically. He sighs. *I can't promise her anything.*

He turns the engine off. His mind is too active to concentrate, never mind driving a car. He peels himself from the seat and decides to walk to the village.

To his left, and through the trees, the Ionian is striking; it has the most beautiful colours, rich in depths of blue but also translucent as if he is looking through glass. As he walks the dust-dry track, the air is clean and warm, and the sea recedes behind him. He can feel a slight burn in his legs as he progresses further, the steady incline of the track twisting before him.

He takes a deep satisfying breath. Around him, the air is pinched in the scent of pines. Now, when he looks, he can see only a hint of the sea.

Being with Elora every day brings a sweet mix of pleasure and pain. It is difficult to reconcile this Elora with the Elora who has been in his head for what seems a lifetime. He wasn't prepared for this.

He knows what she has been through will have made her act in ways that would normally be alien to her. He also knows it must have taken tremendous courage to lay bare her frailties and struggles. It has unbalanced him; he cannot deny that simple fact.

We all draw invisible lines that we dare not cross, that we think we are in control of.

He can identify with her days fuelled by alcohol and the resulting self-loathing that followed. He too has been irrationally angry, losing himself in the spiral of overwhelming grief. There have been times in his life he has felt very broken. Who is he to judge her?

We have both changed. The world has changed. We have found each other, yet we are not the people we once were.

He continues to walk at a steady pace. He is alone. He has not seen another person. Normally, it would not be unusual to meet someone heading towards the secluded beach.

He glances to his left. A gated driveway leads to a single-storey house with blanched shutters and peeling stucco. A dog pounds towards the gate, snarling and baring sharp teeth. It sticks its muscled head through the railings and barks at Brodie vehemently.

Brodie feels an ache. He is missing his dog. Since Jasper has been a puppy, Brodie has rarely been on his own. Jasper always accompanies him; even in the house, Jasper is his shadow. And when he thinks of Jasper, he immediately imagines him running ahead, stopping only to sniff the air and bury his nose deep into a bush or a patch of flowers and then, as always, turning his head to make sure Brodie is still in sight.

Soon, he is passing smart holiday apartments and several small hotels that blend auspiciously into the landscape on both sides of the narrow road.

Further on, he glimpses several houses on the outskirts of the village. He walks next to the cemetery wall and small church. He tucks into the side of a shop to let a delivery van pass and opposite, he sees a chemist. There is a sharp pain across his eyes. At times, it blurs his vision, and he knows he is playing Russian roulette, dismissively and with disregard, every time he pushes it to the back of his mind.

Brodie buys paracetamol and a bottle of water and even before he has left the coolness of the air conditioning, he slips two tablets into his mouth and swallows them with a swig of water.

He enjoys shopping, mostly; he likes the ritual of buying food. He had always done the weekly shop. Every Saturday morning, he would walk the aisles of his local supermarket, packing the trolley until it resembled a mountain range of vegetables, prepacked meats and fish, a selection of fruit, packets and tins, wine, cheese… he rarely diverged from his mental list. He gained a measure of satisfaction from the habitual nature of it, although he rarely unpacked the bags and put the food away. Even after twenty-odd years of marriage, Heather complained, he still did not know that every food item had a place and where that place was.

It's different now. These days, he shops for one on the laptop and gets it delivered to his door. So today is a novelty as he browses the local shops and he delights in one shopkeeper's reaction and the resulting gleam in her eye as he thanks her in Greek.

In the village square, Brodie climbs the steps to the café where he met the priest. The owner remembers Brodie and is genuinely pleased to see him. He orders a beer and takes it outside. He places his shopping bag on the ground and settles into a seat. Taking a sip of beer, he closes his eyes in pleasure and when he opens them, he sees the priest, Nikolaos coming out of the church and talking to a man and woman. Brodie realises he is glad to see him and when Nikolaos starts to walk towards the café Brodie raises his hand in greeting.

'Brodie, I thought that was you.' Nikolaos says as he sits opposite him.

'It's good to see you again.'

Nikolaos nods towards the shopping bag. 'Elora's keeping you busy, I see.'

'I'm cooking dinner tonight so I thought I should do the shopping too.'

Just then, the café owner appears with a coffee and she places it next to Nikolaos. They speak in Greek to each other and then she turns to Brodie and in her Brommie accent asks, 'Enjoying the beer love?'

'It's lovely, thanks.'

'If you need another, like your first one, it's free. Nikolaos is paying love.'

'You don't have to do that,' Brodie points out.

Nikolaos shrugs. 'It's my pleasure. Anyway, Adam suggested it.'

'Adam?'

'Yes. He said, if I saw you again, I was to buy you a beer. He couldn't believe you are staying at Villa Katrina and that you were from Edinburgh. I spoke to him just yesterday.'

'Well then. You'll need to thank him from me.'

'You can do that yourself. He said, when you get back to Edinburgh, he'd like to meet up with you. Him and Georgia. He said it would be great if Elora was there too.'

'I'd like that.'

Nikolaos smiles. 'Good. I told him you would. He also said I should teach you to play chess. And he reminded me how bad he was when he first played. It was not just chess, it was the social aspect he enjoyed. We all did.' Nikolaos smiles at the memory, but his eyes are sad.

A flicker of regret passes over Brodie. 'Nothing is permanent, even traditions change with the times or die out. The only permanence is the memories they leave us. Maybe that's their gift to us.'

'Quite philosophical, Brodie, but I'd agree. I remember those times quite vividly. We used to all go out fishing in this tiny boat and spend most of the day drinking. Adam was just as bad at fishing as he was at chess. I think he came along with us for the beer. Do you fish, Brodie?'

'I dabbled in it when I was younger, nothing serious though. It was the same with golf, but that was a more expensive hobby. I just play now and again.'

'Would you like another?' Nikolaos points to Brodie's empty glass.

Brodie looks at his watch. 'No. I better not. This dinner won't cook itself.'

Elora is standing in the kitchen when Brodie returns.

'I was just about to make a coffee. Would you like one?'

Brodie sets the shopping bag on the tiled floor. 'I'd love one.'

'Did you get everything you need?'

'I did,' he says, pleased with himself.

Elora's gaze falls on the shopping bag. She grins. 'We're almost like a couple. How ridiculous is that?'

'Is it?

She tries to form words, but her tongue sticks to the roof of her mouth. *Is it?* Her breath stops in her mouth.

'We were once,' Brodie says.

There is a murmur of recognition. 'Yes, we were.' She turns and busies herself in making coffee. Behind her, she feels Brodie's hand on the small of her back.

His breath is hot on the nape of her neck. She feels her hair being brushed aside by his hand and then his lips touch her skin, softly, as if it scares him she will break. His hand touches her chin and he tilts her face towards him. He kisses her then; his tongue moves inside her mouth and Brodie is astonished at his sense of relief as Elora turns so readily and runs the tips of her fingers along his face.

When they part, Elora rests her head against his chest.

'I can hear your heart beating.'

Sunlight presses against the white blind. It takes Brodie a moment to process his surroundings and when he rubs the sleep from his eyes, he can feel the soft skin of her leg against him. He turns to face Elora, careful not to wake her, and as his eyes rest on her, he studies her face in intricate detail, as if she is a portrait in a gallery. He can't believe what has occurred between them. He feels shellshocked. It wasn't a dream. He marvels at her hair, curling over her long neck and resting on the pillow. She is real; she is warm, and he can hear her gentle breathing. He can reach out and touch her, trace the shape of her lips with his fingertip, the lips that have touched him, kissed him, caressed his skin. The feel of her velvety lips and her mouth was wonderful. He indulges in the recollection of it. He also feels an alarming trepidation.

Elora stirs and, when she awakes, she immediately smiles at him. 'Kalimera,' her voice is soft with sleep.

'Did you sleep well?' Brodie asks.

'It was the best sleep I've had in… well, I don't know when. A long time. And you?'

'Good. It was… a good sleep.' We're trying to be normal, but it's far from normal. Last night was not a normal night. He must abandon this apprehension. 'I have to ask you, last night, do you regret it, now?'

She touches his face. 'I feel alive.'

He kisses her fingertips, and Brodie can feel every cell in his body tingle. He raises himself onto an elbow and asks her, 'Are you always this beautiful in the morning?'

Her eyes slide from him, and she turns her head away. 'I don't think so.'

He senses her discomfort and tilts her chin so he can lean slightly towards her. He can feel her breath on his lips as they hover tantalisingly close. 'I have always loved you, Elora.'

He can sense something inside her gives, and he lowers his mouth to hers.

Chapter 16

It Feels Like a Lifetime and Only Yesterday

Elora puts her book down, placing it in her lap, and watches curiously as Brodie wheels a bicycle up towards the terrace.

'Look what I found and there's another one in the garage. I didn't know you cycled.'

'I don't. They belong to the previous owner,' Elora says, lifting her sunglasses to see better.

'They're still in good condition, the chains need some oil and the tyres some air, but apart from that, you've got two good bikes. When was the last time you rode a bike?' Brodie asks enthusiastically.

Elora stands and walks over to him. She studies the bicycle and is conscious of Brodie's uplifting tone. 'A long time ago.'

'Do you think you can still ride one?'

'I thought once you learned, you never forgot.'

'There's only one way to find out.'

It was true. She has not forgotten as they cycle through the countryside, along dusty lanes, and olive groves, pine-scented air and fruit-laden orchards.

'I had forgotten how this feels.'

'And how do you feel?' Brodie asks riding alongside her.

'Wonderful and free.'

He has not seen her like this. Elora's face is lit by spreading contentment and he feels they are joined in mutual joy.

They come to a village, and Elora buys ice cream. They sit in the shade, under an awning of branches and tiny leaves. He watches Elora lick ice cream from the cone. He raises an eyebrow and their eyes meet.

Brodie leans into her and kisses her mouth, lacing his fingers around the nape of her neck. She makes a brief sound from the back of her throat and he feels her loosen. Ice cream has melted and has left a trail on her skin. Brodie brings her hand to his mouth and indulgently draws his tongue over her long slender fingers. He kisses a finger and reluctantly frees her hand.

Elora bites her lip. 'It feels like I haven't been able to breathe since last night.' She searches his eyes.

'I've thought of nothing else.' Brodie studies her. 'Do you ever think about how much time we might have together? Months? A year? I've just found you, and it feels each passing day is another we won't ever get back.'

She looks at him, slightly irritated. 'No. I don't.' She reconsiders. 'I try not to,' she says lightly.

They are silent.

Brodie tries to imagine what it was like when they were young and together in Edinburgh. Sometimes, an image will come to him, reeling off others in a spontaneous movement, and he finds it peculiar that he remembers so clearly. The past and present interlinked in a mixture of hope, guilt and loss.

He has questioned himself. Can he do this? Is it just enough that he is with her, after all these years without her? He is delaying the inevitable, and it eats at him each day. There are no other words available to protect her from the blow that will surely come. He knows he is torturing himself. How can he cause her that pain? He wants to scream.

'Are you alright, Brodie?' Elora touches his arm and trails her fingers along his skin.

He looks away and rubs his eyes. She can see they are red.

'I'm sorry,' he says apologetically.

'For what?' She cocks her head, not understanding what he means.

He pushes his hand through his hair. 'I wasn't expecting this… us.'

'And that makes you sad?'

He chews his lip. 'No. It makes me happy.'

'You've got an unusual way of showing it.'

'It's just… well, I think…' With his forefinger and thumb, he pinches the bridge of his nose. 'I think, somehow, suddenly, this all feels real. You know?'

She nods her head. 'I suppose we've both been waiting for this, and really, if we're honest with each other, we didn't really think it would happen. Did we?'

Brodie holds her hand. 'It feels like a lifetime and it feels like only yesterday.'

Edinburgh 1995

Betrayal

'You are fortunate you have someone who loves you.'
　'Yes. I am.'
　'What about Brodie?'
　'What do you mean?'
　'Is he fortunate?'
　'Do you always ask so many questions?'
　'You're avoiding the answer. I wonder why?'
　'Of course, I love him.'
　'That's good. He deserves to be happy. And so do you.'
　'I am... happy.' There was a strange pitch to her voice.
He eyed her warily.
　'I am!' she frowned at him. *What did he think he was
doing?*
　'If you weren't happy, I could make you happy.'
　Elora had envisaged Chris would say something, but to
her astonishment, she hadn't imagined this.
　Chris could feel her despondency and, before Elora
answered, he told her, 'I've seen you together for a long
time and, recently, there's been a change in you. I'm not
even sure Brodie has noticed. Tell me I'm wrong?'
　Elora's lips quivered. Her eyes filling with tears. 'It's
been difficult trying to pretend. Every morning, even before
I get out of bed, the feeling's there. I feel so much guilt. I
tell myself, it's wrong to feel this way, it's not me, it's not
who I am. I don't know myself anymore.'
　The astonishing light in her eyes and the flutter of her
lashes mesmerised him as she blinked away her tears.
　It is a gamble, but one he was prepared to take. 'I like
you, Elora. In fact, I like you a lot. It can't come as a
surprise to you?'

She shook her head. 'No. It doesn't.'

'I wouldn't be telling you this if I thought you didn't feel the same.'

'He's your best friend!' Her words were weak.

'And he's your boyfriend.' He leaned into her.

'What does that make us?'

'We're abandoning ourselves to the truth. We're not pretending any longer. Are we?'

A feathered touch on her cheek and their lips softly met. He withdrew slightly and looked into her eyes, her breath warm on his mouth. He kissed her again, this time longer and deeper, his tongue flicking over hers.

'Elora,' he sighed, kissing at the nape of her neck. His hands glided over her blouse. He felt her rib cage, her warmth seeping through the fabric, as he reached for the buttons. With each one released, he gently slid the fabric from her shoulders. He traced his lips over her skin, a faint and feathered touch, a fluttering in his stomach as her hand moved lightly through his hair and then pressed him against her breast.

He lifted his head and looked into her eyes.

'The bed,' she whispered.

They lay naked in the dim light. Chris turned his head and looked at her, smiling satisfactorily.

As the realisation struck her, Elora tried to imagine the consequences of what they had done. She folded her hands over her chest.

'I love you,' he said.

'You don't. You just think you do,' she said, leaning on her elbows.

'How can you say that?'

Elora sat on the edge of the bed. She drew the sheet over her and stood up. She held the sheet close to her skin, now hiding her nakedness. She walked over to the window and leaned her head against the glass. Outside, a breeze lifted leaves along the street. 'You have to go.'

'Why?'

'Brodie…' she hesitated. The sound of his name on her lips spiked her like a spear. 'He'll be back soon.'

'Then we'll tell him.'

'Tell him what?' There was alarm in Elora's voice.

'About us.'

'No, no!' She turned to face him. 'You can't.'

'So, what do you suggest?'

'That you get out of that bed, get changed and leave, before Brodie gets back.'

'You regret what's just happened?'

'Right now, I don't feel good about it, if that's what you mean?'

'I thought we felt the same about each other?'

Her heart was thumping, the fact that Chris was still here, mixed with what they had just done, ignited her panic.

It took Elora a moment to catch her breath. 'This was a mistake. Just go.'

At that moment, the screen on her mobile phone illuminated into life, vibrating on the bedside table. Elora stared at the name of the caller, 'It's Brodie!'

She looked at Chris with a mixture of worry and hostility and Chris's opposition disappeared entirely.

'Hello, Brodie.' There was a slight waver to her voice.

Chris dressed, his urgency painted over every movement. He pulled his t-shirt over his head. Clumsily, he struggled with a sleeve, worsening his agitation.

'Don't worry about it,' Elora was saying. 'That's fine. I'll see you when you get back… love you too.' Her hand holding the mobile dropped to her side. She took a deep intake of breath, her colour draining.

'You have to go, now.'

'I'm getting dressed as fast as I can.'

Elora stared out of the window. 'He'll be here soon.' She bent down and swiped Chris's trainers from the floor and threw them across the room. 'Hurry up, you don't have time to put them on. Just take them and get out.'

'When can I see you again?'

'Didn't you hear me? This is not going to happen again. This was a mistake.'

Once Chris left, Elora hurriedly put clean sheets on the bed. She stood there, staring at her work, the new sheets crisp and white.

She felt sick.

She wanted to cry.

She just wanted things to go back as they were before.

To be normal again.

To be ordinary.

But this had not been just an ordinary day.

This changed everything.

Chapter 17

All That Matters

Elora scrapes butter over the toast and spreads a generous helping of raspberry jam. She takes a bite and relishes in the sound the crunch makes. With a finger, she delicately wipes a crumb from the corner of her mouth and, humming to herself, she pours a coffee. Wandering out onto the terrace, Elora settles into a chair and lifts her knees to her chest.

She has sensed a certain calmness descend over the house; this has also extended to Brodie and herself. Elora wonders about this. She cannot deny the umbilical pull between them; she has found herself revel in it. Since they spent the night together, they have been less reserved in their affection towards one another. An unspoken restriction has been lifted, and they have given each other permission, through heightened sensation and sense of time.

Being with Brodie has instilled a rush of memories, previously catalogued and stored, which she considers is inevitable. Not only has this brought her joy, but it has also been painful too.

In time, soon, she will explain everything. This has been a barrier between them for far too long. She wants to tell him; she needs to tell him. She knows he is waiting for her to do so. There is an expectation on her part.

And what about her? She has lived with regret, shame and insurmountable grief. Her situation is intolerable. She cannot imagine other realities; she cannot just reconstruct her life and live her days in pretence, for that would mean extricating herself from her past and the truth. And what of the truth? When it is told, she is sure he will leave her. She has told herself it is a price she must pay; it is retribution for past sins. It does not bear thinking about.

Last night she dreamed. This is not remarkable, but it is the first time in as long as she can remember that the dream has not faded and dissolved in the morning light.

The fire is intense, its heat licking and scorching her skin. The smoke billows and rises, blotting the sun, stealing the sky, burning her throat, it fills her lungs that burst and splutter.

She can hear their screams, their panic infects her, boiling her blood and stinging her eyes.

She moves through the house, scanning each room, empty of life.

Hysterical banging rises from the basement and travels through the house. She runs down the hall and shouts out their names. She turns the door handle, hot in her hand. To her horror, it is stuck fast, locked, unbudgeable. Barely audible voices, loud and frantic, escape the basement that encases them. She raps the door with her small fist; the wood is like steel against her skin.

The cypress trees are ablaze, orange torches that spit embers and flames.

She is in the water, the cold sea circling her. The air is hot and thick, blown from the surrounding furnace, snarling like a hungry beast. She gazes around. She is alone under the scorching sky. She is alone… it has always been this way.

Brodie lays a hand on Elora's shoulder and kisses the top of her head. 'Good morning.'

She touches his fingers. 'There's toast if you want and the coffee should still be warm.'

He sits beside her and takes a bite of toast. 'My thighs are killing me. I haven't been on a bike for years. I enjoyed it though.'

'We should do it again.'

'I think we'll need to wait until my legs recover. And my bum, that saddle was a killer; it feels like I'm bruised all over when I sit.'

'I'm fine, not an ache or a pain,' Elora smirks self-righteously.

'You must have more padding than me.'

'Oi! That's cruel. There's nothing wrong with my padding.'

'You have beautiful padding,' Brodie adds gallantly.

Recently, their exchanges have lost the self-censorship and guardedness that previously populated them. Instead, they talk freely, at ease with one another. The usual feelings of apprehension have dissipated with private evocations of their pasts, their intimate thoughts and imperfections. It is a delicate balance that both are profoundly aware of.

'Tell me, Brodie. Have you regretted this, at any time since you arrived?'

'Honestly, in the beginning, I questioned myself and my motives. Sure, I had my doubts, who wouldn't have? It's only natural. It didn't last long.'

'I'm not sure I could have done the same thing.'

'Why not? It's wasn't an easy decision, I'll grant you that, but it was something I had to do. I couldn't live the rest of my life knowing I hadn't tried.'

Elora looks at him as if his words have hinted at something. She is not sure what, maybe she is imagining it. She puts it aside. 'There is no regret on your part?'

'None at all. I choose to be here every day.'

Elora reaches over and laces her fingers through his hand.

This all makes perfect sense. Brodie luxuriates in her touch as he looks over the garden towards lemon trees laden with fruit. He can think of no other place he would rather be.

'What have you got planned for today?' Brodie asks.

'I need to spend the morning writing and then I thought I could show you where I lived when I was younger.'

'Your family home.'

'Yes.'

'I'd like that. Is it far?'

'No. It's about twenty minutes in the car.'

'I'm already looking forward to it.'

They travel north in Elora's car; she thinks it best since Brodie does not know the roads. He can appreciate the surrounding beauty, Elora tells him, and she is right, as Brodie watches the countryside slide by.

Elora parks the car on the outskirts of the village. 'It will be better if we walk; you will see more that way.'

'Has it changed much since you lived here?' Brodie asks as they walk along the pavement hand in hand.

'It has, and it hasn't. It still looks the same, but there's more of it now.' She points over the street, 'There's my old school, where the basketball court is. We didn't have a basketball court. And next to the church is where we used to practise running.'

'You ran?'

'Yes. Did I never tell you?'

'I don't think so. I'm sure I would have remembered if you did.'

'I ran for the Athletics club. I was a sprinter. I once ran in a competition in Athens.'

'So, you were good at it.'

Elora nods. 'I was never going to go to the Olympics, but I'd like to think I was alright, and I still have the medals to show for it.'

'This is weird.'

'What do you mean?'

'This was your home, where you grew up. We didn't know each other until you left to study in Edinburgh.' He leans into her and kisses her lips. 'And now we are here, the two of us. It's funny how life has a way of turning out.'

Elora gives a small laugh. 'The house is just down here.'

They leave the main street and head down what can only be described as a track. They turn a corner and ahead is a cluster of trees.

'I've not been back for years.' Elora tells him. She squeezes Brodie's hand, and he senses a hesitation in her step. 'Remember, when I told you about the fire? Well, these trees were scorched and blackened. The image has never left me.'

The house stands on its own. It has two floors, and a tile is missing from the roof. It is smaller than Brodie has imagined it would be. There is a car in the drive, sheltering under a canopy of branches from a huge tree, its roots, in part, spreading from it like snakes above the dry earth.

'The fire never touched that tree. It saved our house. My mother said it was a miracle. I remember thinking, God must have had a twisted sense of humour. I envied my mother; even out of the most horrific tragedy, she could not speak ill of her God. I admired her steadfastness and her faith.'

'You didn't share it then?'

'No. I gave up on the church a long time before that. When I was fifteen, my mother lifted the compulsory order of attending church on Sundays. I never went back.'

'I was a good Catholic boy until my teenage years, and then I discovered girls, smoking and drinking, and not necessarily in that order.'

'It was something we never spoke about.'

'My mum was devastated when we lived together in the flat. We were living in sin, she often reminded me.'

'Maybe that's another reason why she didn't like me. I was a bad influence, leading you astray,' Elora grinned.

'Has the house changed much?'

'Not much. Although, it looks like it has been neglected. A fresh coat of paint was applied to its walls every year. I think it has been a while since that's happened.'

Brodie can detect the disappointment in her voice,

'Who lives there now, do you know?'

'I've no idea.'

'A house isn't just brick and mortar. It holds memories within its walls. It has seen happiness and sadness, love and hate, birth and death, the whole spectrum of human existence. Thank you, Elora. I'm glad you brought me to see your family home.'

'That makes me happy, Brodie. There are usually just one or two people who hold a family together. My grandmother kept us all together. She was everything to me. When I look at this house, I can feel her near me. It was hard to leave Corfu and go to Edinburgh. I'd never been away from my family before that, never mind moving to another country.'

'I think you did alright.'

'Not always. I've done things I'm ashamed of, that I'll regret till my last breath.'

'Who doesn't struggle just to survive some days?'

'Shall we go?' she asks, cutting him off. Elora looks at the house, she is frowning and Brodie wonders if she is seeing her younger self. She turns to face him. 'Hungry?'

'I am a bit.'

'There's a place just along the coast, we could be there in ten minutes.'

On the way back to the car, Elora is not her usual self. The quiet space between them is unsettling. She doesn't meet his eyes. It is the first time since he has known her that Brodie regrets not being able to find the right words, even asking if she is feeling alright seems somehow inadequate and he shrinks from it.

A sense of dread runs through his body, he feels something has changed.

What has stirred Elora's inexplicable mood? Could it have been the rundown appearance of her old home and the imminent thoughts concerning her family, her grandmother, or was it something else that triggered it?

Brodie thinks back to what Elora said, *'I've done things I'm ashamed of, that I'll regret till my last breath.'*

They both know they are postponing the conversation that is to come.

For a moment Brodie thinks of confronting her, but he knows she must be the one who instigates that dialogue. They have known this since he first arrived. It has always been a matter of time.

During lunch, in a delightful taverna, they go through the motions of polite conversation without asking questions of one another.

They drink their coffee looking towards the sea, where thick foliage headlands steer the eye towards the white masts of sailing boats and the occasional gigantic yacht.

'Have you been in touch with your son or daughter?'

'I've texted them a few times. I'm going to Skype Tom tonight. I'm thinking of telling him about us.'

'Really?' This new piece of information startles Elora.

'Why not?'

'I don't know. Maybe he'll resent me.'

'And why would he do that?'

'Because of his mother.'

'No. He's not like that. He just wants me to be happy.'

'And are you happy, Brodie?'

'I suppose that depends on your definition of happiness.'

She thinks for a moment. 'Wellbeing and contentment with life.'

'Well then, I would say under those conditions, happiness has eluded me.'

'I'm not sure we can be truly happy, not all the time.'

'So, happiness is a fluid state of being.'

'I suppose it is.'

'On another level, if life has meaning, is joyful and is worthwhile, then that is happiness.'

'Okay. If we were to use those to describe what happiness is, are you happy?'

She can see him pondering this.

'Then I would have to say, I'm happy only when I'm with you,' he tells her.

'What will happen when we are drawn back into our own lives?'

'Will we let that happen?'

She runs her fingers through her hair. 'Won't we have to? We're living in a bubble of our own making, after all.'

An awkwardness settles over him. 'Are you content, Elora?'

She wonders at his use of the word and finds she recoils from it. She has been angry and bitter for so long; she sometimes thinks she is incapable of feeling anything else.

He watches as she gestures towards the waiter and speaks in Greek. Brodie assumes she has asked for the bill. His eyes fix on her.

'What?'

'You haven't answered my question,' Brodie gently reminds her.

Around them, the air hints of lavender and the murmur of conversation.

She shrugs. 'Sometimes I am, other times I'm not. I have days when I'm not sure I really understand who I am.'

'I think we can all have days like that.'

Elora bows her head as she stares into her coffee cup. Her pensive expression worries him.

'What happened back there, you seemed overcome with… I don't know. It changed you.'

'It reminded me of what I did to you.'

This takes him aback.

'It brought back the shame and guilt of all those years. I'd betrayed you in the most unforgivable way. I'd left you, the only one I'd loved. I'd run away from what I'd done to you, but I couldn't hide from who I was. That was my punishment. I struggled to live with myself. It took me a long time to be able to start thinking of making a life for myself again.

'When I looked at that house, that had once been my home and a prison of my own making, it shocked me that those feelings came flooding back. And to think, at that very moment, you were standing next to me. There was a time I would never have thought that possible. It would have been unimaginable.'

'Yet here I am.'

'Yes. Here you are.'

He opens his mouth to speak when Elora places a finger on his lips. 'We are not apart and that's all that matters to me.'

Chapter18

Tom

'Hi, Dad.' Tom waves and Brodie responds likewise, waving at the screen of the mobile phone. He is in his bedroom, sitting on the bed.

'Hello, Tom. Where is Lisa?'

'She's having a lie-down. She sends her love.'

Brodie nods.

'Are you enjoying yourself? I looked at the weather app on my phone and you're having lovely weather, it's above 30 degrees Celsius most days.'

'It can get too hot in the afternoon, but I'm sticking to the shade, mostly. What's it like in London?'

'Not too bad, usually around 25, but it's cloudy today. I think it's going to rain later.'

'Good for the gardens then.'

'If I had one. I prefer sitting on the balcony with a cold beer and looking out over the city.'

'You'll have been doing a lot of that if the weather's been nice. Take advantage of it while you can, it'll be a distant memory once the little one arrives.'

Tom presses his lips together.

'Is everything alright, Tom?'

Tom rubs his eyes.

'Tom!'

'Lisa told me not to worry you.'

'Well, you're not doing a good job on that front.'

Tom rubs the stubble on his chin. 'It can wait until you get back.' His voice strains.

'I can see you're upset, Tom. Tell me what's going on?'

'I promised I wouldn't, dad.'

'It's a bit late for that. In a way, you already have.'

'It's the baby. She's lost the baby.' Tom drops his head into his hands.

Brodie reaches out and touches the screen.' Oh, Tom. I'm so sorry.' Brodie's heart feels like a rock inside him.

'Lisa was bleeding. She had these pains in her stomach. We went to the hospital and…' Tom exhales a long breath.

'How is Lisa?'

'Not good. She can't stop crying. I've taken some time off work.'

'That's good. You need to be with each other. I know it doesn't feel like it right now, but eventually, you'll both get through this.'

'It hurts so much and seeing Lisa like this…'

'I know, I know, Tom,' Brodie says gently.

'Lisa has told her mum. She's coming down tomorrow. She could only get a flight to Gatwick at such short notice. I'm picking her up.'

'Are you okay to drive?'

'I'll be fine. Lisa is coming with me. It'll be good to get out of the apartment. We haven't been out for days.'

'Look, Tom. I'll get a flight. I could be there in a day or two.'

'No, dad. Stay in Corfu, you deserve some time away. Besides, Lisa's mum is staying for a few days. You know it's not that I don't want you to.'

'I know, Tom. You're right. Lisa's mum will be more useful than me.'

'You can come and see us when you get back from Corfu.'

'I will, definitely. I'm so sorry, Tom.'

'I know, Dad.'

'I wish I could be with you both.'

'You will be. When are you coming back?'

Brodie sighs. 'I'd booked to stay for three weeks. I've got another two to go, but I could return sooner?'

'No. Don't do that, Dad.' Tom looks away. When he turns back to face the screen, Brodie can see the torment etched over his son's face. 'I was just getting used to the idea, you know. It was silly, I know, but I'd already imagined it being a boy, for some reason, and I'd had all these things in my head that we'd do together, just like we did.' Tom rubs his face and slumps back in his seat.

Brodie's throat aches and tears threaten to spill from his eyes at the mention of Tom's childhood. Tom's look of despondency is almost too much for Brodie to bear.

Tom rubs his eyes with the heel of his hand. 'Enough about me. So, Dad. What have you been getting up to in Corfu?'

It seems trivial talking about this now. 'Oh, you know, the usual holiday thing, some sightseeing, trying out the local food and wine. I've hired a car to get around. The roads are in good condition. Well, most of them anyway.'

'It sounds like you are having a good time.'

Brodie nods. 'I am. I'm missing Jasper. Hana was going to take some videos of him and send them to me. I'll have to send her a text to remind her.'

'Have you met people?'

Brodie hesitates. 'One or two. It's difficult on your own, people either take pity on you or steer clear of you. There are too many people around to feel lonely.' It doesn't sit easy avoiding the truth. Brodie has prepared himself by considering how he will approach delicately the real reason for his visit to Corfu.

He has abandoned this now. He cannot take the risk. Tom is upset. He is grieving the loss of his unborn child. Brodie cannot bring himself to be the one responsible if Tom were to think insensitively or cruelly towards Elora. He could never forgive himself. He has made his choice.

'I hope where you're staying is nice?'

'It is. It looks exactly like the photographs online. Clean and tidy. It's in the old town and perfectly situated. I've got everything around me I need. So, yes, I couldn't have asked for more.'

'That's good. I'm glad and relieved. If there's one thing that can spoil a holiday it's the disappointment of finding the accommodation is of a poor standard.'

'Well, you don't need to worry about that, I'm more than comfortable.' He hates this deceit, and he tries to ease his frustration by telling himself there is a measure of truth in it all.

'Have you told your sister?'

'Jessica knows.'

Brodie sighs. 'I see. How was she?'

'She's busy. Work is full-on. To tell you the truth, I think she's feeling stressed.'

'She shouldn't be stressed at her age.'

'The downside to the modern world, dad. Her job comes at a price. It's the nature of the beast. The City of London breathes it like oxygen.'

'There's more to life than money and nice houses. I worry about her.'

'Jessica's fine, Dad. It comes with the territory.'

'Your mum never liked the idea of her living in London on her own.'

'But she's not now, she has Alex, and she'd probably say she feels more at home in London now.'

'I know she's made a life for herself, as have you, but it doesn't stop me worrying about you both. That's my job.'

Tom smiles for the first time. 'So you keep telling us.'

'I do, don't I?'

'I wouldn't have it any other way.'

'Good, because I'm not about to change. I'll give her a phone after this.'

Tom checks his watch. 'She'll still be at work.'

'Of course she will be. We're two hours in front over here. Once I get back, and once you and Lisa feel up to it, it would be nice if we could all get together, go into town for

a meal, have a few drinks, catch up and you could all stay-
over. It's not as if I don't have the room. I'm knocking
about that house on my own.'

'You should sell it, dad.'

'You know I can't do that. It would be like leaving your
mother behind, abandoning her. We never lived in any
other house. We spent months decorating, knocking down a
wall or two, clearing the garden before we married. We
were paying a mortgage on it for a year before we moved
in. Our friends thought we were mad, but that's what your
mum wanted. She never wanted to live in any other house.
The only way I'll be leaving is in a box. Oh! I'm sorry,
Tom, that was insensitive of me.'

'It's okay, Dad. You don't need to apologise. It's Jessica
who should be apologising. When was the last time you
actually saw her?'

'Two or three months ago. I can't remember.'

'You should, it's important.'

'I've spoken to her on the phone.'

'And who called who?'

'I called her. I know, I know, but as you said, she's
busy.'

'We're all busy, Dad,' Tom retorts reprovingly. 'That's
not an excuse. She can take fifteen minutes out of her life,
surely. That's probably less time than it takes her to walk to
the shops. She doesn't even do that; she gets it delivered.'

'I hear you, Tom.'

'I'm sorry for going on about it. But what has happened
to Lisa and me, well, it has made me appreciate what I
have, to see things in a whole new perspective. Do you
know what is important, Dad? Family, that's important. We
shouldn't take each other for granted. We need to be
making time for each other. Jessica needs to make the
effort.'

'You've got a good heart, Tom.'

'And I take it from mum,' Tom suggests, sighing.

'I've said that before?'

'A few times.'

'Really? Well then, it's true.'

'I don't mean to be like this, it has been a tough few days.'

'You don't need to apologise. I understand. I wasn't taking it personally, anyway.'

'We've decided to try again as soon as Lisa is able to.'

'That's good.'

'It's what we both want. There's no point in waiting. If it is going to happen, it'll happen.'

'It will.'

There is silence for the first time.

'I'll let you get back to Lisa. Tell her she's in my thoughts and give her my love.'

'I will. You take care Dad and we'll see each other when you get back.'

'We will. Definitely.' Brodie circles his forehead with a finger.

'Are you alright, dad?'

'Of course. Just the beginnings of a little headache, that's all. I'm probably not drinking enough water.'

'Well, make sure you do. Bye for now and take care.'

'I will. Love you, Tom.'

'Love you too, Dad.'

Brodie lies back on the bed. The mobile drops from his hand. Above him, the ceiling fan is blurred, the blades distorted, their edges imprecise. A gentle breeze stirs the voile screen, the white linen muted, dulling. It is always like this, the beginning. He knows how it will end.

Chapter 19

Something Has Changed

Brodie rolls onto his back and opens his eyes. How long
has it been? He pulls himself to a sitting position and
massages his temple. This time there is only a dull ache.
When he stands, it is like his brain has turned to jelly and is
wobbling inside his head. The room moves and Brodie
sways. He reaches out and leans his hand on the wall. He
could almost be in a boat on a stormy sea. He considers
sitting back down, but thinks he may feel worse when he
eventually stands again. Brodie wants to close his eyes, but
the need for fresh air is more urgent. Tentatively, he makes
his way out onto the balcony and, resting his hands on the
railing, he inhales deeply, filling his lungs, and then, with
vigour, exhales as if he is blowing up a balloon. His eyes
dare not move from the haze of receding hills as he
concentrates on dispelling his giddiness.

He does this for some time until he is feeling more
himself.

He remembers his conversation with Tom and the pull of
needing to be with him. As he is thinking of this, Brodie
observes Elora below, under the vine-shaded terrace. She is
reclining on a sunbed and reading a book. He observes her
as she fiddles with a strand of hair, curling it
absentmindedly around her finger.

'Is it a good read?' He calls to her.

'There you are. I was wondering where you had gotten
to.'

'I nodded off.'

'I thought you might have done. I could hear your voice
and then it went all quiet about ten minutes ago.'

'I see.' She has answered the question he was just about
to ask. 'I'll come down.'

Elora is wearing her usual hat, white shorts and a loose-fitting cream blouse. Brodie cannot help tracing his eyes over her tanned legs. She removes her sunglasses and smiles at him. 'I was about to send out a search party.'

'Sorry about that.' Brodie says slumping down in the garden sofa.

'Not at all. You can sleep all afternoon if you like.'

'That would be a waste. I don't want to miss a minute of my time here.'

'Ah, Brodie. You might not think that in a week's time. You might be glad to get away from me by then.'

'I don't think so. In fact, you might be the one feeling like that.'

'My legs would be lonely.'

'Oh. You saw me.'

'I did.'

'I couldn't help it.'

'You flatter me.'

'You deserve it,' he says immediately.

She shakes her head and asks, 'How's your son?'

At the mention of Tom, Brodie feels the weight of his guilt press on him. The baby! Tom! The turmoil of Tom's emotion returns to him. Brodie can hardly speak. 'Not good.'

'Oh. I'm sorry to hear that.'

Brodie explains about the miscarriage.

'That's dreadful. You should be with him.'

'That was my instinct. But…'

'Of course, it is. He's your son, he'll need you.'

'He's told me to stay. Lisa's mother is travelling down to be with them for a few days.'

'Okay.' Not only has his decision to stay been the correct one, but the sense of relief in Elora's voice is also reassuring. It is something for him to hold on to.

Elora puts her book down and takes off her hat. She removes the pins from her hair. It tumbles over her shoulders, full, extensive, a radiant auburn.

It has always been the same. Brodie is astonished at how this simple gesture makes him feel. He cannot peel his eyes from her. Elora moves over to the sofa and sits next to him. She shifts slightly and rests her hand on his thigh. She leans into him, her eyes clear and bright are fixed on him. Her breath is hot on his skin sending a quiver deep inside his abdomen. When her lips brush his cheek, he sighs. Brodie lightly brushes several strands of hair from her face. He catches his breath as Elora kisses his mouth. Her lips are soft against his, their kiss tender and protracted.

When they part, Elora's eyes are watery.

'Something has changed in me.'

'What?'

'Don't look so worried, Brodie. You have taken me to a place I never thought I'd be.'

'Where?'

'To a place where I can be happy.'

They are lying upon the bed, Elora's head resting in the crook of his arm. Brodie's finger traces the curvature of her neck, trailing the outline of her shoulder, and where the skin is taut and thin, he tracks the delicate arch of her clavicle. She closes her eyes, her lips slightly parted. Ever so lightly, his fingertip follows the dip of her chest, the descent of her breastbone, gradually outlining the curve of her breast, and then he hesitates before drawing it over her nipple. Instinctively, Elora's spine arches to his touch. He rises above her, lowering his head, he kisses the brown tip and encases her with his mouth. Her breathing alters, eliciting an almost inaudible and soft groan that originates from deep within her.

He kisses the ridges of her ribs and follows along the line of her stomach. He feels the warmth of her thighs and upon

his lips the wiry curl of her hair as he lowers his mouth
upon her.

Edinburgh 1995

Forgiveness (The unbreakable Rule)

Brodie had never hit anyone. For that matter, he had never been in a minor scuffle before. His knuckles were throbbing. Chris was covering his nose with both hands, blood trickling through his fingers.

'You've broken my nose! Christ, it hurts,' Chris cried in disbelief.

The student bar was unusually busy, and Brodie had not expected this. Even though he knew it was not the smartest decision he had ever made, the second he saw Chris, any fragment of restraint deserted him in a burst of adrenalin and blind rage. It did not help that Chris, noticing Brodie, smiled at him.

Now, Brodie was leaning into Chris, his fists clenched, white-knuckled, 'That's the least you deserve, you bastard.'

The second punch smashed into Chris's cheekbone, droplets of blood spraying over Brodie's t-shirt, like the flick of paint from a brush. Chris staggered sideways and, stumbling, fell onto a table, bottles and glasses tumbling with him as he hit the floor. Eyes glazed and wide, an expression of pure fright blazing across his face, Chris raised his arm, attempting to fend off any further attack.

Brodie felt an arm around his chest, and unbalanced, he was dragged backwards, spun around and manhandled towards the exit by two students who had been drinking with Chris.

'You're dead,' Brodie shouted over his shoulder. 'This hasn't finished.'

'Fuck off, Brodie!' The bigger of the two spat as they forced him through a door and deposited him unceremoniously onto the pavement outside.

It felt like he'd ran a marathon. He could feel his heart pounding in his chest as he lay on his back, staring at the sky. He pulled himself up and stood facing the door he'd just been ejected from. It opened and several people stepped outside. 'Hi, Brodie. Where did you learn to punch like that? You would have floored Mike Tyson if he had gotten in your way.' The others laughed. Brodie didn't like his tone but said nothing and was glad when they continued to walk along the street.

Brodie had never been capable of violence towards anyone. He deplored violence and now he had become a perpetrator who had sunk to the levels of blind vengeance and retribution, an animalistic desire for revenge that had become all-consuming. He would not deny it felt good to have seen fear in Chris's eyes. Chris physically recoiled when, suddenly, he realised Brodie knew. And Brodie took great delight in watching Chris's smile dissipate with panic.

Brodie was acutely aware he did what he did, not to defend Elora's reputation, but simply for the self-gratification revenge brought.

He needed to hurt Chris. He intended to inflict pain. Brodie's motivation had been entirely selfish. Also, he would refuse Elora his forgiveness. Tomorrow would have been their second anniversary.

Brodie sat with his head in his hands, rocking slightly.

'How could you have done this? I don't understand.' He looked up at her. 'How could you have done this to me... to us?'

Elora looked away. She, too, did not understand. She could not answer him. There were no words. Her tears stole her words and her silence felt like a betrayal.

'I had no idea you were so unhappy. Why else would you have done this? Was it me? Was it my fault?'

She wanted to reach out and touch him but feared his reaction.

'There were times when you were distant, disconnected even, from me, from your friends. I thought you were just missing your family. I thought you were homesick. I thought to give you space was the right thing to do. I thought...' Brodie shook his head and Elora was unsure if it was because he thinks himself a fool, or he was despairing over Elora's deception.

Her legs gave way, like partial atrophy of muscle and tissue. She knelt before him, her hair spilling around her face. An image of herself praying in supplication as a child asserts itself.

Brodie stands, a rush of anger uncurling his spine. 'How many times did you see him?'

'A few times.'

'How long have you been seeing him?'

'I'm not seeing him.'

'How long?' Brodie rasped.

She hesitated a moment too long. 'It was a few weeks, that's all. Maybe not even that.' She had hoped the short duration would, in some way, alter the impact of what had happened. For a split second, that was her hope. But really, she knew, time was never going to lessen the blow of her infidelity.

'Was he here? Did you sleep with him?' He stared at her intently.

She looked away, an admission of guilt. Everything will be different now. The implicit contract of sexual exclusivity had been violated.

She could hear herself confess, 'It meant nothing, he means nothing to me.' Empty words. She knew it even before they slipped from her mouth. She had to say something, anything that could retrieve even a morsel of hope that Brodie could still have it in him to forgive her.

It had been an unaccustomed hot day for April and the air in the flat was muggy and stifling. She could see a sheen of sweat on Brodie's forehead, as his words impaled her chest.

'You're a slut. That's what you are, a fucking slut.' His eyes spoke of hurt and panic, in that moment, hysteria held him.

She had never heard Brodie speak this way. This was not him. She didn't know this man before her. Elora shuddered; she had done this.

She was sitting on the floor now, sinking into a bottomless emptiness. Nothing could ever hurt as much as this. She pulled her knees up and stooped her head towards them, hiding her face, his words stifling and sucking the air around her. She held her breath, *slut* still stinging her ears, demoralising her, but gradually, her restraint giving way to a rising rage.

She shook her head back and forth. 'I am not a slut. He showed me kindness, understanding. He talked to me, he listened, he was interested. For months, you have been none of these things. You have changed, Brodie.'

He gave a laugh of astonishment. 'So, that justifies what you did?'

'I didn't say that. I'm just being honest. You deserve that at least.'

'Well, if we're being honest, I could never have done that to you.'

Unable to stop herself, Elora's voice rose to a shout. 'We're both to blame.'

'But I didn't have sex with your best friend, did I?' yelled Brodie.

She pulled herself to her feet. When she reached her full height, she looked at him in incredulous fury. 'No. You didn't, I did. I know it's painful for you, but can you imagine what kind of place I was in; I did the unthinkable to the man I loved. It was vile, it was unforgivable, don't you think I know that?' Her voice rose a pitch, almost hysterical. 'If I could…'

'What? You'd turn back time.'

She could feel his eyes fall away from her.

Her arms fell to her side, defeated. She could feel a trembling in her hands. This damage felt physical, like a wound. She felt a blast of sudden warmth creeping over her skin, igniting her neck, spreading over her head, a pounding pulse, like a drum inside her skull. She was exhausted. She had violated the unbreakable rule.

Brodie raked a hand through his hair. 'I can't do this anymore.' He swiped his jacket from the arm of a chair.

'Where are you going?'

'Out! Anywhere but here.'

The front door slammed, shaking the walls with such force that Elora feared they would crack. Standing in the silence around her, in the isolation of her grief, Elora's hands trembled as she tried to catch her breath. And then it came, a churning cry from the pit of her stomach: a resonance, so grotesque, so primitive and raw, the shock of it overwhelmed her. She covered her mouth, doubling over at the waist and, once her tears began, they would not stop.

Chapter 20

An Invitation

Brodie was going to take his car, but Elora is insistent she will hire a taxi instead. She has booked their table in advance and told him the view of the sunset is a striking accompaniment that will live with Brodie for as long as his mind can remember. She is right. It enthralls him.

After the meal, they walk in high spirits, drawn by the intricate patterns of the lights shining gently on the bay. Elora takes Brodie's arm.

'I'm absolutely convinced I don't think I've ever had a better meal.'

'I've never had a bad one yet and I've been going for years,' Elora says, gazing at a display in a jeweller's window.

'Mm, I thought the waiters were unusually friendly.'

She smiles at him. 'Do I detect a hint of jealousy?'

Brodie grins. 'Nonsense. I've no need to be. It was fated by the Gods that we would meet again. It's called Divine intervention.'

'Greek Gods?'

'None other.'

'That's no guarantee. Greek mythology is bursting at the seams with tales of jealousy.'

'Ah, and here's me thinking they were infallible.'

They order a drink at a bar and sit outside at a table. Brodie listens to Elora as she talks. Occasionally, he will answer a question or comment as he watches her gesticulate and run her fingers through her hair. He observes her: the structure of her face, the precision of the eyes, the nose, the full lips and the delicate balance of distance and composition. It reminds him of the Greek woman in her.

'I will be going to Athens next week,' Elora is saying. 'I have a few book signings organised by my Greek publicist.' She tops their glasses to the brim.

'Oh!' Brodie says calmly, although his heart is reverberating in his chest. 'I didn't know you were published in Greece.' Elora's visit to Athens has startled him.

'Of course, in Greek too. My books have been translated into Italian, French, German, in fact most European countries. Have you ever been to Athens?'

'No. I haven't.'

'Then you should come.'

'I had no idea you were going.'

She notices Brodie's surprise. 'I'm sorry, I should have said. To be honest, since you turned up, I haven't thought of such things. I checked my diary this morning. Somehow, I thought the book signing was in a few weeks. It has come as a surprise to me too.'

'How long will you be in Athens?'

'I fly on Wednesday; Thursday is the book signings and I come back on Friday.'

'What would I do?'

'It's Athens, Brodie. You could be a tourist for a day. And we would have time together too. I'll get my publicist to organise it. What do you say? I could see to it first thing tomorrow.' Elora smiles expectantly.

He nods. 'Why not?'

'Good. I feel better about it now.'

'How much of the city do you think I'll be able to see? A day is probably just going to scratch the surface, I would think.'

'You'll be surprised. If you take one of those tourists' buses, you can see far more than if you just walked around all day.'

'I like to walk. You get a better feel for a city that way.'

'Then do both. Take the bus to see the usual sights, the Acropolis, museums, whatever you like really, and then have a wander around. The best of both worlds.'

'I'm feeling quite excited about it.'

'We can meet up later in the day, have some dinner at the hotel or we could eat out if you prefer?'

'I'd rather experience eating out in Athens. I know you've probably done it lots of times.'

'I don't mind. It's your choice. Athens is busy and noisy at the best of times, but at this time of year, it can get too much. I prefer Thessaloniki to Athens. It's right next to the sea, the parks are lovely. You can spend an early evening walking in them or on the promenade.

'It has UNESCO ruins, Byzantine Baths, museums – my favourite is the Museum of Byzantine Culture, and the most astonishing churches, Aghia Sofia is worth a visit. There's plenty of great places to eat too.'

'It sounds lovely.'

'The Ladadika District is beautiful, it's perfect to walk around in and take in the sights. There are some charming tavernas and restaurants to eat in as well.'

'Are you sure you don't have a book signing there?'

Elora laughs. 'Not this time, I'm afraid.'

'That's a pity, it sounds a great city to visit.'

'We should go there sometime.'

'Yes. We should.'

Brodie thinks about this. It suggests a time beyond a beginning; it hints at the possibility of a future. He is hesitant to think about how it will all end. He is afraid to go there.

There is a silence as the night air drifts around them. Elora tilts her head towards the night sky and combs her hair with her fingers. He tries to picture the two of them in a strange city, Athens? Thessaloniki? It does not matter. It is just being with her that is appealing, that is important.

Chapter 21

Fraying Threads

The flight has taken an hour to get to Athens. On their arrival, they are met by a young man holding, at chest height, a card with Elora's name printed in bold black ink. The journey to the hotel feels longer than the flight as they make slow progress through the rush hour traffic.

Once checked in, a well-dressed woman from Elora's publishing company introduces herself. Over drinks in the bar, she goes through the itinerary for the following day and shows Elora the conference room where her author talk and book signing will take place.

Later that night, they walk through the streets of Athens, have dinner at a small and intimate restaurant, where the tables are lit by candles and authentic Greek music is subtly played.

Over coffee, a middle-aged woman sitting a few tables away recognises Elora. She asks Elora to sign a sheet of paper she has ripped from a notepad. Elora obliges and talks for a few minutes before the woman hugs her and returns to her husband.

'It's like you're a rock star. Does that happen often?' Brodie asks.

'Sometimes. It depends where I am. I'm quite well known in Greece, it's one of my biggest markets.'

'You handled it well.'

'It's a privilege. They read my books, it's the least I can do.'

'What did you talk about?

'My books. She's read them all. She asked where I got my inspiration from. She also said she found my husband nice looking.'

'She thought we were married!'

'She did.'
'And you told her we weren't?'
'I didn't want to embarrass her.'
'I'm flattered.'

They step out of the restaurant. Elora holds onto Brodie's
arm as they stroll at a leisurely pace, taking in lively café
bars, reverberating with young people, where tables line the
pavement occupied by people eating and drinking. Shops
are open late into the night where couples meander from
one shop window display to next.
   'Have you ever lived in Athens?' Brodie asks.
   'No. I prefer to visit. That way I don't take it for granted.
The problem with living in a city is you never really get to
appreciate the wonder of the night sky. That's what I would
miss living in a place like this. At home, at night, when I
look at the sky, the longer I look, the more it reveals of
itself, becoming illuminated with stars and, if I'm lucky,
the occasional shooting star or meteor shower. I have it all.
It's wonderful. In a city, you don't see it, you're denied that
wonder because of the city's light. What happens is that
people stop looking, they know the stars are above them,
but they become complacent. You can never become
complacent where I live. I like that.'
   'I never take living in Edinburgh for granted. I can't
imagine living anywhere else. Although, it would be nice to
spend part of the year here in Greece, especially this time
of year.'
   'It's your home. I feel the same about Corfu. When I was
in Paris, I loved the city, but I always felt homesick.'
   'So, even though we've found each other, we're still
separated by place.'
   'It seems that we are. That hasn't changed, has it?'
   'Does it worry you? I mean, wherever this takes us,
could it be enough for one of us to sacrifice living away

from home, or does it mean something entirely different altogether?'

'Like what?'

'That there can't be an us, this is as good as it's going to get.'

She says nothing. Finally, Elora looks at him. Her voice is tight. 'That's what we have to ask ourselves.'

'Can we go there? I want it to be like this with you. I don't know what normal is any more. We've suspended our normal lives; we've stepped away from them. Even you, doing your talk tomorrow, it's different. I'm with you. It's changed everything.'

'Whatever happens, it won't change how I feel. I'm glad we've had this time together. Who would have thought it possible? It has allowed me to get to know you again. Before this, I could only think about you through the lens of the past. I just had my memories of when we were younger. I'm now able to make amends for that time.'

'There's no need,' he says quickly and dismissively.

'There is on my part. It's troubled me that you've never asked about it.'

'I've had nearly a lifetime to get over it. It can't be changed. It is what it is.'

Elora flinches. She thinks he is making light of their past. 'Not for me. It has never been like that.' She thinks of the madness that followed. The remorse, the grey mist of depression that caught her mood and settled upon her. One mistake that changed all possibilities, that ruined the prospect of the life she could have had.

'Elora! I'm sorry. I didn't mean it to sound like that.'

She looks away from him. He can feel her irritation with him. 'You've no idea what I went through.' She turns from him and walks away.

'Elora! Stop!'

Brodie jogs towards her and takes her arm. 'Elora, what are you doing? I'm sorry.'

She wrenches her arm away from him. 'Do you think my house, the books I've written, the money I have, do you think these bring happiness? Do you think, for one minute, they give me closure? I've lived in a state of limbo. I don't have to die to know what purgatory feels like.'

Brodie knows that people are looking at them. There is a slight slurring in Elora's words. He tries to think about how much she has had to drink.

'I'm sorry. I didn't mean it to sound like that. I wasn't dismissing what you went through. I would never do that. You know I wouldn't.'

'Why have you been avoiding the unavoidable?'

'This is not the right time, Elora. Not here, like this. We'll go back to the hotel.'

'I need another drink.'

'You don't.'

Elora's face is white. 'I'll decide what I need.'

'Okay, then just come back to the hotel. Have a drink at the bar. We'll talk there.'

'Just leave me, Brodie. I want to be on my own.' There is a harshness, a finality in her pronouncement. It shocks him. His chest is tight as he watches Elora stride away from him. He is struggling to make sense of what has just happened. He is now fearful, reluctant to put Elora through the pain of the story he must tell her… the fraying thread that links them.

With *Google's* help, Brodie makes his way back to the hotel. He heads for the bar and orders a beer and then another.

When he returns to his room, Brodie checks his mobile, and his heart sinks, she has not texted. It is then he phones her. He is worried now. She does not answer. He hears her voice telling him to leave a message. Brodie paces the room. He pulls back the heavy curtain and peers into the street below.

His forehead is heavy against the glass of the window. *Where are you?* It is then, he thinks of going down to the reception and asking the young woman to phone the police. He sighs. And what will she tell them? They had an argument of sorts and Elora, angry with him, stormed away and he has not seen her since. Brodie shakes his head. The more he considers how the conversation would go, it sounds ridiculous. They will ridicule him; he is sure of it.

He sits heavily on the bed and bends forward, holding his head in his hands. He lies back, feeling the covers beneath him and stares at the ceiling, his eyelids feel like steel and he struggles to keep them open, soon sleep swamps him.

When Brodie awakes, it is light outside. He has slept in his clothes and at some point, during the night, he has gone under the white single sheet. He checks his mobile, *9.00 am* his stomach sinks. He never sleeps this late. What if she has called him or texted? But she hasn't.

He calls her and, as he does so, he opens the curtains. He slides the glass doors open and steps out onto the balcony. As he listens to the dial tone, across the city, he can see The Acropolis. It is his first time, yet the wonderment that would normally ensue is muted. He registers it but, at this moment, all that matters is hearing Elora's voice. He leaves a message; there is panic and desperation in his words.

He showers and gets dressed in fresh clothes. He has no idea what he will do. He takes the lift and wanders into the breakfast area. He gives his room number to the woman who is standing behind a podium. She bends her head and consults her list. She smiles at him and gestures for a waiter to show Brodie to a vacant table.

He has no appetite. As the waiter pours his coffee, Brodie looks out onto the street. A taxi has pulled up outside the hotel and, for a moment, Brodie believes Elora will emerge from the back-passenger door.

It is not her.

He is deflated.

His coffee sits untouched. He has not moved from his seat. It has been half an hour and he has observed every person that has entered or left the hotel from the street outside.

He wanders through the bar area and takes a seat adjacent to the reception. He can see activity down a corridor where the conference rooms are situated. He recognises the woman from Elora's publishing company, the one they had drinks with when they arrived yesterday.

Should he tell her he does not know where Elora is? Or should he wait? She will find out soon enough. Elora is to talk at one o'clock. He will give her time.

The pressing weight of worry does not leave him. He experiences the strange sense there is more to how Elora reacted. Although, as far as he can tell, she has been candid with him, there is something she has not told him. He has sensed Elora's apprehension. Until now, he has ignored it, and this has been the result.

He lets himself into his room. Immediately, he senses something is different. He can hear the rumble of traffic as he walks down the small hallway. The sliding doors are open to the balcony; he can feel the breeze that shifts the fine voile netting. Brodie leans flush against the wall, he will have to crane his head to view the interior. He needs to clear his head and consider the possibilities. The room is on the sixth floor and the door was locked. Did he forget to close the sliding doors? His heart feels like it fills his chest. He tries to summon the courage to move into the room. He can't detect any movement or sound. In his head, Brodie counts. One... Two... Three! He moves swiftly, then he stops abruptly as if he has run into a wall.

'Jesus! Elora.'

She is sitting on the bed, still wearing her clothes from the night before. Elora lifts her face and looks at him as if he is a stranger to her.

'Where have you been? You've been out all night.'

'I... I stayed at a friend's house.' Elora's voice is so anguished, Brodie feels a rush of concern. 'I'm sorry about last night.'

'I should be apologising. It wasn't your fault, Brodie.'

'Why didn't you come back to the hotel?'

'I needed to be on my own. I've known Damaris for years; she has been a good friend to me. She moved to Athens from Corfu years ago. She let me stay the night and she didn't ask any questions as I knew she wouldn't.'

Brodie sits beside Elora and takes her hand.

She takes a deep breath. 'I'm not good for you, Brodie. I'll only bring you pain. My present has always been held hostage by my past. There are things I need to tell you, but you are right; not now, not here. When we get back, back home. That is... if you still want to come back with me?' She pauses. 'I won't blame you if you don't.' She looks at her feet.

'I'm just relieved you're all right.'

She turns her head to him. Her eyes are on the brink of shedding tears. He leans towards her and kisses her softly on the mouth. 'Does that answer your question?'

She nods.

'What shall I do?'

He looks at her, confused. 'What do you mean?'

'The talk. I cannot face anyone, never mind a room full of people. I can't do this. The thought of it makes me sick.'

'You can.'

'I can't. I'm sorry. I can't do this anymore.'

'Trust me.'

She is shaking her head. She doesn't speak.

He stands. 'I'll get you water.'

'No. Don't leave me.'

He bends down and kisses the top of her head.

She is trembling. Leaving her is not a possibility. He thinks awhile. 'Why don't you get changed, we can get something to eat at the bar or I could ring for room service?'

'I can't eat.'

'You have to have something; when did you last eat?'

She wipes her mouth. 'Some soup, then.' She puts a hand to her mouth and muffles her sobs.

'Let it out.' He sits on the bed beside her, puts his arm around her. She presses her face to his chest, and he can feel her tears stain his shirt.

'Would you tell them I'm ill? Please, Brodie.'

'What will happen? People will be arriving.'

She doesn't answer him. She presses her lips together and she shakes her head vigorously. Elora's reaction shocks him.

'I'll go now. I won't be long.'

When Brodie returns to the room, Elora has not moved, she is still sitting where he left her. She lifts her eyes to him.

'It's done. The lady from your publishers wanted to see how you were.'

Elora catches her breath.

'Don't worry, I persuaded her you weren't well enough to see anyone and that I'd phoned for a doctor. She wishes you well.'

'I've even got you lying for me. I'm poison.'

Chapter 22

A Move Towards the Truth

They returned from Athens. There were reports of the cancellation in the local newspapers, a column or two, but nothing more.

Over the coming days, Elora's mood improves, but the incident in Athens lurks in the background as does the anticipation and probability of what is to come. There is the certainty it has made everything fragile.

Elora has wondered for years how this moment will feel. Now that Brodie is here, her mind skips to the possibility that she might lose him. She considers for a split second abandoning her intention to tell him what really happened, the truth of it all. Elora tries to formulate a beginning, a way of starting, but how can she put into words, meaningful phrases that will depict how it was, because that is what Brodie must know; he must know the truth.

It overwhelms her, the prospect of finally relieving herself of this burden. Now that Brodie has entered her life again, it is unthinkable not to tell him. He deserves this. I deserve this, she reminds herself and, for a moment, calmness descends upon her.

Brodie has been observing her as he walks towards the house from the garden.

'I've just been on the phone to Tom.'

'Oh. How is he?'

'Fine. Yeah, he's fine.'

'Then, what is it?' Her scepticism is obvious. She gestures for Brodie to sit. 'Is his wife okay?'

'Yeah. Lisa is as well as could be expected. Her mother stayed with them longer than was first intended. I think that helped them both. They're still trying to get over losing the baby. Lisa is taking it hard.'

'You want to be with them?'

He looks away.

'Don't stay here just because of me. As a father, it's where you should be. They need you.'

Brodie looks at her. 'Right now, you need me.'

'And what about you, Brodie?'

'I have to finish what I came here to start.'

'We both do. I think it's now time we did just that.'

She takes a breath and choosing her words cautiously, she begins. 'There's something you need to know, something I have to tell you. Before I say anything, I want you to know. I never thought I'd get this opportunity, but here we are, the two of us. It's something I'd never imagined would be possible. I remember all the details.' There is a nervousness to her voice which Brodie detects.

She forces a smile and continues; she speaks briskly, to hide her emotion. 'It was fear that made me do it, but we'll get to that in good time...'

Edinburgh 1995

The Truth

She contacted Chris to meet and, to her relief, he agreed. This had to end. What she had done was catastrophic. She feared she had lost Brodie and the life they had made together. She felt it then. It was shocking and surreal. She remembers Brodie's face, how can she forget the pain she watched etch over his face, the disbelief in his eyes. It crushed him. It crushed her.

She heard his voice calling her over. They were meeting in a bar that few students frequented. She chose it for that reason. It was popular with office workers and professional people, a favoured venue for lunch and drinks after work. As Elora scanned the faces of those drinking at the bar and eating at tables, no one was familiar to her. She felt her shoulders relax, but she reminded herself all it would take would be for one person to see them together and things like this spread like wildfire around the campus, bars, and lecture halls.

Elora heard his voice calling her over. As Chris waved, Elora could see he had ordered two drinks. Suddenly, she realised this was a mistake. She sat in the chair opposite him and clasped her hands together, resting them on her lap. Her eyes traced the fiery orange and purple bruise on Chris's face and she immediately thought of Brodie, their snug flat and the laughter and love that had filled it. When she thought of these things, being unfaithful should have been inconceivable.

Chris slid a glass of wine across the table towards her.

'I remembered you liked red wine.'

Elora felt a wave of crazed anger build inside her. She wanted to throw the drink over him. Instead, she pushed it back to its original position. 'I'm not here to drink, or to be sociable.' She took a deep breath. 'And I'm certainly not here to negotiate a compromise over a civilised drink. This is where it ends, Chris. It meant nothing to me, do you understand?'

'No. I don't.'

'I was feeling vulnerable. I wasn't thinking straight… I wasn't thinking at all.'

'It didn't feel like that. I don't believe you.'

She almost laughed. 'I don't care what you believe. I care about Brodie. It's Brodie I love.'

'It's a bit late for that.'

'How do you know that? You know nothing about Brodie and me.'

'Come on, Elora. It doesn't take a genius to know what you've done is irreparable.'

He was enjoying this. It was his smug smile that did it. Elora looked away from him. She tried to keep her frustration under control, but it was boiling inside her. When she turned to face him, Elora stared into his eyes, holding his gaze. 'This is the last time we will meet, speak, or see each other. Am I making myself clear?'

Chris grinned, he slid his finger over the table and then said calmly, 'I think you enjoyed it just as much as I did.'

She would not claim innocence, she was taking responsibility. With a look of pure loathing, she spat out the words. 'I'm embarrassed about it. The thought of it makes me sick. I can't make myself any clearer than that.' Her stomach tensed. She stood up quickly and turned to leave. She felt his grasp on her arm, his nails digging into her skin. 'You're hurting me!'

'You don't walk away from me.'

'Let go.' Elora's heart thumped.

At the next table, the conversation abruptly stopped. A man in a suit observed Elora. 'Are you okay?' he asked concerned.

Chris released his grip. 'It's fine. Everything is fine.'

Eager to leave, she took her chance. Elora hurried towards the exit, and the street outside, without looking over her shoulder.

Elora gulped air, her mouth felt scraped out and her throat dry as sandpaper. I shouldn't have come here. Another mistake. What was I thinking? What is wrong with me? The thought of Brodie made her want to cry. She wiped the tears from her eyes and, fearful Chris would follow her, she ran in no particular direction, she just wanted to get away as far as possible.

Elora found herself in The Meadows, a sizable park area of grass and trees, bordered by the architecture of the city. She sat on a bench, her lungs screaming and aching. A sickly feeling came over her. She gulped compulsively and almost retched, swallowing a slither of acidic bile. A woman walking towards her stopped and asked Elora if she was all right. Her face streaked with tears and embarrassed she had drawn attention to herself, Elora bit her lip and forced a smile, assuring the passer-by she was fine. Unconvinced and reluctantly, the woman went on her way. Elora dropped her forehead into her hands and screwed her eyes shut. She heard the click of the woman's footsteps fade, replaced by another, softer sound. It began to rain, the occasional drop at first, and then suddenly a heavy downpour engulfed her. With a herculean effort, she stood up, her hair already sticking to her face. She sought the shelter of a large tree, the ground dry under a canopy of branches. She leaned against the trunk, suddenly exhausted. She felt her chest through her wet top and pressed her palm over her hammering heart. There was a massive dense slab of grief wedged there and it gave her permission to scream hysterically.

Elora awoke to the sound of rain. She turned onto her side and touched the pillow next to her, where Brodie's absence was a constant reminder of what she'd done.

She rubbed her eyes and looked at the bedside clock. It was still early. On such days, Brodie would make breakfast, toast and tea and bring it to her in bed, on a tray, where they would both eat and talk and sometimes even fall asleep again.

She was unwilling to manage these memories. She thought of them as being in a vitrine. Each time she went over them in her head, the glass became smudged and she could never see the memory as lucidly again.

She ate her breakfast alone at the kitchen table, watching rain slide down the glass of the window above the kitchen sink. The flat was cold, it felt unlived in, even though she hadn't left it for days.

She had an exam that afternoon. She hadn't been to the university in over a week. She wasn't ready to face the inevitable looks, preconceived judgement and the questions of others, especially from her friends. Could she expect their concern and compassion? She didn't know. She didn't care.

She thought she understood why this had to happen. Could she have kept it a secret from him and who would have gained from that? Brodie's was hurt and his agony was unbearable to watch. Elora took a deep breath. It was still unbelievable. She felt like she had fallen into another time zone, another life even. It was not meant to be this way.

She had desperately engaged in attempting to answer what had come over her When she was younger, her mother took her to see a doctor, a specialist of some sorts; she was too young to remember, and her mother never spoke of it. Elora's memory of that time was vague. She remembered feeling different, not in body, but the mind. She still does. She can wake in the morning and immediately feel its presence. She can only describe it as a heaviness that envelops her, shrouding her thought processes, dulling the chemistry of her body and extinguishing the light inside her.

***

She knew he was following her. He was the last person she wanted to see. Lectures had just ended, and students were pouring into the corridor as Elora joined their flow. Around her, voices were loud and frivolous, a flurry of words like bees released from a jar.

Then suddenly, she saw her escape, a fire door. It was raining as she crossed the courtyard, quickening her step. Her eye caught an opened door. Inside, she could hear sawing and hammering and workmen talking. She could taste the dust in the air. She moved quickly, crossing to a flight of stairs, then she hesitated. The door, I should have closed the door. She strode the steps, two at a time leading her to a cavernous room. What now? This is ridiculous, she told herself, glancing around the room.

Elora heard the creak of the stairs and spun around. She stared at the top of the stairs, where moments later, she had entered the room. She saw the top of his head emerge, then his face, his shoulders and her eyes widened as Chris stood in front of her panting in a half-smile.

'Chris, why are you doing this?'

'Because I love you.'

'How can you? You don't mean that.'

'I have done, ever since I first saw you.'

'God, Chris. This is not a story in some romantic novel, it's real life. This is crazy. I've made a mess of this whole thing.'

'You haven't. We can be together now. Brodie has left you. I can make you happy, Elora.'

'No! Brodie made me happy.'

There were bangs and crashes coming from the floor below them.

'But you said it yourself, you were drifting apart. It was only a matter of time. What we did was an acknowledgement of that. I know you felt what was between us when we were together in the flat. When we made love. You could feel the closeness, the bond between us.'

'No! No! No! I've told you it was the biggest mistake of my life. It's ruined my life.'

'You can't mean that? How can something so special, so beautiful, be spoken of like that?'

'Because it's true.'

They could hear footsteps in the corridor and, somewhere, workmen shouting instructions to each other. The rattle of a drill ricocheted off exposed brick walls.

'You don't mean that Elora. If you're trying to protect me from Brodie, if you think that a little scrape on my face will stop me from seeing you, then it won't. I don't care what he does. I only care about you.'

'If that's true, then I'm asking you to stop this now. It's what I want. If you care about me, you will do this for me.'

'I can't.'

'You have to!' she screamed at him.

'I won't.'

'Then you leave me with no choice.'

'What do you mean?'

'I'll go to the police and tell them you're stalking me… and that you've threatened me.'

'Elora, you know I would never do that.'

'I know you wouldn't, Chris, but the police don't know that.'

'I won't let you.'

'Please, Chris,' Elora pleaded.

He moved towards her. In a panic, Elora raised her arms and, with all the strength she could muster, she pushed him in the chest. Chris stumbled backwards, and she saw the last fragments of hope desert his face.

Her heart thumped. Before Elora could even think of her next action, Chris grabbed her by the shoulders and was pulling her towards him. Instinctively, Elora clasped her hands around his forearms, pulling at them. It made no difference; he was too strong. She knew what his intention was then. The look on his face had changed, for it clouded over with anger and resentment. What she did then was intuitive. Fear had taken hold. Chris wrenched her arms away and, with the momentum, with sheer brute force, Elora slammed her palms, once again, into his chest. Shocked, Chris stumbled, releasing his grip. Elora was already running at him, and she braced herself for the impact as her shoulder rammed into Chris's body. It was enough to destabilise his balance. The large window, its old frame rotten and crumbling, shattered. Chris screamed in astonishment and devastation, his hands frantically clawing at nothing but air as he fell from Elora's view.

She was lying on the floorboards and, as she moved, a sharp and hot pain tore through her shoulder. She screamed in agony, and with the realisation that Chris had fallen.

'Oh my God! Oh my God!' She repeated it like a chant. She was shaking, uncontrollably. She scraped her hands over the splintered grain of the wooden floor and clambered to her feet. She felt light in the head and unsteady, as she sluggishly moved one foot in front of the other. She reached the wall and pressed her back against the exposed brick. Tentatively, she craned through the gaping opening where, seconds before, the window had been. In horror, she clasped her hand over her mouth, gasping for air. A stream of dark blood stained the slabs below her. She struggled to breathe, nausea gripping her throat. Her head swam with shock.

Elora could hear the thud of footsteps on the stairs. She looked left and right. There was a passageway at the far end of the room. At the end of the passageway, a narrow stairwell offered her an escape. She looked behind her.

229

Someone was in the room. She scurried down the stairs, the industrious sounds of workmen, somewhere in the building, following her descent. Elora's hands shook, as she pushed through a side door and stepped out onto the street. *So much blood, so much blood.* The image stuck in her head. It was like being in a nightmare, she told herself, as her heart thudded with fear. Panic climbed from her stomach and her thoughts clambered for answers. *Is he dead? It was three floors up. How could this have happened?* She had to leave. Had someone seen her? She looked around, anxiety tugging at her to move, to escape.

Elora was unsteady on her feet as she crossed the street between parked cars. She heard her mother's voice warning her when she was younger, never to cross a street between parked cars. She was programmed to think this whenever she flaunted her mother's warning, even as a grown woman, even now, after what had just happened and, even now, not knowing if Chris was still alive or dead.

Once Elora had made enough distance between herself and the university, she walked solemnly back to the flat. Once inside, she threw herself on the bed and tears filled her eyes. *It was an accident, a freakish accident, but who would believe me?* She remembered Chris's face; she would never forget that abject look of terror. No one could have survived that fall, she convinced herself. She must think of what to do next. And then, it struck her. There was only one way out of this. She could no longer stay in Edinburgh or Scotland. She looked around the modest bedroom and along the narrow hall to the living room. So many memories filled this place. It felt like someone had wrenched her heart from her chest. The pain was suffocating. She could hear a gentle rain falling steadily outside. Suddenly, she yearned for home, for her mother and her family. She longed to feel the sun and bathe her in its warmth, and she would give anything to breathe the air of the only place called home, Greece.

She was standing at the kitchen table, staring at a sheet of paper. She had ransacked her mind for the appropriate words, but none were forthcoming; all were devoid of meaning, the written word was inadequate, none could convey her grief and heartache. In the end, there was only the simple conjoining of two words that mattered; *Forgive me.*

A newly packed suitcase sombrely waited for her in the hallway. Elora regarded the flat for the last time and then stepped outside. She closed the front door and leaned her forehead against its cold surface. She swallowed her sobs and turned the key in the heavy lock. As Elora dropped the key into the letterbox, she flinched at the finality of the heavy thud on the floor. With a leaden weight in her chest, she went down the worn stone stairs and, pulling the collar of her coat around her neck, she disappeared into the drizzling rain.

Chapter 23

A Move Towards the Truth

'It was an accident. You must believe me, Brodie. I didn't know what to do. It terrified me. My life had just imploded. It was beyond anything I could have ever imagined. I've lived with this for so long it has exhausted me. Each new day is like a punishment, it never leaves me. I've lived a lie. I've lived in fear that one day, I'd be found out. I killed another human being. It was awful. I can't change what happened…'

She reads his silence as a shock; he is thrown, he is horrified with me.

She feels herself turning hot with shame. It is mortifying. She has lost him. It is almost unbearable. 'Say something, anything,' Elora pleads.

'I read your note in the flat. I knew then what had happened. I didn't want to believe it.'

It strikes her in the face like a fist. 'You've known all this time, all these years. Why didn't you say something?' Strangely, she feels betrayed.

'I have my reasons.'

'Your reasons, what does that mean?'

He looks away, towards the sea, and then back again.

Elora feels lightheaded. Her heart thumps. 'You weren't there! How could you know?'

He tells her it is an answer she will wish she had never asked for. Elora trembles and for the next ten surreal minutes, as Elora listens, Brodie's story unravels in front of her.

Edinburgh 1995

The Truth

Brodie had seen them as he came out of the lecture hall.
The corridor was bustling with a tide of students, ebbing
and flowing. He fixed his gaze on the back of Elora's head
and, following behind her, screened by the people in front
of him, Chris walked with an air of determination, that
even, at such a distance, Brodie was able to distinguish. If
only he could turn away and reconcile himself to life
without Elora, none of what was to follow would ever have
transpired. His life would have continued as normal but,
when Elora glanced behind her, Brodie knew instantly
something was wrong. He could sense it.

He tried to move at speed but, to his frustration, the sheer
throng of students shifting sluggishly through the corridor
held him back. Elora disappeared through an exit door and,
progressing at a swift pace, Chris followed her.

Unnerved, Brodie launched himself against the wall of
bodies, squeezing through gaps that appeared and vanished
just as quickly. With a sudden panic, Brodie realised, even
though he'd reached the door, he was trapped in a fragile
balance of finding Elora, or of losing her.

Brodie's lungs burned as finally, he stumbled out into the
drizzling rain, the door slamming shut behind him.
Frantically, his eyes searched the surrounding area. He was
in a large courtyard. Sheltering under arches, several people
sat on benches, reading and talking. Brodie ran across the
shiny and slippery cobbled ground. He lost his footing and
stumbled, his outstretched hands breaking his fall.

'Brodie! Are you all right?'

He knew the voice. 'Mark, did you see Elora?'

Mark stood up from the stone bench he had been sitting
on and advanced several steps. He could see Brodie's

agitation. 'Are you sure you're alright? You're in a bit of a state.'

'Did you see Elora?'

'Yeah, a few minutes ago.'

'And Chris?'

'Yeah. Like you, he asked me if I'd seen Elora, and I told him she went inside the building over there. What's going on, Brodie?'

Brodie didn't answer. His growing despair had already propelled him, and he ran, his legs heavy and dragging, as if someone had tied weights around his feet. He was close, so close.

He first noticed, as he entered the building, the interior was in the process of an extensive refurbishment. Brodie hustled from room to room, stepping over workmen's tools and building materials that frustratingly slowed his progress. As he climbed the stairs to the next floor, the anticipation of anguish shadowed him. He realised he missed Elora immensely. He was lonely, even amongst friends. The immense weight of time to come, without Elora, pushed against him.

Desperately, he shouted her name, but the growl of a drill, somewhere in the building, reverberated around him, stealing his voice. His breath came in serrated rasps. He was sweating, moisture shining on his brow. A blush climbed his neck, dispersing over the surface of his face, reddening the skin. He bent forward, resting his hands on his knees. He filled his lungs with minute particles of dust and moist air. From the corner of his eye, he glimpsed another flight of stairs. Satisfied he had combed every space of each room, he rushed towards them. The stairs were wide, and he climbed them two at a time.

He had tried to empty his head of thoughts of him being with her, but it was useless. He could see it now, with absolute clarity. He still loved her. He wouldn't allow himself to think he had lost her. The thought of it jolted in his stomach. He reached the top of the stairs and stood to gaze into a large and expansive room. He could feel a rush of air and then he saw it, fractured pieces of a huge window frame, and jagged glass. A pulse pounded in his ears as he crossed the room. The window had been at least the height of a grown man. He craned his head over the edge and, to his horror, he saw Chris lying lifeless on the ground, a dark red lake of blood seeping from his skull. Someone was crouched beside Chris, while two others, Mark being one of them, lifted his gaze towards Brodie and, in that second, Brodie knew he was an object of scrutiny.

He reeled back into the room, *Jesus Christ, what has just happened? Where is Elora?* The confused heart-pound of fear increased. There was no way of avoiding the raw facts that stood in front of him. He had to find her.

He turned the key in the lock and stepped inside the flat.

'Elora, are you here?' Silence. It was that quiet he could almost hear the blood flowing in his veins. The air around him was chilling, even through his coat. He touched a radiator; it was cold against his fingertips. It felt like there was a window open. The heating couldn't have been on for days. Brodie's eyes flitted from side to side, noting the tired and worn sofa and threadbare carpet. They had often spoken about replacing them once they had both graduated and found jobs. Brodie gasped with the tremendous weight of emptiness.

Had it been two weeks since he left? It felt oddly inexplicable moving through each room, as if he was trespassing and really shouldn't be there. But this had been his home, filled with memories that lingered like the smoke from a wildfire and continued to make him smile. Brodie leaned against a doorframe and then he entered the room that once was their bedroom. He could see the wardrobe door was half-open as if she had left in a hurry. His stomach sank. He knew the interior was empty. He glimpsed several coat hangers hanging from their rail, devoid of her clothes. Brodie noted Elora's make-up bag, her brush and bottles of perfume that usually sat on top of the dressing table were gone, as was Elora. He understood that now.

He slumped onto the bed and trailed his fingers over the sheet and pillows. Something soft tickled his fingertips and when Brodie looked closer, straining his eyes, to his astonishment, several long strands of dark hair lay across the pillow. He took a deep breath and plucked them from their resting place, holding them to his chest. Brodie was struck by the irony that this was the space that he felt closest to Elora as he sat in the cavernous echo of her absence.

'Eventually, I went into the kitchen and that's when I saw your note.'

Elora is devastated deep to the bone. It is unthinkable to her that Brodie knew, after all this time, her darkest secret.

Brodie stands as if mustering mettle for what is coming next. He can see the colour has drained from Elora's face, the shock from his words imprinted like a tattoo.

'There are things I haven't told you about, from the past.'

She wants to be able to answer him, but her throat is momentarily seized.

'This is why I came. Without telling you, there can't be an us.'

It is hot despite the breeze that licks up from the sea. It has become a solace, being able to view the sea every day but, at this moment, nothing else matters to Brodie but the space between them. He draws a long breath.

He tells her, as if it is fresh to him, that he has thought of this moment for a long time.

He stayed in the flat that night. Then, around eleven o'clock there was a heavy rap on the door. He knew who it was. When he opened the door, two men in suits asked to speak with him. The two police officers displayed their identity cards. They informed Brodie he was under caution and asked him to accompany them to the police station.

They interviewed him for hours as he answered their questions: his relationship with Elora, the hostility between himself and Chris, the fight that occurred and Brodie's threat. He was told of the witnesses that placed him at the scene when Chris fell to his death.

Elora covers her mouth with her hand. There is a tightening, it has squeezed a compressing of the space around them as if the air has been squeezed from her lungs.

Brodie hesitates. He knows this will come as a tremendous shock. 'I was charged with Chris's murder.'

'I don't understand!' She is confused

'All the circumstantial evidence pointed to me.'

Elora shakes her head back and forth. The physical sensation is devastating 'No. It wasn't you. It was me. You knew it was me, you have just told me. You knew I pushed him. Brodie, why?'

'To protect you. I did it for you. They were so sure I was guilty. I knew they would not suspect you. I told them you had gone back to Greece. I said you told me this was your intention; you would already be gone. I said, you left Chris and myself together and we argued, and I pushed him. I told them I intended to warn him off, to scare him. It was an accident.'

She opens her mouth as if to speak, but then she looks away. Her eyes narrow. She covers her face with her hands. At this moment, she wants to stop existing. She lowers her face to her knees and enfolds her arms over her head.

In all the variations Brodie has considered, the combination of words he has imagined he would use to tell her, he has not anticipated Elora's reaction. Not this.

Elora sits up and wraps her arms around her body. 'This is wrong. If anyone should have been punished, it should have been me. I was a coward. I was the one who ran away from it all.' The shame she feels is extraordinary.

'You've lived with this for half your life. Is that not punishment enough?' He looks at her, knowing the question is about to come.

'And what about you? Did you… did you go…' her voice occurs as a whisper.

He nods his head.

Her hand goes to her mouth. The sound that escapes her makes Brodie flinch. He moves towards her, but she holds up her hand. And he stands still as if paralysed.

He has just found her, and now, she is slipping from him; he is losing her.

'How long?'

He takes a long breath. 'Five years, but I served three. I pleaded guilty, and the charge was reduced to involuntary manslaughter,' he says as if this final piece of information will lessen the blow.

She tries to process this.

Her heart is pounding.

She registers the hurt.

She is angry with him.

She feels guilty and shameful.

It confuses her.

She wants to scream at him.

She wants to hold him.

She feels a tightness in her head. A lurch in her stomach.

'I'm going to be sick.'

Chapter 24

The Truth

Everything has changed. What is normal is now replaced by the unimaginable. For days, images of cells and uniforms, of isolation and restrictions plague her. It is how the mind works. The reality would have been different from her mind's construction, for how could she imagine what it must have been like for Brodie?

He has not elaborated on that time, and she has not asked. It is too raw. It is enough, for now, just to know. She braces herself just with the thought of it.

She has tried to force herself to focus on the days ahead, but her brain has resisted. She cannot see beyond the present. She contemplates this realisation. Maybe that is what she will have to do, for now; live day to day, circumstance and place, moment to moment.

It has been a few days since they spoke of their pasts and he has given her time to think through the turmoil this has caused. He is unsure if this was the right thing to do as he knows it will have to be revisited and he is unconvinced by Elora's display of normality. Something is nagging at him. There is an underlying tension, and it does not fill him with optimism.

He can see the sadness behind her eyes. Brodie, on his part, is trapped in a delicate balance of trying to reassure Elora and to acknowledge her pure shock.

Sometimes, it feels like nothing has changed. Elora can withdraw into her thoughts and then behave in a way that suggests nothing has happened, as though she has erased the other night from her mind. It is unsettling for him.

The light is fading around them. Brodie and Elora are lounging on chairs outside on the terrace. The sky is intimidating, dark with clouds that threaten rain. It has not rained since he arrived and the thought of it is pleasing to Brodie. He hopes it will clear the air. For days now, at night, it feels as hot as it has been during the day.

He lights a scented candle in a glass bowl. Elora is sitting still, unmoving, her face troubled as she stares across the garden. Brodie senses there is still more to come, it is tugging at him like a child seeking attention. It feels their past has more to tell. He is sure Elora is holding back.

The sound of red wine filling glasses pulls Elora from her thoughts. Brodie hands Elora her drink.

'Thank you.' She takes a mouthful and rests the glass in her lap.

'I think it's going to rain.' Brodie nods towards the sky.

'You could be right. The garden will appreciate it.'

He wonders what would have happened to them if Elora had not left? He knows what he would have done. He thinks it right that he tells her, after all they have been through lately. He worries it might have been   too painful. Still, it was worth it letting her know.

He hesitates a moment. 'I would have asked you to stay, you know that don't you?'

Elora bites her lip. 'I never gave you that chance, did I? It ended so abruptly between us.' She closes her eyes and summons a deep breath. 'And what would have happened if I had stayed? Chris would have still been dead. The police… well, they were not going to go away. We would never have lived a normal life after that. By leaving, I thought I was giving you a way out. I was giving you a chance to get on with your life and I had hoped, in time, you would be able to get over the hurt and pain I'd caused you. I never thought…' her voice cracks. She puts a hand to her mouth. 'But it didn't end for you, did it? It had just started, and I was the cause of it all.'

She has tried to savour every minute with Brodie but since she has learnt of his incarceration, such moments now feel sullied.

'If I had found you in the flat that day, I wouldn't have let you go. I still wanted us to be together. I didn't care about Chris, not then. I just wanted us to go back to how we were.'

'Why are you telling me this?'

'I've asked myself that question too. I couldn't have come all this way and not. I couldn't just choose what I was going to tell you and what I was not. I was doing this for myself. It had to be everything. I hoped in doing so it would bring relief for us both and rid us of the guilt we have lived with. I am to blame for what happened. It was me who made you feel that way, I'd taken you for granted, my actions pushed you away.' Brodie searches her eyes. 'It was a long time ago now. I've lived a whole new life since then, as have you, Elora. I married. I was happy. I had two amazing children. I had a career, a beautiful home, friends, holidays… life went on Elora, it didn't stop, but nor did the guilt and what I still felt for you.'

She is taken aback. 'It would have been better if I didn't know all this.'

'You forced my hand when you began to talk about Chris. I knew there would be a time to speak about it, to face your questions, and I knew the answers would hurt.

'I wanted you to know everything. How could I have kept something like that from you, Elora? I didn't tell you to hurt you or punish you, I would never, ever, have done that. I wanted you to know the truth. I couldn't have lied to you. You mean too much to me.' He tells her this in as calm a voice as he can.

She takes in a sharp breath. 'All I wanted was your forgiveness. There hasn't been a single day that I haven't thought about it.' Elora finishes her wine and pours another. 'Now, I can see how selfish that was of me. I ended your life as you knew it and I started mine anew.'

Brodie watches as she takes a mouthful of wine, his eye settles on the curve of her jaw and delicate contraction of her throat as she swallows.

Elora looks away. She has held herself together until now. Her resolve begins to slacken, fragment and collapse.

'I was just following my instincts...'

'Look at me, Elora.' He leans forward, anxious and impatient. 'You need to let this go.'

'What if I can't? It's different for you. None of what I told you will have come as a shock. You've known all these years. You knew all about me. I was unfaithful, I hurt you, I ran away from it all and Chris is dead because of me, but this, this is different. You went to prison. How can I come to terms with what happened to you, knowing I'm to blame for it? Tell me, how can I?' She finishes the last of the wine in her glass and reaches for the bottle.

Brodie lays his hand over hers. 'I think you should stop drinking?'

'I'll decide when I've had enough.'

'Elora, I don't want to fight with you. I'm worried, that's all.'

'Don't worry about me. This is my normal, my default. If you want to leave, I won't stop you.'

Brodie sighs. He looks at the garden and then straight at Elora. 'I never said that.'

'You're only delaying the inevitable. We both know it.'

She is not herself. He tries to push his frustration from him. 'Why don't you go to bed. You'll feel better in the morning and we can talk then.'

Silver lights, like stars, are now illuminating the grounds around the house.

'No. I'm not tired.'

'This is not you.'

'How would you know? We're basically strangers.'

'Is that what you think?'

'It's not what I think, it's what I know. We're fooling ourselves. What did you expect, Brodie? It's not like a switch you can turn on and off. It doesn't work like that.'

'I know it doesn't. We need to work at it if it's what we both want.'

'And what does that mean?' A defensive tone rises in her voice.

'This was never going to be easy. We both knew that.'

'I'm tired of the complications, the secrets we've kept from one another.'

'Please, Elora.'

'What?'

'This is not achieving anything.'

'It is, actually. It's given me the courage to do what I couldn't do before. There's one more thing I need to tell you. I thought I was able to leave it in the past, but I can't, not after what happened to you. It is to do with when I came home.' Elora closes her eyes and takes a deep breath. When she opens them, Brodie is worried and impatient, she can tell. 'I was pregnant!'

Brodie gives a sorrowful smile. It is not what Elora is expecting.

'I didn't know until eight weeks later. My grandmother, and now you, are the only people I've told. I couldn't tell my mother. It didn't matter in the end.'

'You lost it.'

'Like the others, yes.'

Brodie wonders how Elora has borne such sadness in her life. He is not sure how he feels. He has a son and a daughter. That is what matters. Besides, it was a long time ago, yet still, why does he feel betrayed? To counteract this, he has a sudden image of Heather. A photograph of her with Tom when he was only a few hours old.

'I know what you will be thinking. Was it yours? Honestly, I don't know. It was a fifty percent chance.'

'You mean, Chris.' He feels dazed.

She nods. 'What do we do now?' Her brow frowning with concern.

Brodie unfolds himself from his seat and stands. He leaves the terrace and stops at the garden as it spins around him. He takes in a deep breath of air and tries to breathe normally. Had he looked stunned when Elora told him? Even though it was only a moment ago, he can't remember.

He tries to come to terms with the possibility that even if the baby were born, he would not have seen it grow up. It would have been an adult by now.

Elora watches him as he steps onto the terrace.

'Thank you for telling me. I'd rather know than not. I know all of this is hard for you, it is for me too. It's done now. I hope in time, it will give you some peace, some closure. God. We both need it. Are you all right?'

She shrugs. 'I'm numb to any kind of feeling.'

'I think I'll go to bed. Maybe you should too.'

'I will. Soon.' There is an air of finality about her tone.

'Make sure you do. We can clean up in the morning.'

'Are you sure you're okay?' Elora asks.

'Yes,' he says, but his voice is short of conviction. 'And you?'

'I'll be fine,' she tells him abruptly, reaching for her glass.

Brodie says goodnight and, as he walks towards the house, he turns and looks at her as if he is thinking.

Elora looks up, her hand is trembling as she takes another drink, and he can see tears in her eyes.

'What?' she asks quietly.

'Did you want the baby?'

The question hangs in the space between them.

'Oh. Brodie,' she sighs.

She drops her eyes and turns from him.

Chapter 25

Storm

For several aching breaths, Brodie stands still, his chest heaving, his legs thick with fatigue as he stares into the dark. It is disorientating. He is sweating, his shirt sticking to his back. Brodie tries to calm himself. He listens and strains intently for any sound that will tell him Elora is near.

Around Brodie, there is an eerie stillness. Above him, rain clouds shift, and a silver moon appears, throwing light amongst the shadows. Brodie feels frightened of what might have befallen Elora.

His head pounds as he thinks of the unthinkable, panic rising. He shouts her name, his voice disappearing into the dark, the thicket of trees and beyond.

Above him, the sky opens. Sheets of rain cascade through the trees. He runs, his feet pounding the muddy ground, hurtling through the deluge of water that drenches his shirt and stings his skin. He pushes branches from his face, stumbling through the darkness, his vision blurred from rivulets of water.

Again, he shouts her name. Nothing. Only the thunder of the downpour answers him. He leans against a tree, his lungs burning. A moment to catch his breath and think. She can't be far.

He runs blindly, through undergrowth and bush, not knowing in which direction he is now heading, gasping, rapid breath rapping his throat.

To his alarm, Brodie slips, he stumbles and losing his footing, he is sliding down a steep slope, tumbling through the darkness and with a thud, he crashes into the trunk of a tree. Brodie lies still, staring at an angry sky. The pain he is anticipating, to his relief, is only an ache. He rolls onto his side and pulls himself up.

Sand. He can see the beach. He scrambles through the bushes, and then he is in the open.

He can hear the wash of waves. The rain has stopped, and the moon appears between clouds, illuminating the beach in soft translucent light.

Then he sees something move, or someone. At first, he thinks he must be hallucinating. He makes out a dress, bare legs and arms. Elora! A warm flood of relief moves in his stomach and is immediately replaced with a surge of panic. His body lurches in alarm.

She is already waist-deep as Brodie reaches the shoreline.

'Elora!' His voice cracks into a scream.

He wades through the water, trying to understand what is happening. The light from the moon gleams off the surface of the sea, making it opaque and polished. When he reaches her, Elora is standing still, her dress floating around her chest. Brodie reaches out and touches her shoulder, she doesn't turn. Her skin is icy to the touch and when Brodie moves alongside her, he knows instantly she is not herself. Elora's face is expressionless.

Brodie speaks softly. 'Elora, come with me, let me take you out of the water.'

She doesn't answer him. Brodie takes hold of her wrists and, carefully coaxing her, he guides Elora towards the shore. The surf breaks around them and the sea pulls at their feet in retreat. When they reach the sand, Elora's dress is sticking to her like a second layer of skin. Brodie turns to look at her and gently brushes strands of wet hair from her face. On her breath, he can smell a distillery.

'Let's get you home.' He breathes deeply to still the hammering in his chest.

'I wanted to do it. I really did. I heard you... shouting my name. Your voice...'

The shaking in Elora's body is so intense, Brodie thinks she is near to collapse. A wail soars inside her; it rises to a shrill, a ragged crescendo and, when she screams, she seems to take a bite out of the air.

When they reach the house, the gate sighs shut behind them, and Brodie takes Elora upstairs. In her bedroom, he goes to the bathroom and turns the shower on. He waits until the water is hot and tests it with his hand. When he returns, Elora is still sitting on the edge of the bed where he left her.

'You need to get out of those clothes and have a shower. The water's hot.'

His thoughts are sluggish, but he can still see her in the water, moving further from him. He tries to dislodge the image. He is fearful of leaving her on her own.

'I'm sorry.' Her voice is barely audible, as if her shame, guilt and sadness have swallowed it.

'You don't need to feel sorry.' It occurs to him ,that throughout all of this, Elora has still to look at him.

They are silent for a moment.

Elora crosses her arms across her stomach and rocks, ever so slightly. Brodie feels a peculiar sense of awareness.

'You've done this before, haven't you?'

She sighs and covers her face with her hands.

'I won't judge you,' Brodie says. 'You can get through this. We can get through this.'

'After the first time, I spent time in hospital. I felt safe there, contained, I suppose. After that, I saw a psychologist for months.' She adds softly. 'Talking, talking, talking.'

Brodie sits beside her on the bed.

'What happened that day and the consequences that followed was my choice. I allowed it to happen. Don't you see? You are not to blame. I wanted to protect you. I could never have lived with myself otherwise.' Brodie runs his hand over his face.

'But,' she begins, 'All those years...'

'Listen to me.' Brodie takes her hand and grips it. 'I have never let that time define the rest of my life. You must believe me when I tell you this. Tell me you do?'

She nods her head. 'I don't know how you can stand me?'

'I love you, that's why.'

Chapter 26

Three Weeks Later

Brodie parks the car and reluctantly extracts himself from the warm interior. He stretches his legs before retrieving his jacket from the back seat and slides his arms into the padded sleeves. He zips it up, just below the chin and presses the key fob. The car beeps, flashing amber lights. Brodie wonders how cold it is and thrusts his hands deep inside his jacket pockets and looks up towards a sombre and leaden sky. The air is ice-like, drifting from the north, over the surface of a grim-looking River Forth; it stings his face and nips at his ears.

The structure that is the Forth Road Bridge, an engineering marvel of its day, fills his vision, alongside the elderly but no less spectacular, Forth Rail Bridge. Each one a giant and awesome sight.

When Brodie scans the grey steel structure, it overcomes him with an angst that he knows will never recede from him. It squeezes his chest. Memories crowd in upon him. He can no longer look at the bridge without seeing the tormented face of Isaac and hearing the desperation in his voice. He relives each second, each emotion. It takes the breath from him.

In the distance, Brodie can see a seal gliding effortlessly through the water. It looks beautiful. He thinks it a performance. He wonders how long it will be before it submerges and disappears from his view, and he thinks suddenly of Isaac.

He walks briskly, passed the church that always reminds him of old Italian churches and Tuscany. He turns left and heads towards the high street with its cobbled stone road, café bars, coffee shops and quaint little shops. In the summer and spring months, South Queensferry becomes gridlocked with traffic and visitors. It is a popular venue for weddings, with the happy couple posing for photographs, the Forth Rail Bridge in the background like some prevalent prop. No such obstacles are hindering Brodie's progress today.

Soon, he pauses at the bottom of some steps and he thinks back to the last time he was there, remembering helping Cheryl, Isaac's partner, with a buggy and her son, Zak. He thinks about Cheryl's future, how precarious it might be; he hopes she has found a life for herself and her son.

He stands uneasily at the door to the first floor flat. Brodie rubs his finger over glossy black paint that cracks and flakes in patches. He is only here because of the decision he made that day to walk the bridge. Each passing moment and the outcomes of actions and occurrences perfectly aligned in space and time towards his encounter with Isaac. It is astounding how everything can change in a second.

He holds the brass knocker in his hand, an apprehensive moment passes before he knocks three times. He waits and listens. Nothing. No movement inside, just silence. Voices from below travel the staircase upwards towards him and disappear as the entrance door to the building opens and shuts below him.

He sighs and knocks once more. He can hear the entrance door open and footsteps on the stone staircase.

'Hi. Are you looking for Cheryl?' A young woman, late twenties early thirties, smiles at him. Her cheeks are red with the cold air or the exertion of carrying three shopping bags. She wears a red woollen hat where blonde hair escapes, falling around her cheerful face in curls.

'Yes. I am, but she doesn't seem to be home.'

'She won't be. It's Tuesday. She picks Zak up from the nursery and they have their lunch at The Manna House Bakery, on the high street.'

'That would explain it, then.'

'Are you family or a friend?' she asks, now regretting offering Cheryl's whereabouts so freely.

'An acquaintance, you might say.'

'Oh!' It is not the answer she was hoping for. 'I see.'

Brodie can sense her discomfort. 'I knew her partner.'

'Were you friends?'

'We became close.' She doesn't know, Brodie thinks.

'Cheryl hasn't spoken much about her past.'

Brodie glances at her shopping bags. 'Would you like a hand?'

'No. It's fine. I'm only next door.'

'Well, I'll be off, then. It was nice speaking to you.'

Brodie makes his way down the staircase and catches the young woman glance at him from over her shoulder.

When outside, Brodie takes a deep breath, the chill in the air catching in his throat.

It only takes Brodie a few minutes to walk to the café. Inside, it is busy and warm, the view of the street blurred and concealed by a sheen of condensation.

Brodie orders a coffee and sits at the only vacant table. He glances around and immediately sees her, triggering a cautious happiness.

Brodie watches as Cheryl feeds her son, Zak, who is strapped into a highchair. With a bright blue plastic spoon, she scoops small portions of food from a bowl and gently places it into his opened mouth and simultaneously Cheryl opens her mouth too.

She looks like any other young mother, blending in with those around her. Brodie hopes she is happy, and that she has managed to make a life for herself and her son. A woman walking from the toilet begins to chat with Cheryl. Cheryl is smiling and laughs in response to something she says. Their body language and tactile gestures validate their familiarity with each other.

Watching this scene unfold assures Brodie Cheryl has settled into community life and, more importantly, she has been accepted.

He finishes his coffee and satisfied with what he has seen, Brodie heads for the toilet. Negotiating his way around tables and awkwardly placed chairs, he passes Cheryl and Zak. He is so close to them, if he wanted to and the temptation is potent, he could touch the little boy's head.

He locks the toilet door, the soft click emphasising the silence around him. He leans his head against the door and draws a breath. It is as though it has been years and, at other times, it feels only moments ago.

He thinks of Isaac as he has done a thousand times before, and an inner jolt seizes him as it always does. As if on a loop, he has heard Isaac's cry, as he fell towards the dark, unforgiving water, and he knew then, as he does now, at that moment, his life had changed forever.

There was something in Isaac's eyes, just as the police arrived and Brodie had walked away; *did Isaac think I abandoned him?* Such thoughts siphon a reservoir of guilt. He has hoped today would be a beginning towards the easing of his conscience and finally an end to his torment. Yet, he feels such recompense drain from him. This has not been enough.

Brodie has just come out of the toilet when he sees her. With one hand, Cheryl is struggling with the buggy, the other is holding open the entrance door.

'Let me get that for you,' Brodie offers, taking the weight of the door.

'Thank you,' Cheryl replies as she manoeuvres the buggy out onto the street. She looks at Brodie then, a flash of recognition across her face.

'Have we met before?'

'We have a while ago now.'

'Yes. I remember. I never forget a face.'

Brodie can sense she is struggling to place him. 'I helped you with your buggy at the steps.' Brodie looks at Zak, snug in his snowsuit and hat. 'It's getting to be a habit.'

Cheryl smiles. 'That's right. Edinburgh. That's where you're from.'

'You've got a good memory, as well. That must be over three months ago now.'

Cheryl nods. 'Yes. It was when I first moved here.'

'Have you settled in?'

'I have. They're a friendly bunch around here.'

'That's good. Are you working?'

'I've got a part-time job in the café we were just in.'

'Good for you.'

He can sense a reluctance on her part to talk further. 'Well. I'd better get going. Thanks again.'

'Wait!' Brodie grasps her arm.

Alarmed, Cheryl tries to pull away from him. 'Get off me. What do you think you're doing?'

'Sorry. I'm sorry.' He releases his hold on her. 'I need to talk to you.'

'What?' Her hands grip the buggy.

'It's not what it seems. Look, bumping into you wasn't a coincidence. Neither was the first time.'

Cheryl glances up and down the street, her eyes wide. 'What do you mean?'

'It was intentional, on my part.'

'I don't understand.'

Brodie gestures to a bench across from them that looks out onto the water. 'Please can we sit over there. Let me explain.'

Cheryl shakes her head. 'No. I need to get going. I'll scream.'

'Don't do that, please,' Brodie softly pleads.

There is something in his voice that defuses Cheryl's fear. He has visibly shrunk in front of her.

'I know why you're living in South Queensferry. I know why you are here, Cheryl. Just give me a few minutes. Let me explain.'

She presses her hand to her mouth. 'How do you know my name?'

'There's nothing to worry about. I promise.'

She looks at Zak. 'Did they send you?'

'No. No one sent me. I'm here because there are things I need to tell you. It's my penance you see.'

'Five minutes, that's all.'

They both look out towards the water. On the other shore, a dreary covering of low cloud shrouds Fife. Zak has fallen asleep, his head bent at an uncomfortable angle, his cheeks rosy and round.

Brodie has his hands deep inside his pockets. He shifts on the bench. 'I knew Isaac for a very short time, but he has been with me ever since,' he explains. Cheryl stares straight ahead. Throughout Brodie's account, she does not look at him nor move her eyes from the water. Even when Zak stirs, her gaze does not move.

When Brodie finishes, he hears a sharp intake of breath and Cheryl covers her face with her hands. Her body heaves and her tears and sobs slip through her fingers. Instinctively, Brodie wants to comfort her, to lay his arm around her shoulder, but that same arm feels paralysed. He cannot intrude upon this personal grief.

Instead, he stands and walks to the steps that descend towards the shingled beach with its driftwood and seaweed, rocks and seagulls, and a boy throwing flat pebbles that skim effortlessly across the water.

He does not know how long he has stood there but, when a hand touches his arm, he turns and Cheryl appears by his side, her eyes unsympathetically blotched and streaked.

'Your name was in his thoughts and on his lips until the end.' He pulls from his pocket a brown envelope. 'I thought you might like this. As well as his notes, there is a letter. I never read it. It has your name on it.'

She takes the envelope and places it next to her chest. Brodie thinks she is about to cry again; instead, she takes a deep breath. 'Thank you. I hope you have found what you came for.'

Brodie meets her eyes. Then it occurs to him as he looks at her face, not with pity, but with admiration, 'I think I have.'

Chapter 27

Tom

Her mobile vibrates on the marble surface. She glances at the number on the screen. Brodie! Her heart feels as if it has stopped beating. She hesitates and then picks it up.

'Hello.'

'Elora?'

It is a male voice, but it is not Brodie. 'Yes. Who is this?'

'Hello, Elora. It's so good to hear your voice. I'm Tom, Brodie's son.'

Momentary, Elora is taken aback and confused, her thoughts blurred. 'Tom? Yes. Of course.'

'I know I've probably surprised you and by phoning you'll know by now, Dad has told me all about you. Well, in fact, all about you both.'

There is silence.

'Elora?'

Tears trickle from her bottom eyelids. 'He told you.'

'He did. Everything. I'm glad he did. It was an incredible relief for him. It was obvious he loved you very much.'

The past tense resonates in her head.

'Elora, I'm sorry I have to tell you in this way. I have some bad news for you, it concerns Dad… Dad has passed away.'

At first, the expression, 'has passed away' seems like a strange mixture of unintelligible words.

'He has only been gone a few weeks.'

'It was very sudden. None of us was expecting it was going to be so soon. We thought he was going to be with us…longer than that.'

'No! No! This cannot be.' She puts her hand to her mouth and bends forward. She can see in her mind's eye, Brodie smiling; she can feel his lips on her mouth, his fingers curled around her hand, walking together on sand as white as parchment.

She draws a breath. 'How?'

'It was the tumour.'

'What tumour?'

'God. He never told you.' Tom is not expecting this. He has to think of what to say. It has derailed him. 'He had it diagnosed months before he came to see you. And you never knew. God. I'm so sorry, Elora. You never suspected anything?'

Tom can hear sobs.

'Elora,' he says softly.

'I remember he had headaches; he passed out once. I made him go and see a doctor and he went. He knew even then. He knew all along.'

'I'm so sorry. I thought you knew. When he was with you, I was checking his mail and there was a letter from the hospital. He had been going through tests and they wanted to talk to him about the results. I phoned him to tell him about the letter and he said he'd get in touch with them. He would phone them that very day.'

Elora remembers this. He was in the garden walking towards her and he told her he had just been talking to Tom on the phone. He looked distracted. Had he phoned the hospital then?

'The tumour was inoperable. I think he knew that, anyway. He told me the headaches were getting worse and he was wary of driving as the blackouts were becoming more frequent.'

There is silence. Tom can hear her sobbing.

'Elora.'

'Yes.'

'The funeral is a week today. Obviously, you're welcome. I would like to see you there. We all would. I'll understand if you don't come.'

***

There are so many people in attendance, there is no room in the packed church, and people are having to stand outside. Elora is sitting in the front row with Tom, Lisa, and Jessica; beside them, Jasper is lying in the aisle.

The coffin is draped in flowers, a colourful and bright spectacle that seems at odds with the current sombre atmosphere.

The priest asks Tom to the pulpit. From his suit pocket, Tom retrieves several sheets of paper and places them in front of him. He stares at the words, written by his hand. He tries to compose himself; he has rehearsed this but the tears in his eyes blur the words he has taken time to craft and the ache in his chest steals his voice and tightens his throat.

'My dad lived for his family. It was why he woke each morning and why he breathed for the rest of that day. His family was his life. There were three women in his life he loved unconditionally: his wife, Heather and mother to his children, his daughter, Jessica and… Elora.'

She is taken by such surprise that Elora gulps for air. Lisa takes her hand and gently holds it. As Tom continues to speak, Elora's ears are lost to him. She promised herself she would be strong for Tom and Jessica, but she has never felt such pain, such loneliness. Her cheeks are wet with tears and her hand muffles her sobs. She is no longer amongst them.

Chapter 28

Three Weeks Earlier

'You are beautiful,' Brodie tells her, not quite sure if it is the right thing to say but it is out there.

Elora shrinks from him, shakes her head and tightens the towel around her body. She is not worth his adulation.

He combs his fingers through her hair, still wet from her shower. His eyes drift to her shoulder. Droplets of water sprinkle her skin; it reminds him of the sea, moments ago, wading through the surf towards her. He feels he has been holding his breath ever since.

Elora eyes fix on him. 'I was at my happiest with you. I've been trying to find that happiness ever since.'

She hates what she has done to him. She is ashamed.

'Would you have done it, walked out into the sea?'

'I couldn't move. I felt paralysed. It just became all too much. I thought the sea would take it all away: the guilt, the shame, the remorse. The sea became cold as I went deeper. It seemed to clear my mind. I realised then that knowing what happened to you was in a way a kind of catharsis. I had to know the truth of it if there was ever going to be closure. I was afraid. I was angry… confused. I felt in my bones, the sea had baptized me of my past, washed away the sins of the past. I have a life to live, whatever that looks like, it doesn't matter.'

'I won't always be here.'

'I know.'

'It doesn't change how I feel about you.'

'I want you to stay, but I will not ask you to. I know you can't. It is enough to know we have had this time together. I never thought this would ever be possible. Who knows what the future will bring for us? Life is such a fragile thing, but when I'm with you, I feel insulated and secure.'

Brodie lies his head on her chest.

She runs her fingers through his hair. It soothes, for a moment, his growing despair. Their time together is coming to an end. He finds the thought of it leaves him with a disturbing sadness. Inwardly, an animal has crawled inside his stomach and died. His time is limited.

Elora bends to him and kisses his head. He feels the warmth of her breath and, like a moth to the flame, he can't help himself. He lifts his head and finds her mouth. The towel slips from Elora as Brodie guides her back onto the bed. Elora watches him remove his clothes. He lies next to her and her eyes fix on him. He is on his side, propped up by his forearm.

'I have never stopped loving you, Brodie.' She covers his chest in soft, light kisses. Like a feather gradually trailing his skin. Her touch enthralls Brodie. He inhales the scent of her hair, still wet from her shower. He runs his fingers along the length of her back, over her shoulders and the nape of her neck in soothing motions. He becomes extraordinarily aware of the sensory pleasure, of touching and of being touched.

The intensity of his feelings for her forces him to whisper her name. She makes a soft sound from her throat and it is a response that catches his breath.

'I love you. I love you, Brodie Lucas.' The timbre of her voice is seducing and resonant.

Brodie cups her face between his palms looking into her deep brown eyes. He kisses her longingly, his tongue sliding between her lips. Elora's fingers curl around his neck. He feels like he will disintegrate from his physical need and his longing. He desires every aspect of her.

His hand slides between her thighs and she moves with him, her lips slightly parted, her breathing deep, her eyes closed. He kisses her mouth, her cheek, her forehead, he whispers words of love in her ear as his hand explores the soft fullness of her breast. When she guides him inside her, nothing else matters.

Despite all the odds, he had still hoped to beat it, but the phone call from the hospital confirmed his worst fear and he has been stalling ever since. There is more he could tell her, things he would like to say. He has thought carefully about it, how he can prepare her for his absence in her world. He has never been as frightened as this. He cannot contemplate the possibility that by consciously avoiding telling Elora of his illness, she may at some point find out herself. This has worried him daily. Although it is a choice he has made, he is not entirely comfortable with it and he can't eradicate the constricting sensation this brings.

'Shall we have a bottle of red?'
'Not for me. I'll just have water.'
'You could just have the one you know.'
'I can't. That's my problem.'
'Ah! Well then, in that case, I'll just have a Sprite.'
'I appreciate you're trying to help, but you don't need to abstain just for me.'
'I know. I want to be... be supportive.'
'As long as you know, I don't mind if you do have one.'
'When did you last have a drink?'
'The other night, when you saved me from my inability to see what was straight in front of me.'
'I see.'
'I haven't had a drop since then. Two days now. I can't remember the last time I went that long without a drink. That's how sad I've become.'
'You can get through this. I believe in you. With or without me, it's you and only you who can make that change.'

'I believe in me too. You have to take the credit for that. I wouldn't have been able to do this if you hadn't given me the courage. It's true.'

Brodie shakes his head dismissively.

'Do you think, for one minute, if you hadn't come into my life again when you did, I'd be sitting here without a wine? Well? I can tell you with all certainty there would be a bottle sitting on this table.'

'What's important is it's a beginning. It's a marathon, not a sprint. If you have setbacks, which you might, you can get back up again and continue that race.'

'You see. That's why I need you. Amongst other things, I need your positivity around me. I've often wondered what you are like as a father.'

'A normal one, I imagine.'

'There's nothing normal about you.'

'Well. Like any father, I want the best for them.'

'I bet you played with them, made them their dinner, put them to bed, kissed them goodnight.'

'I did. See, I told you, normal things.'

'Not every father does those things.'

'You're right. My dad was too busy trying to earn enough money to put food on the table and pay the bills. I never really got to know him until I was an adult myself.

'I don't think he could relate to us as kids. He seemed aloof in a way. Not your best father material. He hated Father's Day, saying it was a waste of time and some entrepreneur had probably made it up to make a killing out of people's affinities. It didn't stop him reminding us to get a card for mum on Mother's Day.' Brodie smiles. 'We never had a lot of money. Not for luxuries, anyway. I knew he loved me, in his own way and that was alright, it just took me about twenty years to work it out. You don't talk about your mum or your dad a lot.'

'No. My dad died when I was just an infant. I don't remember him. My mum… I was closer to my grandmother.'

'Why was that?'

'She virtually brought me up. Mum was often in and out of the hospital. Her mental health was… well, not good at times. They say it runs in families. Maybe I caught it from her?'

'It's not something you can catch.'

'I know. I was trying to be humorous. That was my attempt at self-deprecation.'

'Do you see her much?'

'She's dead. She… she took her own life.'

'Elora. I'm so sorry.'

'It was a long time ago. By the time I was twenty-five both my parents were dead, my sister had long gone to London, and it was just me and my grandmother.'

'That must have been difficult for you.'

'As I said to you before, she was an amazing woman. I wish I could be more like her. I know I can be hard work sometimes. At least now you know what you're getting into.'

'And I'm still here.'

'You are and that means everything to me.'

He wants to tell her, and yet, he fears it. The words catch in his throat every time he has spoken them out loud, 'I have a tumour that is going to kill me.'

He wants to spend every minute of every day with her. He wants to never leave this place. He believes meeting her again was fated. Now that he has found Elora, he cannot imagine life without her. The irony strikes him like a bullet.

After all Elora has been through, he cannot bring himself to cause her any more pain and be responsible for the hurt she would endure. The thought is tortuous. He has agonised over this decision since he first learnt of his death sentence,

for that is how he thinks of it. That is what it is, and he
wants to cry, not for himself but for those he loves.

He is troubled with thoughts that concern Elora when he
is gone. It frightens him. He should be with her. He cannot
imagine her being on her own without him. He fears that
when his condition gets worse, he will forget how the touch
of her hand on his skin makes him feel. He shudders at the
prospect that he may forget the sound of her voice, her
throaty and raucous laughter, and the construct and
contours of her face.

A sudden pang of memory, of watching Heather slip
from him. He remembers every detail. It was her, yet it was
not. The finality of it still makes him ache.

The sense of helplessness was overbearing. Sometimes,
that was worse than knowing he was losing her, or even
that her death was imminent. Inside, there was a
hollowness that eventually broke him.

He can distinctly remember all of it.

Brodie cannot put Elora through the same hell. He wants
her to hold onto the memories they have made together,
ones that will, in the days, months and years to come,
remind her of the happiness they found and the intensity of
being loved and to love. They are to remind her that
throughout it all, the short- and long-lived scars and
wounds of their grief, their anger, their loss and lost time,
even as long-buried secrets were unearthed, their love
remained.

This is what he wants Elora to remember.

It is hard to believe he will be leaving her. He has made
her happy; he believes that now. He can see it in her
contented gesture, her small movements, her straight
posture and in her smile.

And she, too, has made him happy, more than he has
ever thought possible. Her vulnerability, tenderness and her
need for him have been like a warm blanket, spreading
contentment.

The broken ends of their lives have finally joined, only to be broken again.

A cat stretches out on the garden wall, and below, another one sits contented, licking its fur in the shade.

'Where did these two come from?' Brodie asks, surprised, as he steps out onto the terrace.

Elora follows his glance. 'I seem to have fostered them. They appear every summer, hang around for a few months and disappear again. Sometimes, they're back again around Easter, but mostly they appear around now.' Elora explains, matter of fact, as she tends to a rose bush.

'Do you like cats?'

'Yes. What is there not to like about them?' Elora asks, answering his question with another.

'They're... temperamental. What I mean is, cats are not like dogs, are they? You know where you are with a dog. Dogs are loyal, they miss you when you're out and they show you how much they've missed you when you get home. But cats?' Brodie shakes his head. 'I've never liked them.'

'You've never met these two, then.'

Brodie observes them, unconvinced. 'Do you feed them?'

'I do. Dora, that's the one on the wall, she's a fussy eater, but Samson, he'd eat his tail if he could.'

'Dora and Samson! You've given them names?'

'Of course. Does this surprise you?'

'I suppose so.'

'I'm fond of them. They don't just lie about all day; they work for their keep. Well, Samson does. He likes the taste of mice. You won't see any around here when he's about. Besides, they're good company. I even let them in the house.' Elora wipes her hands together. Once she is in the shade of the terrace, she tosses her hat onto the table and fills a glass with lemonade.

'Yes. They would be good company, I suppose, if you liked cats, that is.' Brodie grins to himself. He never thought it possible, a cat could bring him such relief as these two have just done. The thought of returning to Edinburgh is still a wrench, but it has given him some momentary relief.

Elora pours another glass of lemonade and hands it to Brodie. The garden is rich in a fragrance of jasmine, laced with lavender and hints of honeysuckle. The trees are luminous, their leaves shining in the sunlight, and the sea, just beyond, a resplendent fusion of light and colour that settles over Brodie in a sense of being bathed in its incantation.

'I'm going to miss this view.'

Elora can hear the sadness in his voice. 'It's not like it's going to be forever. When you return, it will still be there, just as you left it.'

He should tell her now, but he knows he won't.

'I need to take the hire car back before I leave. I'll drop it off and get a taxi to the airport.' A shiver ripples through him. He is talking of leaving. He knew this day would come, but it doesn't make it any easier.

'I'll come with you.'

'No.'

She doesn't reply.

'The thought of you coming back to the house without me would only torment me. Besides, you have Samson and…'

'Dora.'

'Yes. Dora. They'll keep you company while I'm gone.'

'I'm used to living on my own. I've done it for years.' Elora looks away from him.

Samson is plodding along the path that leads to the entrance door to the garden. He sniffs the still air, following the trail of a scent with a newfound eagerness.

'We'll have to take separate cars.'

'And once you drop off the hire car, instead of getting a taxi to the airport, I'll drive you.'

Brodie considers this, he doesn't want to argue the point, his heart is heavy enough.

'Your dog will have missed you.'

'He'll be getting spoilt.'

'He might not want to leave.'

That might not be such a bad idea, Brodie thinks. He will have to make arrangements for Jasper. Would Hana take Jasper? If he were to ask Hana, he would have to explain why. That would be problematic. He will have to consider it. Give it some thought.

The consultant informed him the tumour was in the area of the brainstem which proved difficult to operate on, therefore an option was radiotherapy treatment. The radiotherapy was not a success, the side effects, however, were. He is grateful he only lost some of his hair, and not enough for others to notice.

His consultant called it an astrocytoma; it had reached the level of a 'Grade 4' tumour. It was fast-growing. Only around five percent of people survive five years or more. He had hoped he could hide it from his children, get the treatment and not have to worry them. The consultant mentioned months at the very least. It was at that point he told Tom and Lisa and Jessica.

The headaches and seizures have become more frequent despite the medication he is taking. He has known his vision is changing; in the morning, it is blurred, and getting worse.

'I could come over to Edinburgh, visit your home, see where you live, have a coffee in your favourite coffee shop, a meal in your favourite restaurant, go for long walks around the city. I would love to do all those things. Be a part of your life, just to experience it with you, would be wonderful.'

Brodie feels light-headed.

'Once I've finished writing this book, that's what we'll do. What do you think? I feel excited just thinking about it.'

Brodie does not answer; he is lost for words.

'Brodie?' Elora tilts her head, expectantly.

'Yes,' he eventually says. 'I'd love that.' He deliberately changes the subject. 'How is the writing going? To plan I hope?'

'It is, thankfully. After what happened in Athens, my publishers have been very understanding. They have moved the deadlines back. I feel bad about that, but they said my health is more important.'

'That's good of them.'

'It's such a relief. It has given my writing a new lease of life. Sometimes, what I have in my head becomes totally different when I write it down. I've become excited about my writing again. I'd lost that, but you have helped me, Brodie. I can see now what is important, what has worth now. For too long, I've been blinded by my anger, my bitterness, my deceptions. I'm done with the past. It can't be changed. I never thought I'd be able to accept that or to even begin to think in this way. It's a deliverance, Brodie. And you are the one responsible for it.' Elora reaches over and holds his hand. 'It is now that matters and what lies ahead of me, of us. New beginnings. I feel liberated, and it's all because of you.'

Brodie tenses, an ache tugs at his throat. *I cannot do this. How much should I tell her?* He raises her hand to his lips and kisses her fingers. Her eyes are fixed on him, they are full of light, of life and wonder. He has not seen her like this. He cannot extinguish what she has found. It would be too much for him.

Brodie is still holding her hand to his mouth and, when he speaks, she feels his breath upon her skin. 'When you come to Edinburgh, we can make plans and promises. I'll show you all of my secret places, where I've dreamed of taking you.' Brodie can't remember when he last felt like this. He thinks he never has.

'I'm getting goosebumps just thinking about it. Together, we have our whole lives in front of us.'

He tries to smile, but he can't help thinking, his lifetime is now an episode of shrunken time, racing towards him, which he cannot stop.

Chapter 29

Three Weeks Later

'I'm glad you came, Elora.' Tom says as he sits beside her.

'There must be over a hundred people here.'

'I hope the buffet lasts. Would you like tea or coffee, a drink perhaps?'

'A coffee would be just fine. I'll get my own.'

'You sit there, and I'll get you one. How do you like it?'

'Just black.'

'Just like Dad. He liked his coffee black and no sugar.'

'I know.'

'Of course, you do. I'll just be a tick.'

Elora sits with her hands clasped together in her lap. She glances around the large room and is suddenly aware she doesn't know anyone. She wonders if others are asking about her and her connection to Brodie? She is wearing a dark skirt and suit jacket, offset by a white blouse. Her hair lies across her shoulders. She did think of tying it back, but then remembered Brodie always commented on how he liked it this way.

When Tom returns, he places her coffee on the table, and she can see two biscuits balancing on the saucer.

'Thank you, Tom.'

Tom sits down with a heavy sigh and sips his tea.

'Are you okay?' Elora asks and for the first time that day she notices how tired he looks, his eyes sunken and heavy.

'It's been a tough few weeks.'

'I'm sorry about the baby, it can't have been easy.'

'We're getting there.'

Just then, Jessica and Lisa approach them. 'Do you mind if we sit?' Jessica asks.

'Of course, not at all.' Elora tries to smile.

They both have a glass of wine. 'I wasn't going to have one, but then I thought why not? It's not that good, actually.' Jessica screws her face up as she takes a sip.

'Are you coming back to the house, Elora?' Lisa asks.

'I'll just get back to the hotel, I think.'

'You must come back, Dad would have been mortified if he though we left you on your own,' Tom insists.

'I don't want to intrude. You need to be together as a family.'

'Then it's only right that you should be with us too.' Tom smiles.

Elora tries to swallow the brick in her throat.

'It's expected that we should mingle,' Jessica says, taking in the room and physically shrinking in front of them. 'I'll have another one of these, even though it's rank.' She tips the last of the wine into her mouth. 'Another?' she asks Lisa, holding up her empty glass.

'Not for me.'

'I'd better say hello to a few people,' Tom says, rising from his chair.

When Jessica and Tom leave the table, Lisa asks, 'Which hotel are you in?' She crosses her legs.

Elora's mind clouds. 'It's in Charlotte Square.'

'The Kimpton?'

'That's it. I stayed there the last time I was in Edinburgh.'

'The book festival?'

'Yes. That was when I met Brodie...' She has tried so hard, but the mention of that time is too much for her. She covers her sobs with her hand and is grateful when Lisa reaches into her handbag and offers her a tissue.

'Thank you.' Elora wipes her eyes. 'I'll be a mess now. My mascara will be running everywhere.'

'It's not. You look beautiful too.'

Elora blows her nose. 'What! I don't think so. I feel a mess right now.'

'Believe me, you're not,' Lisa says warmly.

'I don't think Jessica likes me.'

'She does. She just needs some time to get used to the fact that you were her dad's secret.'

'Yes. I suppose it must have come as a shock to her.'

'Give her time. She'll come round.'

'I hope so.'

'How long are you staying for?'

'Just today and tomorrow.'

Lisa nods and raises an eyebrow. 'Anything planned?'

'No. I'm lucky I got here. I'm amazed I got a flight and hotel at such short notice.'

Tom appears at Lisa's side and sits down heavily. 'Uncle Harry's going to be pissed if he keeps knocking them back like that. He's already beginning to slur his words. Does anyone want any food? The buffet has just opened. The wraps look nice.'

'Not for me, but thanks.' Elora's appetite has deserted her.

Tom looks expectantly at Lisa.

'I'm fine. I might have a slice of that cheesecake with a cup of tea later.'

'More coffee, Elora?'

'No thanks, Tom.' She looks at her cup, undisturbed and still full of coffee. None of it feels real. She feels suspended in a surreal limbo. Brodie had only left three weeks ago, and they were making plans for her to visit. *Why didn't he tell me? I could have... I could have what? I was so wrapped up in my own little world, feeling sorry for myself and, all that time, Brodie knew he was dying. Even when he left to come back to Edinburgh, he knew then. I'm angry with you and broken hearted. What must you have gone through and all that time you kept it locked up inside? Why couldn't you share it with me? All I have are questions and the precious time and memories you left me with.*

The car draws up to the house and, beyond the hedge and garden gate, she can see a dominant black door.

'We're here,' Tom announces. He turns the engine off and glances in the rear-view mirror. Elora musters a smile, and it's enough to reassure Tom that inviting Elora was the right thing to do.

Once inside, Lisa heads for the kitchen, 'I'll put the kettle on.'

Elora follows Tom over the antique tiled floor of the entrance vestibule and into the hallway, under high ceilings. She rubs her forehead and takes in the tiled floor, the staircase at the far end and the framed paintings on the walls. As she looks closer, they are not paintings at all but black and white photographs of Edinburgh. *He should be here with me; it was what we planned. I shouldn't be in Brodie's house, not like this, not now.* She brings her hand to her mouth, muffling her stuttered gasp.

'Are you alright, Elora?' Tom rests his hand on her shoulder.

'It's just a bit of a shock, being in his house, that's all. I'll be fine.'

He leads her along the hall and into the kitchen where Lisa is filling the kettle under the tap. It is bright and spacious; the kitchen is modern, which surprises Elora. She imagined Brodie's taste to be more conservative, traditional even. Then Heather comes to mind, this is her influence. Two glass doors offer unobstructed views of the garden, where Elora's gaze is instinctively pulled.

Tom glances at Elora as he removes his jacket. 'Dad said you liked gardening.'

'I do.'

'Do you have a big garden?'

'It's big enough for me. I just potter really.' She remembers the morning walks Brodie would take in the garden. He often commented on the scents of the flowers and herbs infusing the air around him, each area expelling its unique fragrance as he moved from one part to the next.

She wraps her arms around her stomach, her grief drags inside her, it is intolerable. She closes her eyes. She fears she will forget the sound of his voice, the contours of his face, the way his touch could melt her.

She is in his home, amongst his possessions, yet he is not here. She could never imagine such a possibility.

The front door opens, 'It's only me,' Jessica calls.

Elora wipes her eyes and turns to meet her. Jessica appears at the kitchen door. It is evident she has been crying, her eyes are red and puffy. She walks over to Tom and falls into him. He wraps his arms around her.

'I still can't believe he's not here,' she gasps between sobs.

'I know. I know.' Tom inhales deeply.

Elora averts her eyes and looks out into the garden. Her mouth tightens and she clasps her hands tightly together. Suddenly, all she wants is to escape outside into the garden.

Lisa presses a mug of steaming coffee into her hand. Elora lifts her head. Lisa's eyes are kind and warm.

'I'll show you around the garden if you like?'

Elora nods and is sure Lisa can sense her relief.

The grass has recently been cut, it still has the shaded lines along its length and Elora wonders if Brodie thought about her as he walked up and down the lawn cutting the grass. Her eye is snagged by a rubber bone and a tennis ball, both lying where they were dropped.

'Where is Jasper?'

Lisa sips her tea. 'Hana has him. I suspect that's where he'll stay for now.'

'What will happen to him?'

'We're hoping she'll offer to take him. Jasper knows her and has stayed at her place, so it wouldn't be such a big change for him.'

'I'll take him. He can stay with me.'

Lisa's jaw loosens. 'Really? You live in Corfu.'

'If he's chipped, which I presume Brodie would have had done, all that is needed is the appropriate certificates, rabies certificate, the EU vet health certificate and an airline health certificate.'

Lisa tilts her head. 'How do you know all this?'

'I did some research into it for one of my books.'

'Ah! I see. Hana is away a lot with work. Maybe it's not such a bad idea, after all.'

They reach the end of the garden and sit on a bench under the protective branches of an old Sycamore tree. Elora cradles her mug in both hands, she blows over the coffee and takes a sip.

'I think Brodie would approve.'

Lisa touches her lightly on the arm and nods eagerly. 'Yes. He would.'

Elora brings her hand to her mouth. 'Jasper! Is he okay with cats?'

Lisa curls her lips. 'He was brought up with two as a pup. Besides, he's too good-natured to be bothered with cats. Why?'

'I sometimes have two that visit now and again.'

'Oh, I see, I think.'

Just then, Tom and Jessica walk down the garden towards them.

Tom shakes his head. 'We've just checked the fridge, there's nothing but a few microwave meals and some eggs, I'll need to go to the supermarket if we're going to eat tomorrow.'

'What about tonight?' Jessica says as she sits on the grass. 'I don't fancy spaghetti bolognese from the microwave.'

'We'll get a takeaway, later.' Lisa suggests.

A faint whiff of smoke blows across the garden, through the fence, in the next garden, Elora can see a man prodding a small fire with a stick.

'Dad was never the adventurous type,' Jessica is saying. 'When it came to food. He could stretch to a Chinese, an Indian at a push, but that was it really.'

'I managed to get him to experiment a little. At breakfast, I'd give him figs, honey and yoghurt. He wasn't too keen on the figs though. If we went out for a meal, he'd often try the local dishes.' Elora tensed. She hasn't meant to, but she has just contradicted Jessica and now she is expecting a reprisal. She fingers the rim of her mug.

'Jesus, Elora! Dad must have loved you.'

There is no bitterness. It is not the response Elora is expecting. Jessica is smiling at her.

Elora straightens her back. 'And I love him.'

'I'm glad he eventually found you and I'm sorry I've been standoffish with you. I've been selfish, I know. We're all grieving. Can you forgive me?'

'There's nothing to forgive,' Elora says softly.

Jessica smiles shyly, knowing she's been let off the hook.

A few minutes later they are all back in the house. There is talk of the days and weeks to come, the arrangements to be made, visits to the lawyers, the breaking up of the house, who will get what, objects and belongings that have been promised to family members down the years by word of mouth.

Such discussions do not concern Elora, and she wonders should she even be present while the details are gone over.

She taps her fingers on the arm of the black leather sofa and tries to divert her attention by taking in the sitting room. There is a large bay window with white wooden blinds. A lofty ceiling supported by cream walls, except the wall where a decorative fireplace takes centre stage wallpapered with a fashionable design, not to Elora's taste. It probably cost a fortune. The fireplace, on the other hand, she finds compelling and wonderful. It wouldn't look out of place in her house back in Corfu. A substantial glass wall

opens onto a patio and into the garden, flooding the sitting
room in sunlight. She would have given anything to have
sat in this room with Brodie. Her heart is strangled by an
inconsolable ache.

'Elora, there's something I want to show you,' Tom
announces as he rises from his chair.

Elora follows him along the hall. 'Just in here.' He opens
the door into what she can see is a study, Brodie's study. A
large desk sits at a window with views of the garden. A
black high back leather chair sits in front of an Apple iMac.
On each wall are shelves with books, hardbacks and
paperbacks, personal nick-nacks, a bust of a Roman
Emperor and framed family photographs. Elora notices one
that piques her interest. Brodie with his arm around
Heather, and she is smiling into the camera.

Tom's hand slides over the back of the chair. It is a
gesture Elora knows; it conveys his loss, his need.

'I was in here the other day, tidying dad's things and
really, if I'm honest,' his voice strains. 'To be close to
him.'

Elora bites her lip. She reaches out and gently touches
his forearm.

'Dad spent a lot of time in here. When I was younger, it
was just a space to store things in, before he turned it
into… his space.' He rubs his eye with the back of his
hand. 'It's just over here.'

Tom takes a box from a bottom shelf and places it on the
desk. He turns and faces Elora. She stands with her arms
wrapped around her chest to stop them shaking.

'I'll leave you, now. If you need me just call.'

Elora nods, her eyes falling on the box.

Tom closes the door behind him, and Elora stands in the
silence around her. She lowers herself into Brodie's chair
and takes a deep breath. She slides the box towards her; a
mixture of intrigue, fear and anticipation seep from her and
she hesitates.

She lifts her head, sits forward and gazes out of the window. It is the view Brodie would have seen a thousand times. The sycamore tree owns the garden, it is the focal point, towering above everything else, magnify its grandeur. Sunlight edges between the leaves of the sycamore tree and Elora tries to absorb every second and every detail, for she has no idea what the next few seconds will bring.

Elora slides her fingers over the surface of the lid and taps it gently. She takes a deep breath to calm the hammering in her chest and gently, she lifts the lid.

Her eyes grow wide, and her breath catches in her throat. She curls her fingers around a stack of envelopes and places them in front of her on the desk. They are tied together with string. She counts fifteen. The first envelope has her name written on it in black ink and a date, *12th September 1996*. There is something else in the box. She peers inside and takes out a folded sheet of paper, yellowing at the edges. Her hands tremble, she instantly recognises the sheet of paper for what it is. She unfolds it and her eyes fall on the words still as visible as the day she wrote them, *Forgive Me*. What she is not prepared for is her plea for forgiveness has been answered. Under her words is written, *Always*.

She puts her hand to her chest and tries to steady her breathing. The letters of the words blur in front of her as her eyes flood with tears, her chest heavy with heartache.

She restrains the urge to devour each letter. Instead, she wants to absorb every word, every sentence, every detail and let it seep into her. She craves the luxury of it.

I have looked at Corfu on a map countless times and wondered what you were doing, what were you thinking and feeling. Do I occupy a space in your mind? Another day lost; another week passes, and I am without you. I am desolate. I have a photograph of you; it was taken in The

Meadows. June, I think it was. I keep it beside me at night, and when the lights are turned off, and the cells become still and silent, I can still see your face…

Elora does not know how long she stayed in the study but, during that time, she felt so close to Brodie, he could have almost been sitting next to her. Tom insisted she keep the letters, and she was engulfed with gratitude. Before she left, they promised to keep in touch and Elora gave an open invitation for Tom, Lisa and Jessica to stay at her house in Corfu whenever they wanted.

Epilogue

Her world had become enclosed within the walls that surrounded her house. She retreated from social life and refused to attend the promotional activities or give interviews to the media for her new book.

Each new morning, her grief was etched on her face and her pain devoured her, her heart clawing at her lungs. At night, she would lie in bed and, breathing harsh sobs, prayed that sleep would find her.

Each space, each room resurrected a memory. Sometimes, they unfolded unsuspectingly, and it stopped her like a sting from what she was doing, demanding all her attention, and she gave it willingly. The outside world could wait. It was the inner domain of thoughts and recollections, of wonder and imagination that concerned her.

She often recalled the last time they lay together. She was deliriously happy then; she had always loved him, and she knew she would never love another again.

Her heartache crushed her, at times, it was unbearable. All day, she was blinking back tears of grief, of anger, of self-pity and for the loss that brought a pain so extraordinary, profound and deep, it was possible she was losing her mind.

It was what she deserved.

She was flawed.

She was ordinary.

She was real.

That was then.

***

The woody scent of thyme drifts towards her on the warm breeze. Elora takes a sip of the cold lemonade in front of her. She can see him, silhouetted against the bright sunshine and vast blue sky. He plods towards her and rests his head in her lap, his eyes fix on her and they are warm and shining; there is something unconditional about them, Elora has his utmost attention.

She tickles him behind his ear. 'Hello, Jasper. Let me guess, it must be time for your walk.'

Jasper's tail wags, fanning Dora the cat who is sleeping and lying stretched out beside Elora.

Elora rises from her seat. 'Come on then, let's get your lead.'

The sun is warm on her face as Jasper chases the murmuring surf, rolling in and out. She takes her sandals off and delights in the feel of wet sand, where each footstep slightly sinks.

She is writing again. She is energised with her newfound routine, rising early, writing until lunchtime and then, a long walk, Jasper by her side.

Sometimes, she can feel a hand press lightly on her shoulder, she can hear his voice, close to her, feel his breath upon her skin.

She has taken comfort from knowing that she and Brodie found each other and, in her mind, she tries to savour every second. Treasured time permanently suspended. She is left with her imagination. It is something precious. She has tasted happiness; it is intense and magnetic. It leaves her exhilarated.

Her mobile vibrates in her pocket. She takes it out and shades the screen with her hand. It is a text from Tom. They will arrive next week, as they have done, every few months, for the last three years. He signs off by telling her little Brodie cannot wait to see her and spend time with his favourite aunt Elora again.

Elora feels animated in her sense of great contentment. She holds the mobile close to her chest and tears fill her eyes. She is not sad; she is smiling.

Acknowledgements

Heartfelt thanks to Sheona, my wife, for her continued support and constant encouragement. Thanks to Tracy Watson, Maggie Crawshaw, Anne Clague and Lisa Richards who have been with me from the beginning. Also, thanks to Dilys Killick. As my advanced readers they have given me invaluable feedback on this novel. Finally, I am indebted to Katrina Johnston for her editorial skills, advice and time.

About the Author

Dougie lives in Dunfermline, Fife, with his wife, daughter, son and golden retriever.

A Moth to the Flame is his fifth novel.

Thank you so much for taking the time to read my novel. It really does mean everything to me. My novels are inspired by my favourite city, Edinburgh and my passion for Greece, her islands, people, landscapes, sea, light and ambience, all of which are important themes and symbols in his writing.

My books encapsulate themes such as love, loss, hope, coming of age and the uncovering of secrets. They are character-driven stories with twists and turns set against the backdrop of Edinburgh and Greece.

I never intended too, but seemingly, I write women's contemporary fiction and since 95% of my readers are women, I suppose that is a good fit.

Since all my books are set in Edinburgh and Greece, you will not be surprised to know that I identify with a physical place and the feeling of belonging, which are prominent in my writing.

Edinburgh is one of the most beautiful cities in the world, it is rich in history, has amazing classical buildings, (the new town of Edinburgh is a world heritage site) and it also has vibrant restaurants and café bars.

Greece occupies my heart. Her history, culture, religion, people, landscape, light, colours and sea inspire me every day. There is almost a spiritual quality to it. I want my novels to have a sense of time and place, drawing the reader into the social and cultural complexities of the characters. I want my characters to speak from the page, where you can identify with them, their hopes, fears, conflicts, loves and emotion. I hope the characters become like real people to you, and it is at that point, you will want to know what is going to happen to the characters, where is their life taking them in the story.

The common denominator is, I want my novels to be about what it means to be human through our relationship with our world, our environment and with each other. Most of all, I want them to be good stories that you, as a reader, can identify with and enjoy.

Printed in Great Britain
by Amazon

84668620R00164